GREENSWORD

GREENSWORD

A TALE OF EXTREME GLOBAL WARMING

DONALD J. BINGLE

FIVE STAR

A part of Gale, Cengage Learning

GALE
CENGAGE Learning

Detroit • New York • San Francisco • New Haven, Conn • Waterville, Maine • London

GALE
CENGAGE Learning

LIBRARY OF CONGRESS CATALOGING-IN-PUBLICATION DATA

Bingle, Donald J.
  Greensword : a tale of extreme global warming : a novel / by Donald J. Bingle. — 1st ed.
    p. cm.
  ISBN-13: 978-1-59414-728-9 (alk. paper)
  ISBN-10: 1-59414-728-0 (alk. paper)
  1. Global warming—Fiction. 2. Environmentalists—Fiction. 3. Protest movements—Fiction. 4. Criminals—Fiction. 5. Malibu (Calif.)—Fiction. 6. Tragicomedy. I. Title.
PS3602.I545G74 2009
813'.6—dc22   2008039751

January 2009.
Published in 2009 in conjunction with Tekno Books and Ed Gorman.

Printed in the United States of America
2 3 4 5 6 7 12 11 10 09

For Linda, who is cleverer, better-looking, and much, much greener than I will ever be.

ACKNOWLEDGMENTS

Anybody can make fun of the guys on the other side of a debate. The question is: Can you make fun of the guys on your side of the debate, too?

I went to college and law school at The University of Chicago, an institution that considers itself the home of the "reasonable man." While I was there, I also participated in, and later coached, parliamentary debate, an activity that asks its members to debate, at almost a moment's notice, any side of any question. Such debates, as a whole, give the debaters an appreciation of the strengths and weaknesses of arguments from the perspective of those with different agendas and beliefs. But the goal of each individual debate, as it occurs, isn't understanding others. The goal is to persuade an audience of people who don't already agree with you to join your side of the argument. I particularly liked the debates where the audience was physically divided on opposite sides of the hall at the beginning based on whether they agreed or disagreed with the proposition and then people got up and moved to the other side of the aisle if you convinced them to change their mind while you were speaking.

Unfortunately, persuasion is not the purpose of political debate anymore. Political debate is now targeted on riling up the people who already agree with you so that you can get more fund-raising or votes out of them. This leads to exaggeration, extremism, and polemics, further polarizing the already-not-too-civilized state of discourse on important topics. Global warming is now one of those topics. Consequently, any evidence that does not contribute to one extreme view or the other is routinely belittled, subjects that are logically related but don't fit the political agenda of the proponent (nuclear power, population control, genetically-modified crops, etc.) are ignored, and reasonable voices that speak of such things as cost-effectiveness and no-build zones are silenced in favor of those who prefer, on the one side, to pursue an anti-industrial agenda or, on the other side, to blindly march forward, denying that anything has ever changed or should ever change.

My goal in all this is the goal of all good pieces of speculative fiction, most especially those which are darkly comedic: to entertain you while nudging you to think critically about important questions.

Special thanks to all of those people who read and made comments on all or part of this book while it was in progress, including: Bill Dolan, Dewey Frech, John Helfers, Kerrie Hughes, Randall Lemon, Jean Rabe, Beth Vaughan, Tim White, Mary Zalapi, and the members of the St. Charles Writers Group, led by Rick Holinger. Despite their help, anything included or excluded from the final draft (including political views, real or imagined) is completely my fault, unless the copy-editor ran amok after I approved the galleys. Also, special thanks to Linda Bingle, Cheryl Frech, my extended family, and my friends from my writing life, my gaming life, and my work life for their encouragement and support during this entire process. My editor, John Helfers, and the fine people at Five Star Publishing have been incredible, as always (insert shameless plug for my earlier novel from Five Star, *Forced Conversion,* here).

I originally wrote this story as a screenplay, which is an interesting piece of trivia for those of you curious about the writing process and a critical piece of information that I desperately want to convey to any film producers, directors, actors, or agents out there. Call me. Please. No, I really mean it.

By the way, as far as I know, this book will *not* be printed on recycled paper, so if that kind of thing bothers you, start feeling guilty now. On the other hand, if instead of reading this book you were eating a chili cheese dog (methane, first from the cows, then from . . . uh . . . you), driving a car (carbon monoxide), or even ogling dancing cats or other nefarious content on a flat-screen monitor while you surf the Internet (which, according to one recent news report of unknown credibility, now consumes, with its associated computers, 9.4 percent of the electricity in the United States), your carbon footprint could be even larger. Nobody said environmentalism was easy. Me, I'm not worried. Since this is a small-press publication, I figure I'm only killing one tree—I'm just hoping that it is a really, really big tree.

Action is great, whether it's planting trees or planting ideas. But listening and thinking are great, too. Let's keep them all in the equation. And let's keep a sense of humor along the way.

Thanks for buying, or at least reading, my book. Let me know what you think. Contact me at www.orphyte.com/donaldj bingle or through www.greensword.org.

Aloha.

Donald J. Bingle
May 2008

PROLOGUE

Brandon shivered. He was cold, miserable, and tired beyond belief. Worse yet, the task before him was enormous, almost infinite.

Yet it had to be done.

He shouldered off the black Terra 40 backpack he had gotten from The North Face in Berkeley years ago and pulled out his clipboard to make notes on his day's meager progress in protecting the environment. He tallied up with some satisfaction the number of invasive plants he had uprooted—mostly *Clidemia hirta*, otherwise known as Koster's Curse. Yet a quick scan of the montane bog spread out below him showed he had barely made a dent.

He sometimes felt that he alone stood between mankind's uncaring neglect and the almost certain extinction of Greensword. His logical, calculating mind also nagged at him, telling him again and again that there had to be a better, more efficient way to go about this task. It was folly to rely on the almost-futile actions of a single individual like him being repeated often enough by a sufficient number of people to make a difference.

Brandon had been in this same position before, and his inner voice had been right: there was a faster way.

Of course, the fallout from that particular shortcut was why he was here now, tired and chilled to the core, providing manual labor to protect the environment. Brandon had no future here, but an endless series of days uprooting *Clidemia hirta* in an ef-

11

fort to save the few *Argyroxiphium grayanum*—the endangered Greensword plants—that remained in this remote place.

But then, he had no future anywhere else. No future at all. Not after what he had done.

Somehow, it had seemed like a good idea at the time. The rest of the guys in the group had all agreed. Everyone had helped in the planning, too. Even then, they knew that they were about to save the world; they just didn't want to get caught doing it.

CHAPTER 1

Dalton stood on a low bluff on the California shore, just off the coast highway. He tried not to let the woman wailing a dozen yards away distract him from his work, but his eyes involuntarily flicked over to where she huddled, wrapped in a soaking-wet, flowered bedspread. Her head was pressed against the T-shirt-covered, flabby chest of her balding husband, who stood stoically as the tableau nearby played out. The woman's eyes stared wide at the same scene Dalton was trying to capture for posterity . . . or at least the evening news. Her tears mixed with the spray of the surf carried by the gusting wind, leaving her face uniformly wet and, no doubt, numb.

He tore his attention back to his task, cleaning off the lens of his digital video equipment. The expensive camera was pointed across a narrow inlet at the adjoining lot, the lens angled as downwind as he could manage and still get the shot. He checked to make sure the tripod remained steady and positioned himself surfside of the camera, shielding it as best he could from the keening offshore wind. He looked back at the van.

Griffin Gantry, KQZJ's current star investigative reporter, sat in the front passenger seat calmly reading a magazine and sipping a West Coast Caffeinators grande double mocha cappuccino.

Dalton tried waving, but Griffin just turned the page on the latest issue of *Maxim* and took another sip of caffeinated heaven. Dalton took a quick glance over his shoulder; he needed Griffin out here. He grabbed at the Nextel in his right coat pocket and fingered the push-to-talk button. He brought it up to his face just as the late afternoon sun peeked through the clouds for the first time in days. Seawater splashed over his athletic shoes as a particularly forceful wave crashed against the nearby cliff side. The splash was, of course, accompanied by yet another thunderous roar of the surf, but this time at the crescendo there was a sharp crack and a prolonged groan of wet timber bending.

"Griffin, get out here, would you? It's any minute now."

Griffin looked up lazily from his magazine and glanced toward the coastline in back of Dalton. He shrugged minutely and reached languidly toward the dashboard to pick up his own Nextel. "Looks the same to me."

"Yeah, well, trust me, it looks different from out here . . . where the story is. I've had some experience in this kind of thing before, you know."

Griffin looked at him sharply through the dust- and spray-streaked windshield of the van. "Cut the 'experience' crap, Dalton. You work for me. I didn't get to be where I am today by doing things the way they've always been done. . . ."

Dalton dialed down the volume on his Nextel while Griffin launched into his usual rant. The cameraman had heard the whole youngest-principal-field-reporter-for-an-L.A.-network-affiliate spiel before. He not only knew how long it would last, he could practically recite it word for word. He hoped he wouldn't hear it again . . . at least not again today. Dalton dialed the volume back up just as Griffin finished in full bombastic mode, ". . . and that's why I've got an Emmy and you've got an enemy if you don't do what I say."

Dalton didn't press the talk button on his phone immediately. Instead, he feigned an abashed look of employee remorse with as much faux sincerity as he could muster. All the while he was looking contrite, though, he was fantasizing about marching over to the news van, reaching in to pop the gearshift into neutral, and watching in gleeful delight as the van rolled over the bluff and plunged into the sea carrying Griffin with it. Naturally, in his mind's eye, the van exploded into flames on the way down, just like cars did in bad movies.

Finally, Dalton smiled exaggeratedly at the van. Press. "Just trying to do my job as field producer, boss."

"You do that. Remember, this is your frolic and detour. You practically hijacked me. We're supposed to be covering that protest group way the hell up in Malibu."

Dalton sighed. Why did he have to get assigned to this asshole? He fingered the button on the Nextel. "They'll wait."

"What if they don't? We'll have spent the entire afternoon at the beach and have no story. That'll be on your head, not mine, Dalton."

"Whaddaya mean 'no story'? You already talked to the family." Dalton jerked his head toward the couple huddled nearby.

"Which is useless, if nothing happens while you're shooting." Griffin poked his Nextel toward the windshield at the clearing sky to the west. "It's getting late. The eco-fanatics could leave anytime and we've still got a thirty-minute drive."

Dalton looked at his watch. "Five more minutes, boss." Griffin started to shake his head, so Dalton kept his finger on the 'talk' button, so he could continue to make his case without interruption. "People with an agenda always wait for the camera. Real news happens when it happens." Now he released the button and waited for a reply, but Griffin just stared at him in silence, so he pressed on. "All the great photos in history are the result of either incredible patience or incredible luck."

Griffin jabbed at his phone, his impatience apparently reinvigorated. "And all the great *interviews* are the result of the people actually being there for the interview. Pack it in, Dalton. That's an order."

15

Dalton flipped off the phone, jamming it back, deep into his pocket. He turned away from the van, partly to begin disassembling the tripod, but mostly so Griffin wouldn't be able to read his blue lips as he set about following orders. Another wave shuddered against the coastline, the spray whooshing up the cliff-face to drench his shoes yet again. The big wave was clearly the last straw, because suddenly what Dalton had been waiting for—praying for in the sick way that afflicted all news hounds and other vultures of unhappy events—happened.

There was a loud, sharp crack, like setting off an M-80 in a basement. The crack was still reverberating when it was followed by a jumble of groans and rumbles, accompanied by the sharp tinkle of breaking glass.

Just to the north of where Dalton was waiting, the house on which he had focused his camera for the past two hours shifted sickeningly. It hung awkwardly for a moment as if pondering its fate, but there was no stopping it. Half-undercut by the erosion of the surf, there was an unnatural angle to the massive home's once architecturally classic lines that could not hold. As the giant wave of the El Niño–driven storm receded back into the churning malevolence of the surging tide, the western two-thirds of the mansion joined it, tumbling and crashing and sliding down into the surf, racing the mud and rocks of the cliff side into oblivion.

Dishes and knickknacks and furniture and groceries tumbled over each other, spilling out the sudden gaps that appeared in the walls and flooring as those surfaces folded downward and split apart into a mass of twisted splinters. The homey detritus that had once been the structure's contents catapulted downward into the foamy, gray water as the waves gathered themselves together and again began to assault the bluff. A large, well-maintained aquarium slid along the angled floor of the wrecked residence and then dropped through one of the gaps and fell

16

intact all the way down to the rocks, where it smashed, depositing its pampered residents into an unwelcoming sea.

Dalton adroitly panned back to catch the full expanse of the showy destruction even as it was occurring. New wails of anguish from the huddling couple and the continued roar of the hungry surf provided more poignant commentary to the scene than Griffin ever could have.

And then it was over.

The flotsam of the collapse quickly succumbed to the turmoil of the sea, sinking out of sight—a lifetime's possessions sucked into the murky depths of the surging ocean.

Dalton looked back at the van. Griffin had opened the door to get a better view, but still sat inside, where his blazer would stay dry and his hair would not get mussed. Then he shut the door and went back to casually ogling the bimbos in his laddie magazine. The reporter showed no more sympathy for the distraught homeowners than had the waves.

Dalton wanted to say something to Griffin, but held his tongue. Instead, he stepped over to the couple to mumble a few quick words of condolence and hurried back to his equipment before Griffin did something even more boorish, like honking the horn in impatience.

There was no reason for the team to tarry here any longer.

Dalton disassembled the tripod with efficient ease and stowed the equipment in the back of the van, before climbing into the driver's seat.

As he dropped the gearshift into reverse, Dalton looked over at Griffin, who, of course, had been too busy "reading" to have bothered to help with the equipment. Dalton let it slide. He jinked the van into a three-point turnaround and began to guide it back to the coast highway. As he pulled away, Dalton saw the owners of the destroyed home in his outside rearview mirror, still shuddering against one another in shock and grief. His eyes flicked away from the rear view to the turn ahead onto the highway. Their problems were not his. Their images had already been captured. Their story was over as far as TV news was concerned.

He glanced over at his current problem. Griffin Gantry. He didn't want to argue, but he didn't want a long ride in grumpy silence. He decided to try casting their earlier . . . discussion . . . in a positive light. "It all worked out for the best. Incredible patience *and* incredible luck. You know, Griffin, you've got three pieces of luck you don't even know about."

"What're those?" said the reporter, without bothering to look up.

Dalton eased the van around the curves of the scenic highway as he spoke. "One, Mother Nature doesn't take orders."

Griffin's eyes remained glued to the curves in the magazine. He shrugged absently.

"Two, we don't use film anymore. We use digital video."

Griffin looked up, arching one eyebrow. "I know that, Dalton." His eyes flicked over to the equipment. "Everyone in the biz knows that. I'm a television professional, not an idiot. But I am surprised to hear that *you* think it's fortunate. I thought all you would-be directors preferred film. Richer texture . . . blah, blah, blah."

"Film is expensive and finite. You can't afford to just point at something and let it run until the house crumbles or the gas tank explodes or the hostage makes a break for it or whatever. With digital you can aim and wait. You can dependably get shots that were just lucky before, if you're patient."

Griffin turned back to his magazine. "Nice footage, Dalton. But you shot for almost two hours. And what did you get? A snippet that is maybe twelve seconds long? Even with the sniveling family footage, it's not even really a segment."

"Don't worry. Your third piece of luck is that you got me. I'll hold it back from the editing crew at the studio and inter-splice it with a montage of traffic jams, belching smokestacks, heavy equipment bulldozing the rainforest, parched desert ground, strip-mining, wildfires, aerosol cans spraying, garbage dumps . . . all the usual environmental flash images. It'll be great."

Griffin put down the magazine and stared through the windshield as Dalton steered the van up the coast highway toward the tony beach houses of Malibu and the promise of a useable environmental protest. As he did, the network's youngest field reporter mused softly, "Man versus nature. Nature wins. Film at eleven. A Griffin Gantry exclusive." He turned to Dalton. "Step on it. If we get some good blurbs from the protest group, I can step this up from a segment to a feature."

CHAPTER 2

Zeke surveyed his handiwork with pride. Sure, the group of twelve environmental protesters was a bit ragged-looking. And it was true that some of the signs they carried had smeared somewhat from the spray, especially earlier, before the sun had come out. But the protest march still was worthy of respect. For one thing, numbers weren't everything. Fervor was important. And every single person in the group was dedicated to the cause. Dedication to the cause always filled Zeke with pride.

Everything in life was transitory—apartments, clothes, hobbies, even friends. But the cause . . . the cause was an eternal struggle for a future that preserved the past. He was a foot soldier in that cause, a squad leader in the perpetual battles on behalf of Mother Nature. The fatigues he wore from the Army/Navy-surplus store down on Alameda Boulevard weren't just a physical manifestation of his commitment to recycling and his disdain for the waste that accompanied the fads of high fashion; they were a reflection of his soul.

As a minor leader in the environmental movement, he relished the thought of his small band of true believers making a difference in the world. Today was a notable skirmish in that effort; the twelve protesters trudged along the narrow beach near a fabulous, post-modern house jutting out from the cliff side. They carried signs that he and Brandon and Milo had made that very morning, protesting the El Niño–fueled storms that were ravaging the coastline and would soon undercut and imperil the magnificent beach house. Global warming fueled the storms. The owner of the beach house, movie star Matthew Barrington, fueled his environmental group, GreensWord.

Barrington gave GreensWord money, visibility, and the kind of star-appeal that drew media coverage and a constant supply of part-time volunteers. A large number of the recruits were women in their thirties who worried what the future held for their kids. They had flexible schedules that allowed them to spend an afternoon walking in circles. Of course, most of the middle-aged hausfraus were also, quite frankly, anxious for a chance to be associated with, and maybe even meet, a real movie stud, even one who could no longer open a picture as a leading man.

The protesters began another one of their series of singsong chants: "Global warming is no treat; Washington should feel the heat."

The wind and, eventually, the sun, had reddened their skin as they struggled along in the sand, but they trooped on despite the adversity, despite the fact that nature struggled to thwart their efforts to help her. Zeke read the signs again as they passed by, regarding their prose in the basking self-satisfaction of all writers. The signs ranged from the straightforward "Stop Global Warming," and "Save the Earth," to the self-promotional "GREENSWORD," to the catchy whimsy of "El Niño is Hot Stuff" and "Mother Nature is Really Pissed Now," to the stern "The Earth is One Big Superfund Site," and culminated in the blatant emotional appeal of "How Hot Will It Be For Our Children?"

Zeke's reverie of self-satisfaction was, however, interrupted by the sound of a slamming door and the sight of GreensWord's chief benefactor stalking past his sunbathing girlfriend, bounding down the deck stairs, and trudging across the deep sand toward him with a scowl on his famous face. Barrington was

stockier than he looked in the movies and not nearly so pleasant, even when he wasn't as pissed off as he apparently was
right now.

"I give you ten thousand dollars and this is what I get? Ten
lame-ass protesters and no news coverage?"

Barrington had moved in close, invading Zeke's personal
space, no doubt for dramatic effect, and was louder than he
needed to be, despite the stiff wind tearing at his words. But the
overall effect was nothing like it would have been in the movies.
For one thing, Barrington was a full head shorter than Zeke;
the star's going nose-to-nose with Zeke's sternum was really not
that intimidating.

Zeke tried to dial down the mood before he cracked a smile
and really pissed off the group's deep pocket.

"Twelve," he said casually, flexing his knees slightly to
decrease the difference in height between the two of them
without being obvious.

"What?" Barrington fumed, losing a bit of his head of steam.

"Twelve lame-ass protesters . . . all of them committed
environmentalists and . . . of course . . . Matthew Barrington
fans. Besides, I'm sure the press will be here any minute so they
have live coverage for the early evening news."

Barrington glanced over at the sign-toting protesters, apparently sizing up the women among the group, but did not seem
to be impressed by what he saw. He turned back to Zeke. "And
what's that going to accomplish?"

"Well, social awareness is the first step in a comprehensive
approach to. . . ."

"Blah, blah, blah, blah, blah. Is that all you have to say? I
don't have time for social awareness!" Barrington gesticulated
wildly, first flinging his arms at the thin strip of beach and the
waves that unceasingly assaulted the sand's tenuous purchase,
and then shoreward and upward toward his ostentatious abode.

22

"See that? See that house? That gloriously stupendous, but unbelievably expensive beachfront house? I did two fucking, crappy B-movie sequels . . . in the Czech Republic, for God's sake . . . to get that damn house. And it's going to fall into the fucking ocean if this erosion keeps up." He paused his tirade, as if waiting for the thunderous crash of an accommodating wave to punctuate his declamation, like it would have in the movies, but the timing was off.

Zeke would have smiled at the ridiculous rant and the mistimed crescendo, but this was his organization's main money man. He had to placate the guy. "Yes sir, Mr. Barrington. Y'see, the rising ocean temperatures cause a condition known as El Niño, which causes increased storms because of the high rate of evaporation of equatorial surface waters above eighty degrees. . . ."

Techno-babble apparently wasn't going to do the trick this time, because Barrington interrupted, twisting back towards him, inadvertently drilling his feet into the sand and losing a bit more height. "And what are you going to do about it?"

Zeke soldiered on. "Well, Mr. Barrington, climatic conditions like El Niño are long-term phenomena that can be reversed by a commitment to systematic change in industrial, transportation, and lifestyle habits. By acting now, global warming can be checked, even moved towards reversal, over the next two or three generations."

Barrington convulsed in anger, his arms flailing wildly, but his feet remained oddly stationary, caught by the soft sand. He lowered his voice, but focused it directly at Zeke. "Do I look like I give a damn about future generations? I'm a movie star! If I cared about future generations, I'd join the Peace Corps or teach retards or something."

"Differently-abled."

"What?" replied Barrington with a sharp, but confused look.

Zeke shrugged crookedly. "They don't call them retards. It's differently-abled."

Barrington's eyebrows tilted inward and he gave Zeke a steely, distasteful stare. "Look, retard, I didn't give you a bunch of *my* money so you could scratch your ass while you saunter along *my* beachfront ogling *my* girlfriend while giving *me* a hard time." Zeke started to reply, but Barrington cut him off. "You said you could do something about my problem."

Zeke made a deliberate effort to slow and calm his own speech patterns. He had seen on the Discovery Channel that doing so worked when you were approaching wild animals and he figured has-been movie stars were pretty much the same. "Well, yes," he said, his voice even and soothing, "I think mankind can make a difference if we all just join together. . . ."

"Screw that!" shouted Barrington, almost overbalancing himself as he gesticulated. He struggled for just a moment to loose his feet from the grip of the sand before continuing, gesturing broadly back toward the imposing, trophy mansion. "Twenty million dollars worth of glass and stucco is going to fall into the goddamn ocean unless something happens soon. Soon, do you hear? Can you solve my problem or not?"

Zeke could almost picture Barrington's money floating away on the brisk ocean breeze, flittering off into the hands of some slick, monstrous, corporate-style environmental group—the kind that produced glossy calendars and hired Washington lobbyists and practiced partisan politics . . . all in the name of the cause, but which did not feel the fervor of the cause the same way he and his little band of misfit environmental adventurers did. He couldn't let that happen.

"Absolutely, Matthew . . . er . . . Mr. Barrington. I'm sure we can come up with something that will make you very satisfied in an acceptable time frame."

Before Barrington could respond, Zeke's colleague, Milo,

sauntered up. Milo's long hair was bleached in splotchy streaks of blonde on brown by the sun and surf and tangled by the wind. He wore a garish Aloha shirt and wrinkled, khaki pants. The cheap, loose-fitting clothes made him look even more bedraggled than did Zeke's Army/Navy-surplus. But Milo, as always, seemed unconcerned about his appearance. Taller than Zeke, Milo would easily have dwarfed Barrington, but he casually stopped seaward, and thus downhill, of both of the others. He jerked his head over his left shoulder toward the public beach access a few hundred yards to the north. "Dude," he said laconically to Zeke, "the reporters are here."

Zeke screened his eyes on the shore side and looked up the beach. "Looks like Griffin Gantry and a cameraman." He turned back to Barrington, but the star of the silver screen had already dialed up a broad smile and was smoothing his hair into place as he headed toward the publicity.

Milo smiled slightly. "Dude, I told you that the reporters would wait 'til late afternoon for more oblique lighting from the ambient sunlight. It makes us look wild-eyed to the cameras, man." Milo opened his startlingly blue eyes wide, wagged his tongue, and shook his unruly hair.

Zeke smiled back, welcome for the break in the tension that had been building with their benefactor. "Is that what it is? Here I thought 'Movie Matty' was just mad as hell."

Milo looked over Zeke's head, where Zeke had seen Barrington's stunning playmate sunning herself on the deck of the actor's extraordinary house. Milo shrugged. "Nice digs. Nicer bed warmer. What's he have to be so ticked off about?"

Zeke shook his head in amazement. "Jesus, Milo, the environment! He's mad about the environment. That's why he gives us money, lots of money, because he wants something done about the environment."

Milo seemed to pull his gaze back from the curvaceous starlet to his organization's leader, but Zeke didn't have the impression that all of Milo's attention came along for the ride. "Well, yeah. But we're the ones schlepping around on a surprisingly rocky sand beach carrying these totally non-ergonomic signs around in the wind . . . for a career, man. The guy should show some appreciation. Seriously."

For the millionth time, Zeke wondered what GreensWord would ever do if he wasn't around to lead it. Everybody lost focus so readily; they didn't appreciate the practicalities of running an organization. He was about to say something when Brandon, the third core member of GreensWord, ran up.

Better dressed than Milo, Brandon wore tan slacks which sported a crease, a button-down shirt, and penny loafers without socks. His somewhat conservative haircut had been gelled into place—it remained perfect despite the wind. The out-of-date preppy fashion look was decidedly marred, however, by both the slightly apprehensive look on his face and the ever-present clipboard he was carrying. The result was something like a cross between a Sears summer catalog model and a Wal-Mart management trainee.

Once a geek, always a geek, thought Zeke. But, of course, the movement embraced everyone . . . except Republicans.

Brandon ignored Milo and looked directly at Zeke. "Anything special you want me to say to the cameras, fearless leader? They're practically set up." He motioned toward the north, where the cameraman was fiddling with a tripod, the camera mounted so that it would get the protesters in the background behind Griffin Gantry.

At least Brandon had some organizational skills, some enthusiasm, and was able to take direction. Zeke smiled re-assuringly. "Just the usual shtick. And get rid of that clipboard. You're supposed to look like a concerned citizen, not some advance man for Ralph Nader."

Milo interrupted. "Can Ralph even afford a clipboard?"

Dalton framed the shot with casual expertise: waves to his right; house to the left; protesters center back—close enough so the viewing audience would be able to read the signs, but far enough so the protesters' simplistic chanting wouldn't drown out the rich baritone of Griffin Gantry smooth-talking his way to a feature. Dalton positioned Griffin on the ocean-side of the interview subjects, which gave the star reporter's face even light and featured Griffin's supposedly good side—not that Dalton had ever seen a good side to the pompous newsie. The setup put the interview subjects squinting into the random flashes off the water caused by the setting sun and tumultuous surf, so they were lit from beneath, shadows flitting over their faces as they spouted whatever crap they were selling.

As everyone waited for him to check the light and sound levels, Dalton wasn't surprised that Griffin was ignoring the protest group's spokesperson and was instead chatting up Matthew Barrington. No doubt young Griffin was banking points for a future entertainment segment or trying to score an invite to a post-awards-show gala or somesuch. Funny, the production videographers, the guys who actually found the news and shot it, never got invitations to swanky parties with *foie gras* and bevies of buxom bimbos eager to please—that stuff was reserved for the talking heads . . . the talking empty-heads.

Finally, everything was set. Dalton gave his usual I'm-ready-when-you-are throat clearing and settled in behind the camera. Griffin adroitly concluded his private conversation with Barrington, checked his hair, smiled his professional best, and looked into the camera, one eyebrow arched just so.

Dalton used hand signals to count down the cue as Griffin adjusted the microphone in his hand with practiced ease so that the station logo would face toward the camera. He began.

"We're here with Brandon Connoway of the environmental action group, Green Sword."

The Connoway guy leaned in toward the mike in front of Barrington to interrupt. "That's Greens Word."

Crap, couldn't Griffin even get the organization's name right? There was five minutes' worth of editing to smooth that faux pas over, for sure. He should just call for another take, but Griffin would chew him out for disrupting his flow. So, for now, Dalton just let the camera run.

"I see," said Griffin in a smooth, even tone, arching his eyebrow further to mock the earnest young man, before he continued with just a tinge of condescension in his voice. "Greens Word. Of course. And what is the point of today's protest, Mr. Connoway? What is the Greens' word for the day?"

Connoway still leaned in toward the mike too much for Dalton's liking, but the guy at least moved quickly into his canned spiel—avoiding the "ums" and "ahs" and sentence fragments that so bedeviled news editors everywhere. "The point is that global warming is a fact and that mankind will not survive if it does not take steps now—meaningful, substantive steps—to reverse this march toward global extinction."

Dalton was not at all surprised when Gantry, having gotten a useable quote out of the no-name nerd, quickly shifted his attention to the more high-profile interview subject. Dalton tightened the shot to a "two frame" and motioned Connoway to move away to the left so he would not still be in the shot when Dalton widened it again for the closing wrap. Griffin's easy tone glided on just as smoothly as Dalton had smoothly adjusted the shot: "Matthew Barrington, star of the mega-blockbluster *Failed Mission,* is also here with the protesters today. Mr. Barrington, do you agree with Mr. Connoway?"

Barrington's posture was impeccable. Dalton noted that the actor stood on a small mound of sand, apparently pushed together during setup so as to make the diminutive star appear taller, but the posture was the real trick of a professional for simulating height. The movie star let the microphone come to him, trusting the technical crew to adjust sound as necessary back at the studio in post-production. When Barrington responded, he looked directly into the camera, rather than at Griffin—a nice, professional touch.

"Absolutely. Drastic action is needed. Extreme action. And we just can't wait any longer."

There was some more. Griffin asked a number of the usual softball questions about the environment generally tossed at celebrities at fund-raisers and independent film festivals, with only slight variations in theme. Barrington, naturally, responded with typical blather, delivered with a dollop of conscientious eco-fervor. Griffin, of course, nodded sagely during the answers no matter how devoid of content. But all that back-and-forth didn't really matter. Dalton already had what he needed. The rest was just for coverage, in case the equipment had glitched or the sound had over-peaked and they needed to fall back to a different response.

Finally, just before they lost the light of the setting sun, Griffin turned away from his interview subject and gave the camera his best "trust-me-I-know-more-about-this-subject-than-you-will-ever-know" look. "And so, nature continues to punish the Southern California coast for the environmental sins of both the past and the present, but a few hardy volunteers and their supporters and champions sound the clarion call for action before it is too late. Will our nation heed the call? Or will it stick its head in the eroding sand until it is too late? Only time will tell whether our grandchildren will live the California dream or suffer the penalties for our lives of excess. This is Griffin Gantry, protecting the environment. Protecting your future. Back to you in the studio."

"Stick its head in the eroding sand?" Gack! How was he going to edit around that atrocity? It was in the damn wrap and the sun had just set, meaning they had lost the light necessary to do a second go-around. It was getting so that these young talking heads couldn't even talk, couldn't even ad lib a simple wrap. One thing for sure, though, a phrase like "stick its head in the eroding sand" was bound to be a Griffin Gantry exclusive. No one short of George W. Bush could mangle a metaphor quite so badly, at least now that Dan Rather had quit the biz.

Dalton knew better than to say something, of course. He just stuck his head in the eroding sand, smiled artificially at his kid-boss and started disassembling the equipment. He had a long drive and lots of editing to do before the late news. He could plan out his tasks as he drove, if Griffin didn't whine the whole way back. The talent always whined if you gave them any excuse at all.

Zeke opened up the back of the ancient Minibus so that Brandon and Milo could toss in the signs the protesters had been carrying. Despite the smearing from the surf, some of the placards were reusable and all of the wooden sticks were. GreensWord was on a budget. That same budget, or lack thereof, was why Zeke, Brandon, and Milo, the three core members of the group, were still riding around in a junker van from Woodstock days.

As Zeke slammed the creaky back doors of the van shut, he noticed yet another rust-hole expanding on the door panel. He sighed and vowed to plaster an environmental bumper sticker over the hole, just like they had done with every other rust spot on the junker. They sported more "Save the Whales," "Make Love, Not Landfills," and "I Brake for Small Animals" stickers than he could count at this point. But the powerful glue on the stickers held like steel after a few weeks in the California sun and, given the van's age and the salt air, there was damn little real steel in the Minibus anymore.

Zeke walked around to the driver's door and got in. Brandon was riding shotgun, as usual, and had already buckled up for safety. Milo was sprawled in the back, playing some kind of hand-held video game, while he listened to tunes on his ever-present iPod. He dressed like a bum, but he always seemed to have money for portable electronic toys. Without taking off the ear buds, Milo gave Zeke a thumbs-up. "Not a bad day's work," he said, unnaturally loudly.

Brandon nodded in agreement. "I thought it went very well."

Zeke gave a brief nod in return, but grimaced as he did it, remembering his encounter with their benefactor. "Yeah," he said, "but we have a problem. A big problem." He looked back at Milo, but he, of course, appeared not to have heard anything. He just gave another thumbs-up sign and grooved to his tunes. Zeke brushed off Brandon's quizzical look with an "I'll tell you later," turned the key, and headed the van away from the tony neighborhoods with their spectacular views of the coast. He cruised inland toward GreensWord's dumpy headquarters, where the property values were low, at least for California, and the views were always depressing.

Something needed to be done.

CHAPTER 3

Milo slouched in the old, swivel desk chair in front of the screen of GreensWord's boxy, beige computer. He had one leg draped over the chair's worn arm as he leaned back with the keyboard in his lap. His other leg idly rotated the chair back and forth as his left hand ran nimbly over the keys and his right hand worked the mouse on the low table next to him with abandon. The computer was a low-end Quompat that Brandon's mom had gotten Brandon for his birthday eight years ago.

Milo hated it.

Given the pace of advancements in electronics, eight years was an eternity. Any computer that was eight years old was a piece-of-shit in Milo's mind, and this particular beige box hadn't even been the top of Quompat's line way back then. It was the kind of computer only a mother could love, with tinny little speakers and a crappy 3.5-inch-floppy port. The bulky fifteen-inch CRT monitor had a blink-rate that gave Milo a headache after six or seven hours. Worse yet, the computer was preloaded with the slow, buggy version of Macrosurf's god-awful operating system that had been about to go obsolete when the computer was purchased eight years ago from a cable shopping channel for twenty percent above what it could have been bought for at an electronics superstore.

The Quompat also lacked a decent sound card, an acceptable graphics card, and any capability to handle MP3s. Milo was forced to download the music for his iPod illegally at the university library like a damn freshman foreign exchange student. Even the illicit downloading wasn't likely to last much longer. His fake college I.D. was becoming less and less credible as he got older. Someone on the staff had even noticed he'd been coming in for more than four . . . now five . . . years at this point. He kept asking if Milo had switched majors.

Milo longed to chuck the Quompat, or at least upgrade the damn thing with parts that he could scrounge from better computers that other people were already tossing out in favor of state-of-the-art equipment, but Brandon didn't want him fussing with his mom's gift. Milo had surreptitiously over-clocked the processor to get a little juice out of the thing, but that was about it. Accordingly, he always got a bit crabby when his net-surfing was slowed down by the thing's pathetic lack of power.

The news story flickering in front of his eyes on the Internet news site didn't help his mood either. It featured the despised Macrosurf logo. He read the press blather with disgust.

"I can't believe that asshole, Nakajami, is trying to claim a patent on voice recognition technology. I don't care if he does have seventy-three billion freaking dollars. . . ."

Zeke looked up from the genuine Naugahyde recliner where he traditionally did his paperwork. The chair, Milo reflected, was three times as old as the computer and probably worth twice as much if they hauled it down to the flea market at the old drive-in movie parking lot. But Zeke didn't say anything about the comfy chair. He simply said "Eighty."

"What?" said Milo in confusion.

Zeke set down his papers. "Eighty billion dollars. The man has eighty billion dollars. The market is up. It's been up all month."

"Whatever," grumbled Milo.

"Look, I just figured if you are going to have a sworn enemy—a nemesis that haunts your every waking moment—you

33

might not want to underestimate the guy . . . or, at least, his fortune." Zeke glanced at his cheap digital wristwatch as Brandon wandered in from the kitchen. "Besides," Zeke said, "I thought we were going to watch ourselves on the news together." Their leader flipped on the television facing them all and tuned in the news, but left the sound muted.

Milo couldn't let the subject drop. "Seventy-three, eighty. It's clearly too much." He gestured at the undersized, yet bulky, CRT screen of the computer setup. "And now Macrosurf is suing Apple for infringing its patents in software developed for Macintosh users! Duh! As if anybody would rip off the crap Macrosurf foists on the world." His lip curled in a snarl. "Fascist dick-head!"

Zeke folded his arms and looked at Milo with a calm, penetrating gaze, the way Milo's Aunt Sissy used to when she caught him reading comic books when he was supposed to be studying. Zeke also spoke with the same condescending adult tone Aunt Sissy had used when mildly reprimanding him, but used words that never would have passed Aunt Sissy's Christian lips. "We are all, I quite assure you, fully-fucking-aware that you believe Goro Nakajami, software billionaire and principal owner of Macrosurf Technology, is a fascist dick-head. Now, can we focus on the damn cause, instead of our petty personal agendas, and watch the news together like civilized people?"

Milo would have let it go, even though he hated the whole greener-than-thou tone of leadership Zeke put out at times like these, but Brandon decided to jump in to defend Milo.

"Besides," said Brandon, "Nakajami's really evil act was buying the Seattle SuperSonics and renaming the team the Netsurfers."

It was like having your kid sister jump to your defense by quoting your frightened words of bravado to the school bully.

Zeke looked confused. "Evil? The 'Protesters Unlimited'

newsletter said the name change was yet another indication of the shift of industrial America from traditional manufacturing . . . such as building airplanes, hence the Seattle SuperSonics . . . to the new service economy of Internet America. A sad reflection on America's place in the world today, but I don't know why that would make the name change evil."

Milo could hold back the gathering diatribe no longer. "Never trust the media, dude. Not even the liberal media." He sat up in the desk chair, his left leg slipping off the arm, as he focused his energy on the debate. "Actually, the NetSurfer name is a play on the fact that us serfs carry the largest net burden of taxes to support the military industrial complex, while fat cats like Nakajami hire shysters so they pay nothing in taxes. . . ."

He was just getting into it when the argument ended the same way his arguments with the guys always ended.

"Shut up, Milo," said Brandon and Zeke in unison.

Milo glowered for a moment. Maybe this time he wouldn't just let things drop. But, then, Zeke pointed to the television screen and thumbed off the mute.

"Hey, enough propaganda. I think we're next." Zeke sat back in the recliner as the picture showed a graphic behind the local anchorman which read "Environmental Beach Protest."

All three of them leaned forward to savor their moment of notoriety, their noble blow for the cause, but their posture of anticipation went unrewarded. No beach scene appeared on screen. Instead, the anchorman suddenly said: "We were going to take you to an environmental protest in Malibu, but this breaking news just in . . . a high-speed chase on the Ten is. . . ."

Zeke muted the drivel to come and slammed down the remote control. "Great. That's just great. Barrington wants results. Now. And we get bumped for some drunk low-life who didn't want to be stopped for changing lanes without using his blinker."

Milo stared at the television screen. He loved this chase crap. It was just like one of his video games, except a lot slower and with a lot less carnage—though one could always hope. "Hey, man. Watch it. That could be my dad you're talking about."

Brandon took a step toward Zeke and picked up the remote. He started flipping stations, checking the other channels to see what was on. Milo started to protest, but there was no need. They all showed the same thing, just from slightly different perspectives.

"I don't believe this," said Brandon with disgust. "All the local networks are following the same stupid car chase."

Milo waved at Brandon. "Go back to KQZJ. They had a better angle from their chopper."

Zeke picked his paperwork back up with a weary sigh. "He's getting more press coverage than we got."

Brandon continued to fume. "I don't know which is more ridiculous, that the moron driving the beat-up Ford Taurus thinks he is going to escape with four helicopters and seventeen police cars watching his every move or that this is considered a newsworthy event. You'd think the news would cover stuff that actually mattered to people's lives."

Zeke looked up from his papers at Milo, whose eyes were still glued to the Trinitron screen. "Brandon has it right, big guy. These guys in the car chases are morons. There have been hundreds of these things broadcast in L.A. alone and do you ever, I mean ever, remember someone getting away?"

Milo flicked his eyes away from the spectacle for just a moment. "Well, no. . . ."

Brandon apparently chose to switch sides for the latest dispute. "Zeke's gospel. Criminals never plan ahead. I mean, look at DNA evidence—you'd have to be practically brain-dead not to know it exists, what with the O.J. trial, the death row reversals those kids from Northwestern got, and all the CSI-type forensics shows on TV—but crooks are always getting caught because of blood or hair or some microscopic piece of dust or something at the scene of the crime."

Milo responded without taking his eyes from the chase. Yeah, they'd replay anything good in slo-mo, but nothing beat seeing the chase develop live. "Dude, there's gotta be a way to beat it."

Brandon tapped his fingers idly. "No way. You can't help but leave something behind."

Milo shot Brandon a dubious frown. "Hey, O.J. got off, didn't he?"

Brandon winced. "Yeah, but I don't think that the guys robbing the local fast-food joints are rich, famous ex-football stars with expensive defense teams and unemployed actors staying in their guest houses."

That last phrase distracted Milo from the chase for a moment. "Hey, did Kato have a sweet deal or what? Very *Magnum, P.I.* Hang out in the guest house of a rich dude and wait to be discovered. . . ." It was everything Milo craved in a lifestyle. "Do you think Barrington would take me in? Sauna, veranda, heated pool—all very chi-chi. He probably has a kick-ass computer network built in. Wireless, dude, wireless! I could access the Net from poolside and take a dip to cool off whenever I wanted."

Zeke harrumphed from the easy chair. "I think Barrington would drain and refill his pool if you fell in it."

Brandon put down the remote. "Look, I'm sure the news will pick up our protest at eleven. That's what's important. No one watches the early news anymore anyhow. They're either at work or it's on against Oprah. The guy in the rusting Taurus will crash or run out of gas by eleven. And I thought our bit was pretty good copy, even if I do say so myself. Even Barrington came off as committed."

Milo continued to watch the chase as he talked. "Yeah, what

was it he said? 'Drastic measures, man. Extreme measures. Now.' He is the king of short sentences. Very demanding."

Zeke put down his paperwork again. He looked serious. "But that's what I haven't told you guys yet. Barrington is demanding. He's going to cut our funding if we don't get results. Soon."

Brandon waved a hand lightly in dismissal. "Don't worry, fearless leader. The clip will be on at eleven. That's a major media coup. Do you know how many people in greater L.A. watch this station for late news?" He pulled out a clunky calculator, the kind that you got for free from credit card companies if you paid four-ninety-five in shipping and handling—a gadget so uncool that Milo knew it must have been another present from Brandon's mom—and began to punch in numbers as he continued. "If even ten percent of them make one less car trip because of this, why . . . why it will mean. . . ."

Zeke reached out a hand to stop the useless calculating. "That's not what he means by results. He doesn't want a slight reduction in car trips among watchers of KQZJ in the Southland. He wants results. He wants global warming to be stopped. Now."

Brandon stopped ciphering, but didn't put the calculator down. "Look, in the next two decades. . . ."

"Now!" said Zeke with finality. "He was very insistent. He needs to see something meaningful now or we lose our funding."

Brandon shrugged, showing no concern. "So, we'll get other funding."

The topic had taken a turn that was suddenly more interesting to Milo than a Ford Taurus' lazy weaving through surprisingly light traffic on the Ten. "Man, I can't work for any less." He pointed at an open can perched at a precarious angle on a pile of papers near the computer. "I'm eating dolphin-safe tuna fish as my dinner entree now."

Brandon chimed in with his usual dig. "Carnivore."

Milo took the bait. "Damn straight. Besides, all your tofu and vegan crap is expensive."

Brandon looked at Milo with an air of superiority. "Principles, my friend, are always expensive. But a lack of principles is even more expensive." Milo sneered slightly in response, but said nothing. "Besides," Brandon continued, "what's the big deal? So, maybe we get jobs in the real world for a couple of weeks until some new funding comes through."

"It could be more than a few . . . ," started Zeke, but Milo cut him off.

"Jeez, dude! Why do you think I do this? The real world is controlled by feudal lords like Nakajami, sucking the life out of their toiling serfs."

Zeke moved quickly in an apparent effort to subdue Milo's coming rant. "Milo, I've told you a million times. It's Macrosurf . . . S-U-R-F, not serf, S-E-R-F."

Milo would not, however, be so readily quieted. "That's what they want you to believe, man. Their little joke. I'll bet he's laughing his ass off right now in his sixty-room house in the shadow of Mount Rainier."

"Sixty-five," said Zeke with preternatural calm. "He's got a sixty-five-room house."

Now Milo really was pissed. "Whatever. Look, all I know is that this is my life, man. No chick in SoCal will go out with an unemployed computer jockey, not since the post-bubble tech revival. They figure he must molest kids or be a has-been from a reality show or something or he'd have a real job. Even wanna-be actors have real jobs—waiting tables or some other minimum-wage crap. But an environmental warrior for Greens-Word . . . that excuses the natural appearance, the small apartment, the encouragement of going dutch. We gotta do something. Now."

Brandon looked at him earnestly. "For the good of the planet," he said, with stolid environmental fervor.

"Whatever," said Milo, his diatribe winding down. "I just need to get laid regularly or I get cranky." He picked up a plastic fork and chased down the last chunk of tuna in the opened can, then snatched up a Twinkie for dessert.

Zeke spread his hands, palm down in an apparent motion to quiet his two colleagues. He looked as if he wanted to speak, but was resisting the urge. Finally, he shut his file folder, set it on the coffee table, and got up. "Look," he said with clearly faux casualness, as he grabbed his cap, "take the weekend off. Think of something. We'll regroup on Monday." He hesitated for a moment before continuing. "Me, I'm going to watch the eleven o'clock news from home."

Milo watched Zeke depart. The dude always took their banter too seriously. He always took everything too seriously. The guy was gonna get an ulcer or go postal or turn into a jerk or something else bad if he didn't watch it. As the door shut, Milo turned to his friend Brandon.

"Zeke is way too tense, man."

Brandon shrugged. "Hey, that's why he's in charge. If you were in charge, nothing would get accomplished."

Milo looked at Brandon. "Never let your work become your identity, dude," he said, as seriously as he had ever said anything. "Nothing good can come of it."

CHAPTER 4

Brandon's weekend routine never varied. On Friday nights he watched *Monk* on television while he paid his bills and tidied up his apartment, although he wasn't really expecting any visitors. He watched the late news, then went to the basement to do his laundry. Rather than running up and down from his place to change loads, he usually brought along a book and sat in one of the indestructible, molded plastic chairs scattered about the fluorescent-lit, concrete-block room to read.

On Saturdays, he rode his exercise bike while watching reruns on TV Land, then visited his parents. He almost always took his mom shopping at the mall nearby, then browsed through one of the mega-bookstores while she had her hair done at an overpriced salon where everyone spoke with an accent, real or affected, that Brandon couldn't understand. After dinner with his folks, who clucked disapprovingly about his vegan habits, he stopped by the local Blockbuster and rented a few DVDs.

On Sundays, he watched the morning political interview shows over a breakfast of hot Kashi and organic orange juice, then went to his parents' Lutheran church. Afterwards, he ran errands and dropped by the local library to read some more and pick up a book or two for the week.

The high point of this particular weekend was seeing himself, albeit fleetingly, on the late Friday news, sandwiched between a story on the disintegrating Russian economy and one on health code violations at various fast-food chains. Unfortunately, his

41

mom and dad had missed his big appearance—they went to bed early—but he taped it and left them a VHS cassette when he went over on Saturday. They couldn't watch it right away—his dad had run the VHS with the dust cover on again and fried the thing—but they promised to watch it as soon as they got their machine fixed.

He finished up a book on statistics and returned it to the library, along with a book on self-help techniques he had read earlier in the week. He started reading a volume he had picked up on public-relations strategies.

Both Saturday's DVDs and Sunday's sermon were predictable and forgettable, just like the rest of his life, except, of course, what he did for GreensWord. That, he was convinced, would make a difference in the world.

Zeke's weekend routine never varied. On Friday nights he went over GreensWord's financial reports, which Brandon produced for him every Thursday, printed crisply on 100-percent-recycled paper. Then he went to bed depressed.

On Saturdays, he went to the university library to read all of the latest research on environmental matters. Sometimes he would hook up with a girl and head for a local coffeehouse that featured live folk music, but he usually ended up at whatever activist rally or documentary film festival was posted *ad nauseum* on the various kiosks and bulletin boards around campus. Whether at the coffeehouse, a rally, or the university auditorium, the evening always ended the same—talking activism and politics into the wee hours of the night with anyone who would listen.

On Sundays, he ran errands and did the minimal chores he needed to do in order to maintain his simple life, then spent the rest of the day planning GreensWord's upcoming efforts while the Discovery Channel showed nature videos in the background.

This weekend, he had gone over the details of the declining financial position of his organization while he watched Brandon and Matthew Barrington on the news, read a portion of a Carl Sagan biography, watched a Discovery show about the volcanic eruption at Krakatoa, and chatted up one of the leaders of the campus women's alliance, who had ended up more interested in talking about the effectiveness of mass demonstrations than in either the coffee or him.

Life sucked and was getting suckier all the time. He knew most protesters were, by necessity, unhappy people. Contented people didn't complain. But if things kept going the way they were headed, he was going to be one damn-fine protester.

Milo's weekend routine never varied. Fridays, Saturdays, Sundays—they were all the same to him. All he wanted to do was blow things up and get laid.

Accordingly, he spent more than half the weekend glued in front of his computer terminal, playing *Deaf-Mute Commandos* and *Terrorist Threat,* first-person shoot-'em-ups that left his thumbs calloused, his eyes red, and all of his opponents nuked out of existence.

Whenever he finished a level or got bored—day or night—he would rummage around his pile of laundry for a Hawaiian shirt that smelled reasonably clean, then go find a place to pick up women. The places varied: ice cream shops; the beach; the mall; dance clubs. It didn't matter. Milo had an easy charm and a non-threatening attitude that worked with women of a certain age, from about twenty to twenty-four or so: women who were experienced and confident, but not yet settled down with a family or beaten down by the numbing forces of the workplace.

Just like in his computer games, Milo liked the chase and he liked to score. Saturday's score? Three levels in *Terrorist Threat* and two romantic liaisons—a receptionist who had been rollerblading near the beach and a wanna-be actress from a new ice cream place where they mixed the toppings into the high-fat frozen confections while singing show tunes.

CHAPTER 5

Zeke sat on the worn couch at GreensWord's headquarters and dispiritedly shuffled through the organization's financial statements one more time. His mind had been churning all weekend, but the prospects of the group, his group, were bleak and getting bleaker. Not only was it a distinct possibility the group would fold—he couldn't afford to pay even minimal salaries to the three of them for more than a few more weeks—but he had not garnered enough attention, enough headlines, to generate interest from other potential backers. Nor had he established enough of a personal profile or demonstrated sufficient leadership abilities to market himself as a credible activist organizer for one of the bigger, corporate environmental groups, assuming he could stomach it.

He couldn't sell out even if he wanted to.

Worse yet, GreensWord had not yet made a difference in the world, had not yet had a perceptible impact on the cause, and that is what he burned for. If something didn't happen soon, his group, his livelihood, and his cause—all he ever lived and worked for—would be lost.

He looked again at his staff and his depression grew. Milo was at the computer, as usual, fighting cyber-monsters in some stupid game world. Brandon was sitting at the kitchen table, reading and tapping a pencil against his ever-present clipboard.

"Jeez, Brandon" said Zeke with more edge to his voice than

he really intended, "tell me again why you aren't a school teacher?"

Brandon looked up at him, matter-of-factly. He shrugged his shoulders as he began to answer. "How many people does a school teacher influence over the course of their career? Hundreds, maybe thousands?"

Zeke simply stared at Brandon. It was just like Brandon to answer a rhetorical question with statistics.

Brandon continued before turning back to his book. "It's not enough to have any real impact on the world."

The simple, offhand statement struck Zeke with a primal force. Brandon was a true believer. He wanted the same thing from GreensWord that Zeke sought. It gave Zeke a moment of hope.

But then Milo glanced up from the computer, swinging his scraggly hair back from in front of his face. He looked around the room, as if he were counting people. "Oh, yeah, man. You're sure influencing more people with this gig."

And there it was. A bald statement of Zeke's failure as a leader, as an environmentalist. His hope, his pride in his work, crumbled back to unmitigated despair.

Zeke nodded slowly in admission as he started to reply to Brandon. "Here you have a rapt audience of. . . ."

The tinny sound of an explosion vibrated out of the Quompat's speakers, a rolling bass punctuated by static. Milo whipped his attention back to the screen. "Bummer! The terrorists just fried my commando team. Time to reset." He grabbed the plastic joystick that dated from the days the Quompat was produced, punched a button, and immediately started manipulating the controls furiously.

Zeke's eyes turned away from Milo and back toward Brandon. ". . . one," he whispered.

Brandon raised his head from his book, a look of mild confusion clouding his countenance. "I'm sorry. Did you say something?"

"Nothing important," said Zeke, his voice soft and tired. He sat upright with a weary groan and waved his arms a bit to gain the attention of his companions before continuing, speaking more loudly, in his best "boss" voice. "Okay guys. . . ." He gestured dismissively at the computer. "Milo, turn that off, will you?"

Milo hit a control on the joystick that made the action freeze in mid-explosion, then reached over to the computer terminal and pressed a button. The gory animation disappeared and the screen went dark.

Time to be a leader, thought Zeke. "Did anyone discover something new over the weekend?"

There was a long pause.

"Anything?" pressed Zeke, sounding a bit desperate, even to himself.

Milo raised his hand to draw Zeke's attention. "I . . . uh. . . . Yeah, I . . . uh . . . think Rocky Road is an aphrodisiac."

Zeke exhaled heavily. Brandon rolled his eyes.

"Something," Zeke corrected, "relevant to our problem."

Brandon, ever so eager to please, spoke up. "Well, according to some of the material I've been reading recently, if the average adult repeats something twelve times, it becomes ingrained as a habit."

"Is that why they're all called 'twelve step' programs?" Milo riffed.

"I'm serious," Brandon responded with a huff. "If you repeat something twelve times. . . ."

"The Candyman shows up," joked Milo, "or maybe the ghost from *Beetlejuice*?" He smiled broadly, obviously having a good time at Brandon's expense. "Or maybe. . . ."

Zeke shot Milo a look that said "Shut up, Milo" as clearly as if he had said it out loud. Milo closed his mouth and folded his hands on his lap.

Brandon had waited for both of them to look at him before he continued. "Look, all I'm saying is that psychological studies show that if we could get millions of people to do something small, but meaningful, for the environment twelve days in a row, then they'll likely keep doing it out of habit and we'll have a measurable impact on the environment in our lifetimes."

Zeke despaired. GreensWord had trouble getting someone to do something small for the environment once, much less twelve times. This didn't sound helpful.

An apparently chastened Milo, however, now seemed to be making an effort to take the conversation seriously. "The question then, Brandon, is: How do you get millions of people to do something twelve times?"

There was another pause. This wasn't getting them anywhere.

"Add it to the steps in the *Macarena*," said Zeke, oozing sarcasm. Nobody laughed, so he quickly continued on to cover the silence. "Guys, I don't think that this is what we are looking for."

Brandon straightened his back slightly, looking perturbed that now both of them were ganging up on him. "It's statistically significant according to my reading."

Zeke spread his hands in conciliation and softened his tone. There was no reason to piss off the only two people in the world who actually considered him to be an environmental leader. "It's just that. . . . Look, unless you are going to get millions of people to start walking to work every day, I can't see how we could have a measurable impact in a decade . . . much less before Barrington gets tired of waiting and decides to cut off our funding."

Milo bobbed his head in agreement. "He did seem pissed when I came over to you guys on the beach, man."

"Yeah," said Zeke to Milo. He turned to Brandon. "People aren't going to stop driving their cars or do anything else that inconveniences them. People are selfish and lazy."

But Brandon didn't back off. "It doesn't have to inconvenience them."

Milo responded without hesitation. "That'll be a first for the environmental movement."

Brandon furrowed his brow in concentration. Milo started playing with a rubber band—a sign that he was in full think-mode also.

Zeke was surprised. He had somehow managed to stumble his way into the most serious discussion of environmentalism that the group had had in months. Everyone was participating and thinking . . . and coming up with exactly nothing.

Finally, Brandon broke the lengthening silence. "There is this guy at a think-tank that says the greenhouse effect can be reversed by painting things white."

"Huh?" said Zeke and Milo in unintended unison.

"It's really simple," said Brandon, shifting into a stilted, professorial tone. "The earth's got a low albedo. . . ."

"The earth's got a low sex drive?" blurted out Milo. Zeke shot him another look and he quickly shut up.

Brandon took the question seriously. "Not a low libido . . . a low albedo. It's dark in color and therefore soaks up most of the sunlight that falls on it."

"Clouds are white, man. There are lots of clouds," murmured Milo. Zeke would have given him another stern look, but he believed the goof was actually being serious for the moment.

Brandon again took the point seriously. "Not all the time." He stood and began pacing back and forth behind the kitchen table as he talked, punctuating his points animatedly as he got into it. "Look, according to what I read, the trapping effect of all the greenhouse gases ever produced is equal to one-thousandth of the incoming solar energy. If the earth's albedo could be changed so that it reflected back one-thousandth more of the sunlight than it is reflecting now, then that extra amount of reflection would balance out the impact of the greenhouse gases. It would eliminate the effect of greenhouse gases on global warming. If even more extra sunlight could be reflected, it would begin to actually cool the planet."

"We could have a cool planet?" asked Milo in faux innocence.

"Absolutely," declared Brandon without irony.

Milo apparently decided to press on. "Dude, are you sure this isn't some bullshit idea of the white supremacist movement to justify killing off the black man?"

Brandon clearly didn't know when he was being mocked. High school had probably immunized him. "I don't think the total reflective surface represented by the tops of people's heads is statistically significant, especially . . . ," he said with apparently mounting glee at having discovered an effective counterargument, ". . . especially when most people are indoors most of the time. Besides," he finished with a flourish, "most people have dark hair anyway."

Milo turned to Zeke; he seemed to be trying to bring Zeke in on the fun. "Dude, you realize that this means that blondes are actually good for the environment?"

Zeke smiled condescendingly at Milo. "Hoody hoo!" he said sarcastically. "Peroxide rules." He turned back to Brandon. Maybe Brandon had something here. Maybe GreensWord could change the world. Maybe he wasn't a complete failure. "How much reflective surface do we need?"

Brandon thought for a moment. "I think it was about a thousand square feet per person. That's a fifty by twenty foot square."

"That's bigger than my apartment, dude!" blurted Milo.

Zeke motioned yet again for Milo to be quiet. "Yeah. But

maybe we could start small."

There was a prolonged silence as all of their minds churned, searching for the idea that would save GreensWord by saving the world from global warming.

"What faces up all the time?" murmured Zeke softly.

"Roofs," said Brandon in a brief moment of excitement. "Roofs face up."

"Yeah," agreed Zeke, "but shingles are made out of tar, aren't they? I've never heard of white tar."

Another moment passed in silence, as their excitement began to wane.

"Car roofs," said Brandon, his excitement rekindled. "We get people to paint all their car roofs white."

"That would work," agreed Zeke, "but how do we do that?"

Milo leaped up from his chair, sending the ancient joystick for the computer skittering across the floor until the cord brought it to an abrupt stop.

"Dudes! I've got it! The idea that will save the world!"

Four helicopters fly low over an L.A. expressway, tracking a white stretch limousine speeding down the highway. The first, a police chop-per, flies at a higher, safer altitude, from which it can see not only the stylish limousine, but also the upcoming traffic and ramps, as well as the phalanx of police cars following close behind the limo in hot pursuit at speeds in excess of 110 miles per hour. The other three helicopters are news choppers. They jockey and vie for the best angle to cover the high-speed chase. All three stations' cameramen do their best to keep the roof of the speeding, weaving car centered in their video lenses, as close-in as they can.

Printed neatly on the roof of the car, in glittering, golden, sparkling paint are the words: "If all cars were white, global warming would end. GreensWord"

All over the Southland, televisions are tuned to the dramatic scene.

Millions of viewers are enthralled by the chase—there's never been a pursuit with a limo before, nor a chase this long, at least not at these breathtaking speeds. Live feed streams to the networks for inclusion in the upcoming evening news. Griffin Gantry and his news brethren provide a constant patter of commentary on the chase and, as it continues into its fifth hour, an increasing amount of commentary on global warming and this simple solution for saving the world. The scientist from the think-tank is contacted and brought into the studio to explain the theory. Graphic artists at the news stations design diagrams to explain the concept of albedo and the impact of reduced sunlight on earth's climate. Environmental groups are brought in to endorse the concept and sing the praises of GreensWord and its enlightened leadership.

Hundreds of thousands of people turn out to line the roadway and cheer the limo onward. They carry signs and placards mimicking the message on the limo. Others, far from the site of the chase, race from their homes and grab buckets of paint from their garages and car ports and begin painting the roofs of their cars. Global warming is stopped, then reversed, and GreensWord becomes world renowned. Griffin Gantry remembers how to pronounce its name and, better yet, GreensWord receives the Nobel Peace Prize for preventing the extinction of the human race without the need for expensive or controversial measures. As the award is announced, billions of citizens rush outside—all of them have bleached their hair blonde—and shout in unison: "Milo! Milo! Milo!"

Zeke looked in bafflement at Milo, who was jumping up and down on the couch and gesticulating with wild abandon as he concluded his story. "Dude, why are they shouting your name? The albedo thing wasn't even your idea."

"Yeah," piped in a clearly irritated Brandon, "and your sign wasn't even accurate. It's an exaggeration. Car roofs alone aren't big enough to create the effect needed."

Milo stared at them dumbfounded. "It's advertising, dude. No one expects it to be literally true. Expand your mind. See the possibilities."

Zeke shook his head briefly. "I don't know. . . ."

"Dude, be a leader, man. It's for the movement."

Zeke knew Milo was pushing his buttons, but damn it, he knew what buttons to push.

"Okay, for the movement."

CHAPTER 6

"Who'd of thought we would have to wait two days for sunshine, dudes? I mean, this is California!" Milo sat on the roof of the Minibus, a can of white, latex house paint teetered next to him. He was slathering the milky white liquid on the roof with a rag, a wide grin on his face. The van sat on the driveway short of the carport to the GreensWord headquarters—actually a tract house in a relatively run-down suburban subdivision. The sun beat down from a clear blue sky that tinged brown toward the horizon from pollution.

Brandon looked at the messy scene with disgust. The paint was rolling over the curved slope of the roof and dripping down the sides of the van. He backed off a few steps to make sure that he didn't get his Dockers spattered, even though he knew the paint would clean up with soap and water. He wrinkled his nose as he answered: "If you hadn't bought such cheap, crappy paint, we wouldn't have to worry so much about the weather. And besides, moron, the El Niño storms that are causing the bad weather are why we need to stop global warming." Milo dunked the rag in the paint can and slopped it back onto the roof with a wet thud, splashing paint onto Brandon's loafers. "I really wish you would pay attention to what you're doing," continued Brandon.

Milo bobbed his eyebrows and shoulders in unison, apparently unconcerned. "Someday soon, the entire world will pay attention to what we're doing. Besides, I'm almost done here.

We'll be ready to roll in less than an hour."

Zeke, who was watching from the shade of the carport, looked up. "Don't we have to wait for the white paint to dry before we can do the lettering for the sign?"

Milo smiled as he finished up his slathering and slid off the car roof holding the open can of paint, sloshing some onto the cracked, concrete driveway. "No problemo, fearless leader." He put down the paint container and strode toward the door which went from the carport to the house. "I had to do something while it was raining. I got stalled on the ninth level of *Terrorist Threat*. Brandon's crappy computer has such slow reaction to that stupid joystick that I just can't off the gang that takes over the passenger train; no matter what I do, it ends up derailing. It's like the bad guys got Uzis and I got a freakin' crossbow or something, it takes so long between shots."

Milo passed Zeke and reached into the doorway, pulling out a piece of white poster board with lettering from a black marker in Milo's inimitable, messy penmanship. He also grabbed a roll of silver duct tape. He held the sign up proudly for Zeke and Brandon to read.

"White . . . white . . . something or other . . . stop global warming: GreensWord," read Brandon aloud. "What's the second word? It's completely illegible."

Zeke squinted at the sign and nodded in apparent agreement.

Milo looked down from above at the sign he was holding. "Roofs, guys, it says roofs. I can even read it upside down."

Zeke tilted his head heavily to his left side. "That does help," he said quietly.

Brandon folded his arms and gave Milo a squint-eyed look. "How is this supposed to promote our cause if it can't even be read? Aside from the atrocious penmanship, the sign's tiny in

55

comparison to the van roof. How will anybody in the choppers read it?"

Milo sauntered toward the van, tossing the sign up onto the roof atop the already clearly drying paint. "Dude, you have to think dramatically. It'll drive the newsies crazy trying to figure out what it says. Griffin Gantry will prattle on about it for twenty minutes. Viewers will pause their DVRs and zoom in to try to figure it out. We'll not only give them a chase, we'll give them a puzzle—a virtuous message wrapped in a complete entertainment package!" He grinned broadly as he used the back bumper to boost himself up onto the van roof again and began tearing off long strips of duct tape.

Brandon looked dubious. "I don't know. It's still pretty small. . . ."

Milo chuckled. "A phrase, my man, that I am not familiar with. Besides, dude, the whole point of this is that the roof of the van is white. The message is lost if the white roof is practically obliterated by black lettering."

Zeke bobbed his head up and down. "He's got you there, Brandon. Besides, this is Milo's scheme—he's the one looking at jail time for not stopping for Highway Patrol—it's his call."

"See," said Milo to Brandon, "my call, man. You just get in your mom's car so you can provide blocking when I need it." He jumped back down from the Minibus and shoved his hand into the pocket of his decrepit, paint-spattered jeans, pulling out a walkie-talkie. He pushed down the talk button and spoke into it. "It'll be just like *Smokey and the Bandit.* That's a big Ten-Four to you, good buddy."

Milo's voice boomed from the front pocket of Brandon's Dockers, along with a squeal of feedback and a burst of static. Brandon winced and started heading for his mom's Oldsmobile at the curb without responding. He fished out his walkie-talkie and tossed it through the open driver's side window onto the dash before getting in.

Zeke followed, looking back over his shoulder at Milo before he got into the old-fogey-mobile on the passenger side. "Don't waste the batteries, okay?" He snatched up the walkie-talkie from the dash before buckling up at Brandon's insistence.

Milo jammed the walkie-talkie back into his jeans and clambered into the Minibus, adjusting the seat for his lanky frame and popping in the ear buds for his iPod.

Brandon waited for Milo to pull out of the driveway and start down the block before he followed. "You know," he said to Zeke as they got up to speed, "I expect GreensWord to pay for it if my mom's car gets damaged."

Zeke closed his eyes for a moment, so Brandon wouldn't see them roll. Nobody focused on the big picture. He took a deep breath and counted silently to ten, before replying. "Sure, Brandon."

"And it would be polite to top off the tank before we return the car."

Zeke sighed. "Fine, but we're not springing for premium. All that octane hype is bullshit."

They followed the Minibus for several miles down residential streets. Brandon let Milo get a couple blocks lead, just like, Zeke was sure, Brandon had seen so many times on cop shows on television. Unfortunately, that meant that Zeke and Brandon didn't see the problem right away, when Milo stopped at the light at the edge of a commercial district. The bright green grass at the Wendy's on the near right corner should have been a giveaway, but Milo somehow missed it. The heavy metal on his iPod meant he also missed the sound of the water falling onto the van as the overactive sprinkler system angled onto the van from the right rear, before hitting its stopping point and reversing course.

It was a long light and pale white water was trickling down the back of the van before Zeke was even sure what was happening.

Zeke shouted into the walkie-talkie for Milo to get out of the spray, but he got no response. Brandon caught on and gunned the Oldsmobile in an attempt to catch up, but then the light turned green and the Minibus lurched off. Grayish white water flowed off of it as it made the turn.

Milo was looking forward to his moment of glory. He had imagined it all in his head. Now he turned onto one of the main commercial drags in the area and gunned the feeble Minibus motor as he approached a highway overpass. There was a doughnut place nearby that saw to its security needs in the iffy neighborhood by plying the patrolmen with free coffee. There was almost always a cruiser parked beneath the underpass with a couple bored cops sipping hot joe while they waited for speeders.

He pressed the accelerator to the floor and attempted to shift into third as he approached the ramp to the expressway. He would pick up some mild g-forces as he wheeled onto the curve of the ramp, but the Minibus wasn't top-heavy like the current SUV death traps. It wouldn't roll over and he would have good speed for commencing the highway chase.

Unfortunately, the Minibus's aging transmission balked at going into third and he lost momentum as he struggled with the gears. He laid on the horn as he passed the cops in order to bait them, but the Minibus just made a tinny squeak. He would have yelled at the cops—something witty like "Oink, oink" sprang to mind—but when he turned to his right to shout, he noticed that the passenger window was closed. Strangely, it seemed to have milky water droplets on it.

★ ★ ★ ★ ★

Brandon did a rolling right turn on red at the light and gunned the big car. It wasn't a sports car, but it clearly had the muscle to overtake the anemic Minibus. Zeke kept shouting in the walkie-talkie and Brandon laid on the horn to get Milo's attention as they passed a doughnut store near the underpass. As Milo steered the Minibus onto the ramp, Brandon cut over from the left lane to follow. He saw the red lights flash on atop the police cruiser as they passed it. The siren followed in quick succession. Brandon swerved onto the acceleration lane as the Minibus pulled away. Meanwhile, Zeke was yelling "Abort! Abort! Abort!" into the walkie-talkie like a crazed squad leader in a bad action flick.

As the police officers approached the car, Brandon raised his hands and put them behind his head. "Put down the walkie-talkie and keep your hands in sight," he urged his camouflage-wearing companion in a low voice, without turning toward him. "I'm not getting shot over this. I'm letting my mom kill me, instead."

Looking into the rearview mirror, Milo saw what was happening. He snatched the ear buds of his iPod out. The words "Abort! Abort! Abort!" and a burst of static sprang muffledly from the area of his groin. He heeded Zeke's instruction and let up on the accelerator. After a bit of effort and a certain amount of weaving across lanes as he fished in his pocket to dislodge the walkie-talkie, with its protruding, stubby antenna, from his jeans, Milo tried calling back, but no one answered. So he got off at the next exit and circled back to GreensWord headquarters, disappointed.

It was almost dusk before Zeke and Brandon returned. Brandon was clearly pissed and Zeke was just as clearly tired of putting up with Brandon being pissed. Zeke plopped down on the couch with a grunt as Brandon stormed up to Milo, who had used the intervening hours to shower and change clothes and was now snacking at the kitchen table.

"Three tickets! Reckless driving, failure to signal a lane change, and a noise reduction violation for improper use of a horn!" Brandon flung the citations down on the kitchen table.

Milo picked them up, but didn't really look at them. "Don't worry, dude. If you send in a check, even for a lot less than the actual fines, the flunkies that process the mail will probably just mark 'em off as paid. Less paperwork for them; higher productivity."

"That's . . . that's dishonest," Brandon sputtered.

"No duh," replied Milo with a smile.

"I'm not adding fraud to my rap sheet," squawked Brandon, "and, besides, the *money* isn't why I'm pissed."

"Ohhh," drawled Milo. "Don't worry about the plan. We'll try again tomorrow."

"I'm not," Brandon fumed, "trying again tomorrow. I'll be lucky if my mom ever lets me borrow her car again."

Milo looked perplexed. "So don't tell her, dude. You have to learn to deal with your parental units."

Brandon just glared at Milo. Zeke cut in to explain. "The Highway Patrol called his mom. He wasn't driving his own car—they had to make sure it wasn't stolen. Why do you think this took all afternoon?"

"Oh," said Milo, momentarily chagrinned. He shrugged it off quickly, however. "So, we'll do it without the chase car. It couldn't go any worse."

"Not for me, maybe," snapped Brandon, "but it could for you. Maybe something like. . . ."

A lone police helicopter tracks a beat-up Minibus as it careens at a moderate pace down a side-street. The telephone lines and overhang-

ing trees force the copter to fly high to remain safe. A small, white rectangle on the top of the roof has smeared, almost illegible black writing, which, in a blowup of a police photograph introduced into evidence at trial, is later shown to read: "White [something freaking illegible] stop global warming: GreensWord." The message is lost, however, amongst the innumerable environmental bumper stickers which hold the rusting Minibus together and are peeking through the partially washed off paint-job like teenage acne through Clearasil.

Police blockades and the Minibus's balky transmission conspire to keep the vehicle off of any major thoroughfares. When the police surge in from the front, back, and sides to make the stop, a panicky Milo Stanczyk, who is already wanted in four states for sending illegal e-mails to computer wunderkind and billionaire Goro Nakajami, jumps the curb, veering into a park, tearing up the begonias and running down a nine-months pregnant woman . . .

. . . pushing a baby carriage . . .

. . . with identical twins . . .

. . . adopted from Sri Lanka . . .

. . . after surviving the tsunami . . .

. . . while she is on a charity walk to raise money to fight cancer . . .

. . . among the homeless . . .

. . . from New Orleans.

Griffin Gantry does a thirty-second bit on the early news about how a loving mother and two orphans were brutally run down by a scruffy radical who deserved much worse than merely a criminal conviction for multiple counts of vehicular homicide. Homeys in the joint decide Stanczyk is a white supremacist and end up making him their bitch. He eventually ends up getting shanked in the shower by a humongous wanna-be gangsta' rapper named Titanic Ice Berg and bleeds out before the hot, steaming water runs out and his naked body becomes visible to the uncaring guards. His last thoughts are that he hasn't gotten laid—not by a girl, anyway—since he was arrested and that he'll probably never have Rocky Road ice cream again.

61

No one comes to his funeral, which is picketed by homeless cancer patients and both of L.A.'s native Sri Lankans.

Certainly not me; I don't come to the funeral.

It's not just that I won't cross a picket line; it's that even three years later, I'm still not allowed to borrow my mom's fucking car!

CHAPTER 7

Zeke leaned back on the couch in despair. Who knew that mild-mannered Brandon had such a flair for the dramatic when pushed too hard?

Of course, this wasn't the first time that Brandon had paid the price for one of Milo's harebrained schemes. They had all gone along a year ago when Milo had suggested chaining themselves together to block a logging road that went into an old-growth forest in the northern part of the state. They'd recruited some enthusiastic college students to join them and were just finishing shackling everyone together when one of the coeds got skittish and ran off.

Milo, of course, had bolted to "comfort" her. When they didn't return, Zeke had gone off in search of them, just in case they had gotten lost or hurt. Their groans led him to them, but they hadn't been hurt. They were, according to Milo, just enjoying nature by doing what comes naturally. Or, as Brandon, an Errol Flynn fan, later put it: "celebrating in pirate fashion."

Just a few moments after Zeke discovered the trysting couple, they all heard the local sheriff on his bullhorn in the distance ordering the protesters to disband or be arrested. Zeke, Milo, and the embarrassed sorority pledge skedaddled (after Milo and the coed got fully dressed), making a successful getaway. But Brandon had gotten arrested with the rest of the college kids.

Brandon had made a show of shrugging the incident off when they bailed him out, but there was obviously still some anger beneath the surface. Zeke couldn't allow that to get in the way of the organization and its goals. Sure, things had looked promising for a few days, but the whole car roof project was rapidly devolving into bickering and silliness, perhaps worse.

Zeke made a leadership decision. "We're not going to try this again. I . . ."—he spread his hands in conciliation—"I appreciate the effort, but we never should have even gone down this route. We'll brainstorm some more tomorrow evening. In the meantime, go home. Unwind. Whatever."

Brandon calmed down, but it appeared to take some effort. Finally, he simply turned to Zeke and said, "Fine. Milo can have the van. I'll drop you off before I take the Oldsmobile back to my mom." He headed back for the door.

Zeke got back up and joined him. "Nah, I'll go with you to your folks' place and talk to your mom. This is my responsibility. I run this organization, after all."

To hell with going home. Milo needed to get laid. On bad days, he needed to get laid to cheer himself up. On good days, he needed to get laid 'cause it was the perfect way to keep the good times rolling.

Milo always needed to get laid. Fortunately, he was good at it.

He stopped by a local gas station with an automatic car wash and punched in random codes at the payment panel at the entrance to the bay 'til the cars behind him began honking and the attendant back in the gas station's mini-mart punched in an override code just to keep the line moving. Milo figured that eliminating the evidence of the day's disaster would help placate Brandon in the morning. Who knew the wuss could be so vehement when he got riled?

Milo hoped this wasn't still about the damn logging protest. Jeez, it was only a misdemeanor and it was more than a year ago. Brandon needed to learn to let go and mellow out. An arrest was a badge of honor in some protest organizations, not that Milo had ever been caught.

The car wash completed, Milo headed the van toward a strip with several dance clubs, figuring to hook up with someone and go back to her place. At the second club, he succeeded, catching the eye of some minor starlet whose blonde hair, he figured, was as fake as her boobs.

He knew the starlet, Mitzi, looked familiar, but he couldn't place her until she drove the BMW convertible into the driveway at a Malibu beach house . . . the Malibu beach house.

She laughed when she saw his eyes widen. "Don't worry, baby. He's at some film festival 'til tomorrow afternoon."

The next morning, Milo wandered out of the magnificent bedroom of Matthew Barrington's beach house, down the hall into the great room toward the kitchen, wearing only his boxer shorts and a look of contentment. He found Mitzi, similarly contented and wearing a short, silk robe. She was singing lightly and buttering a croissant at the kitchen pass-through to the great room. Through the great room windows, the slate sea roiled to the shore with unending perseverance.

She finished her tune and smiled at him. "Hey, baby, do you want any coffee with your croissant?"

Milo sneered briefly. "Just another addiction meant to keep the serfs in line."

Mitzi laughed a gentle trill and passed a plate with a buttered croissant to him through the opening to the high-end kitchen, toppling a stack of mail so it slid, spreading out on the horizontal surface. An envelope with bold red lettering on the outside reading "Final Notice" caught Milo's attention. He put down the croissant plate and picked up the envelope. The return address read "California Homeowners Insurance Company."

He couldn't believe his eyes.

"You mean Matty—arrogant, movie star Matty—pays his own bills? Or should I say 'doesn't pay his own bills'?"

Mitzi frowned, a sexy little starlet pout. "Poor Matty. That's what happens when you switch accountants. Everything gets messed up."

Milo sighed. "The rich and famous have so many things to do."

He tossed the letter back toward the stack of mail. It slid across the stack and fell off it, on the kitchen side of the pass-through. He heard it drop with a hollow, metallic echo, but he didn't care. His full attention was on Mitzi, who was a good-enough actress to make her sexy pout quiver just so as she undid her silk robe.

"And so little time to do me. . . ."

Milo was a lackadaisical guy about many things, but not about sex. He moved with a purposeful stride toward the kitchen and swept her up into his arms. "Luckily I'm here to do you for him," he whispered throatily as he carried her back to the bedroom, she giggling in anticipation.

He vaguely remembered he was supposed to be doing something else over the weekend, something for work. Whatever. He'd get to it eventually if it really was important.

Sex, now that was important.

Never let your work become your identity, dude. Nothing good can come of it. That's what he had told Brandon and he had meant it. He lived by it. He always followed his own advice. Besides, it was good advice.

The sex, it was better than good.

CHAPTER 8

The next evening, as Zeke had requested, they were all back at GreensWord's headquarters. Almost a week had gone by since the beachfront protest, and they were no closer to solving the problem. Yesterday's tension was still present, but Zeke was pleased that nobody was screaming at one another, at least not yet.

They were in their usual positions. Milo sat at the computer, sullenly playing his game. Brandon sat at the kitchen table, clipboard in hand and calculator on the table ready for use. Zeke found himself fidgeting a bit while sitting on the well-worn recliner.

"Look," he finally said. "We may not be able to eliminate global warming overnight, but we at least need to do something dramatic in that direction. If we can get some results fast, maybe that will be enough to keep Barrington funding us."

"Yeah, even Matty's girlfriend said he was . . . uh . . . oriented to quickness."

"How would you . . . ," began Brandon, but Zeke cut him off.

"All I know," he said, "is that Barrington's money pays the bills: the payroll, the rent, everything. And Mr. Moneybags is pissed."

Brandon, no surprise, resorted to his usual problem-solving mode. "Maybe we could cool him off by getting him more favorable press on his concern for the environment. Movie stars love press."

"Maybe," said Milo with a look of disdain toward Brandon, "*we* could get his girlfriend to withhold sex until he agreed to continue our funding. Movie stars love sex."

"Nah," replied Brandon, "he'd just get another playmate."

Zeke reasserted his leadership. "Practical suggestions. I need practical suggestions."

Milo wrinkled up his nose for a moment and started playing with a rubber band again. Finally, he tilted his head to one side and beamed at his two compatriots.

"We could blackmail him into giving us the money," he said casually as he stretched out the rubber band.

There was a moment of stunned silence before Milo's rubber band broke and flew across the room toward Brandon, who flinched even though it fell well short. The rubber band seemed to get Brandon's juices flowing even more than it had Milo's.

"Don't you have to . . . I don't know . . . do something bad, or at least embarrassing, before somebody can blackmail you?" sneered Brandon. "What could we accuse him of that we would have hard evidence of?"

Zeke tried to interject before they both started up again. "Guys, this isn't really what I had in. . . ."

Suddenly, Milo jumped up, raising his hand in the air and waving it frantically, spilling the joystick onto the floor yet again. He looked Brandon square in the eye.

"Dude, I know. We say that you're his gay lover."

Brandon reddened fiercely. "You be his gay lover," he shot back. "I don't want to be his gay lover."

"Who'd believe that, dateless one?" Milo threw out his chest in a gesture, in Zeke's eyes, of both pride and confrontation. "*I* got laid this weekend. Twice. By different chicks. Both hot. *I* got laid last night, while mommy was grounding you. *I* have a reputation." He looked Brandon up and down, with a dismissive, contemptuous glare. "*You*, on the other hand, have a clipboard and a compulsive attention to detail. You're already anal. . . ."

Brandon dropped the clipboard self-consciously and quivered in anger. "Hey, I've put my mother and father through enough this week. I don't think they'd appreciate being. . . ."

"Everybody's got a mother and father," retorted Milo.

"Yeah, yeah," continued Brandon, apparently bringing his emotions in check and moving to the offensive. "But my parents actually know and care where I am and what I'm doing."

That last remark, Zeke knew, had cut deep. Milo slowly sat back down, clearly both deflated and hurt. Brandon seemed to realize he had gone too far, too, and tried to lighten the mood.

"Besides," Brandon said, "accusing Barrington of homosexuality would just get him better service at expensive restaurants."

"Yeah," said Milo, with a weak smile. "No wonder school kids graduated to guns. The old standbys just don't pack the same punch they used to."

Zeke smiled. The three of them got on each other's nerves from time to time, but underneath it all they were a tight team. Maybe he should be prouder of his leadership skills than he thought. "I'm glad we settled that," he declared.

"I know," said Milo with a joking tone of enthusiasm, "we'll cut off Brandon's ear and send it to the cops and tell Barrington that we're going to turn him in for Brandon's murder if he doesn't continue our funding."

Even Brandon smiled at that. "Hello! I'm alive, thank you, and I intend to stay that way."

"No problem," replied Milo with a shrug. "You can just stay out of sight 'til we score on the funding."

Brandon glanced around at the messy headquarters. "You want me to hole up in here indefinitely?" He wrinkled his nose.

Milo sat forward in his chair, his enthusiasm obviously growing for real. "It'd be like a vacation, man. You haven't even gotten off the first level of *Terrorist Threat*. You could entertain yourself for weeks! It's got totally awesome graphics and killer stereophonic sound, if you don't mind the static from the crappy speakers."

Brandon shook his head. "Killer stereophonic sound would be somewhat ineffective if I only had one ear! Besides, what about my parents, you know those people who bought the computer you are always complaining about? Why am I even discussing this lame idea?"

It was clear to Zeke that Milo was beginning to push Brandon a bit too far yet again. "Look, we're not going to blackmail anybody. . . ."

"Breaking the law for the greater good is well within the traditions of the environmental movement, dude," chirped Milo, with a nonchalant lack of concern.

Zeke continued to try to diffuse the situation. "So, you've read your Thoreau. . . ."

Brandon cut him off. "I'm not cutting off my ear, even for the movement." He seemed, though, to realize that Milo had just been goading him. He backed off. "I got nipped once at the barbers and it hurt like hell."

Zeke welcomed the gesture. "I agree. No ears being cut off. No blackmail. Legality isn't the issue. Effectiveness is. Blackmailing Barrington doesn't solve the problem; it just postpones it. We need to show some measurable impact on global warming . . . fast."

"But, Zeke," said Brandon, "even the Kyoto Accord talks in terms of decades. You can't cool down a planet overnight."

"Well, you can," interjected Milo wryly, "but only half at a time. It's always daytime in the other half. Sun keeps shining somewhere, no matter what you do."

"Yeah," said Zeke. "Where's a good volcanic explosion when

you need it?"

"Huh?" said Brandon and Milo in unison.

"Oh, it's just something I saw over the weekend. Volcanic explosions have a cooling effect on the planet. Tons of particulate matter in the high upper atmosphere make less sunlight come through. Kind of the same thing as the white car roof thing, but on a gigantic scale. The sunlight never gets to the surface in the first place, so it doesn't need to be reflected back up. Less sunlight means the planet cools down."

Milo rolled his chair as far from Zeke as it would go and held up his fingers in a cross, like in old vampire movies. "Get back, Satan. It sounds like you're saying that we need more industrial smokestacks churning out even more crap into the air. Isn't that what got us into this mess in the first place?"

"Nah," said Zeke with calm certitude. He knew more about the technical aspects of the movement than either of his compatriots ever would, he was sure. "The stuff that industry pours starts out pretty low in the atmosphere. The gases rise and deplete the ozone, but the particulates hang low and just end up in the groundwater when it rains. Volcanoes are different. The particulates literally go sky high, get picked up by the jet stream and stay aloft a long time, reducing the ambient sunlight."

Brandon seemed skeptical. "Do they really have that much effect?"

"Oh, yeah. Even Mount St. Helens had a measurable impact on global temperatures. Krakatoa, Vesuvius, Tambora; they all had a noticeable impact on global temperatures for years."

"Interesting," said Brandon, "but not really useful. Eruptions are infrequent and unpredictable. Too bad you can't mimic that effect with something man-made. That would get Barrington off our back."

"Well," said Zeke, drawing out the word while he thought.

"You can. Carl Sagan's thesis. . . ."

". . . had billions and billions of typos?" interjected Milo, doing his best, sonorous impression of the departed television host.

". . . was on nuclear winter," continued Zeke. "If enough nukes go off, the temperature of the planet plummets and we have a global cooling."

Brandon folded his arms. "So, there's our solution."

"No. I don't think so," replied Zeke, appalled that he was being taken seriously. He gestured at himself, Tarzan-style. "Us environmentalists. Hate nuclear stuff."

"Yeah, man," Milo added. "Besides, it sounds like it would take a shitload of nukes."

"Not to mention the minor problem of destroying the planet with nuclear weapons in order to cool it down a bit." Zeke was taken aback. It was an obvious point. Couldn't Milo and Brandon see that?

Apparently Milo couldn't.

"There are parts that are expendable." Milo looked up, as if searching for a sample. "Madagascar, for example. Does anybody know anybody who cares about Madagascar?"

The ever-practical Brandon spoke up. "It would put a serious dent in worldwide vanilla production," he said, once again demonstrating to Zeke a grasp of information that was useless in attracting women, but might someday win him a spot on *Jeopardy*.

He might win, but he would never score.

"Point taken," replied Milo with a nod. "Aside from people who like boring ice cream or Classic Coca-Cola, does anybody know anybody who even knows anybody who cares about Madagascar?"

Brandon started to speak, but Milo stopped him. "I mean,

aside from computer-animated penguins in crappy kids' movies."

Brandon stalled. Zeke knew it was because he hated to be stumped. "Statistically speaking, Kevin Bacon does, maybe a couple of people more removed."

"Nuke it from orbit," intoned Milo. "It's the only way to be sure."

"Spoken like a true movie buff, Milo," interjected Zeke, "but that wasn't Kevin Bacon. It was Bill Paxton or Michael Biehn or somebody."

"Besides," said Brandon, "we don't even have enough in the budget to print fliers. I don't think we can afford several billion dollars to start building our own nukes."

Milo shrugged his shoulders in his usual, casual way, as if the details of the plan, any plan, were not an issue. "If hundreds of meth labs operate undetected in greater L.A., I don't see why you couldn't hide a uranium enrichment facility."

"We don't even have a basement in this place," cried Brandon, with obvious exasperation, "and you want to start handling high-level radioactive material?" He glanced down at his waist. "I might want to have kids someday!"

"Good luck with that," zinged Milo.

Zeke tried to shut down the discussion before the two could really go at each other again. "Forget this. Go back to your games or whatever. It's my responsibility. It's my job. I'm just going to have to tell Barrington that he has to be patient."

Milo smiled. "Dude, we can go back to the ear thing."

"Shut up, Milo!" came the familiar refrain in stereophonic sound.

CHAPTER 9

The surf thundered with mind-numbing monotony. The beach house vibrated in rhythmic harmony. He tried to ignore it, to turn his attention to more pleasant thoughts, but the beat always permeated through into his consciousness.

Roar.

Shudder.

Plunge.

Matthew Barrington enjoyed being a movie star. He loved the attention whenever he came into a room. *Roar.* He noticed the subtle deference whenever he expressed an opinion. He smiled inwardly every time some fan without a real life pleaded for his autograph. *Shudder.* He calculated his portion of the take whenever he saw long lines of fans snaking outside of suburban multi-plexes to see his action flicks. *Plunge.* The money was excellent and the demands of the job were minimal.

Roar.

Shudder.

Plunge.

But most of all, he absolutely adored what stardom and the trappings that came with it—the fame, the beach house, the fancy cars, the fashionable clothes—did for his love life. *Roar.* He didn't believe for a minute that if he had not been plucked from obscurity in a cattle-call casting session for the sleeper hit *After the Prom,* that he would be where he was today. *Shudder.* No, he would instead be just another height-challenged drone working in advertising or accounting or, God forbid, sales. *Plunge.* And women, drop-dead gorgeous women willing to put out at the wink of an eye, never came up to salesmen as they were having coffee or chatting with friends so they could slip them a phone number or a room key.

Roar.

Shudder.

Plunge.

Sure, you had to watch out for the crazies, the stalkers who didn't understand that casual sex was really supposed to be casual, the groupies who wanted to have his baby, and the social-climbers who craved his fame and his bank account. Those women were why he had a vasectomy (no kidding!), a security service, and a high-powered attorney. *Roar.* Sure, not all of the women were as gorgeous and as simple as his current bed-mate, Mitzi, but the plain-Janes were eager and easy to please. *Shudder.* Even a simple photo of the two of them together snapped by a star-weary waiter with Jane's picture phone was enough to send many a touristy hausfrau into orgasmic hyperventilation. *Plunge.* He usually patted their rears as they scampered away, so they'd have a story to tell when they e-mailed the picture to all their stay-at-home-mom girlfriends back in the Midwest. Sometimes he wondered if he'd patted enough rears to explain his two People's Choice Awards.

Roar.

Shudder.

Plunge.

Finally, something snapped. He raised himself up, looking about the bedroom of the Malibu beach house: two robes and four slippers lying in a haphazard tangle on the floor; the surf surging in the moonlight outside the sliding glass doors to the veranda; burning candles nestled on the nightstand between the old-fashioned, corded phone and the sleek, modern, stainless steel alarm clock reading 11:04 p.m. in cool, blue digits. He looked forward, at the rich grain of the headboard of his oversized teak bed. Then, he looked down at Mitzi, naked and soft beneath him.

"I just can't stand this rhythmic pounding anymore!" he shouted, panting from exertion and exasperation.

The beat continued. *Roar. Shudder.* But Matthew had stopped keeping time to the music. Mitzi looked confused by his outburst and disappointed that no plunge had followed the latest roar, the latest shudder.

"But I like it, Matty," she said, her voice all girlish and pouty.

Matthew resisted her charms. "That's not what I mean, baby," he said to soothe her, but his voice quickly took on an exasperated edge as he continued. "It's the cadence of the waves. It pervades everything. It gets into your head, like *It's a Small, Small World.*"

Mitzi made another pouty face. "Is that bad? I had an awfully good time on that ride once. . . ."

Matthew rolled off the starlet and sat on the edge of the bed, facing away from her toward the night surf, toward the view that had added millions to the cost of the house, toward the ocean. At first, he had loved the gentle sound of the surf outside, but with the erosion of the beach, the action of the waves on the shore had become increasingly irritating as it thrummed through the support pillars beneath the house. Truth be told, in the last few months, the ocean had become the bane of his existence.

"It's driving me crazy," he said simply. His tone hardened and his words quickened as he went on. "It never gets any faster. . . . It's like trying to make love to *Bolero.* It doesn't get faster; it just gets louder. It just keeps going . . . on and on at the same pace."

Mitzi leaned toward him and reached out to stroke his arm.

She made no effort to cover herself. Her musky aroma, her look, her touch all whispered "fuck me" seductively. Either she really wanted him or she was one hell of an actress. "That means you just keep on going and going and going," she purred breathily. "Like that rabbit. I love bunnies. C'mon, Matty, let's fuck like bunnies."

Okay, a great actress who needed a writer.

Matthew turned toward her, with more anger than he knew she deserved. "This isn't about you and what you like," he snarled. "It's about me and what I like. I'm a star! I shouldn't have to put up with this!"

Suddenly, the numbers on the digital clock flickered off and the ceiling fan above the bed clicked softly and began to slow with an uneven wobble. The power had failed. Again.

Matthew leapt to his feet, the sheet falling to the floor, leaving him naked in the dim, candle-lit bedroom, as he lifted his right fist and raged at the ceiling, overacting as usual.

"California's supposed to be better than this!"

No sooner had he offended the gods with his outburst, than a loud ringing responded from somewhere in the darkness.

"What the fuck is that?" he yelled, before the nature of the sound could fully register.

Mitzi sighed and lay back on the bed, covering herself with the sheet. "It's just the phone," she said with resignation.

Matthew grabbed the receiver. "Yeah . . . yeah. What do you mean my insurance expires at midnight?" He began to pace next to the bed as the conversation continued. "Look, my accountant must have messed up again. You think you might have given me a little warning." He stopped pacing. "I didn't get a letter." He started pacing again. "What the hell am I supposed to do now? It's the middle of the goddamn night, at least it is here. Who the hell knows what time it is in India."

Matthew sat back down on the bed wearily as the accented

voice, trained in dealing with irate customers, made the responses mandated by the insurance company's customer service call book. "My voicemail was full," the star responded with growing aggravation, "I was at a premiere. I didn't get the message." Finally, he could stand the bureaucratic flak-catching no longer and just slammed the receiver back into its cradle on the nightstand.

He turned toward Mitzi seeking comfort, but her eyes were already closed and her breathing regular.

"Can somebody please tell me why the phones work during a blackout?" he said to no one in particular.

Only a damnable roar and shudder responded.

There was no way he could get someone else to insure the beach house now that his current policy had lapsed. The agent would take one look at the thong-sized strip of beach between the veranda and the restless sea and smile politely, but shake his head and walk away. Matthew had to fix this problem himself. Drastic action was needed. Extreme action. And he just couldn't wait any longer.

He got dressed and drove his BMW into the night, his hair tousled by the wind.

Brandon hated these all-night planning and bull sessions. They disrupted his routine. But Zeke and Milo were definitely night owls, so whenever anything big was going on with GreensWord, the strategizing tended to occur at night. They had gathered at ten p.m., but hadn't really gotten down to business until close to midnight. They took care of their usual, mundane tasks—paying bills, updating the list of volunteers, etc.—and then rehashed recent events for a while, before Zeke had opened the floor for new ideas.

When no one responded, Zeke had sighed heavily and plopped down on the big recliner, snatching up a bag of Milo's cheese curls and drowning his frustration with audible crunching. Now he sat slumped in his traditional Army-surplus fatigues, with fluorescent orange fingers on one hand and both lips, like a hunter wearing a bright orange safety vest over his camouflage gear. Milo, of course, sat sideways in the chair at Brandon's computer, playing a game that entertained through ersatz violence.

Despite the late hour, Brandon knew that the session wasn't over. So, he sat on the couch, his posture impeccable, his hand extended with the remote, flipping channels, waiting for something to happen. He was on his fourth pass through all one hundred and twenty channels, when Zeke finally spoke again.

"Jeez, Brandon. You've been through the channels a dozen times." Zeke had a tendency to casually exaggerate, especially when he was trying to make a point. "I don't think there are any more ideas there."

"Well," said Brandon, trying not to show his exasperation, "we've got to do something."

Milo looked up from his game, his fingers still twitching commands, whether from mere muscle memory or an actual ability to play the lower levels of the game without having to look at the screen, Brandon was unsure. "We already have three good ideas."

Zeke sat up a little, and wiped off his mouth with the back of his sleeve. "We've been through this, Milo. The car roof thing was a good idea in theory, but it just won't work in practice. And I don't think it would save GreensWord as an organization."

Before Milo could respond, Brandon cut in. "And don't even start up again with the ear thing."

Zeke nodded at Brandon, then turned back to face Milo. "You said three. What was the third?"

Milo smiled. "Adding something to the *Macarena*, man."

The response was immediate and predictable.

"Shut up, Milo," droned Zeke and Brandon.

Milo looked irked, but then something seemed to catch his eye outside the living-room window, back and to the left of where the couch and easy chair faced. "Fine," he said surprisingly cordially. "I'll shut up, but you're going to have to tell the dude something soon."

Zeke looked puzzled. "I can take a couple days to get back to him. I'll think of something. That's my job."

Suddenly, there was a vigorous pounding on the door. Brandon got up and looked through the peephole, which he had insisted on installing last year. Barrington was outside. He was dressed nicely enough, a tan sports coat over a striped button-down shirt, and fashionable dress pants. No doubt he wore expensive shoes, too. But his hair was askew and he had a crazed, fierce look on his face—the kind of look you saw only in drunk-driving mug shots or right before a paparazzo got punched out. Brandon turned back to Zeke, an adrenaline surge making both his voice and his manner urgent. "Think fast, noble leader. Our benefactor has come to see us. And he looks really, really pissed."

An adrenaline shot apparently surged through Milo, too, because he dropped the joystick and stood abruptly, his eyes flicking toward the side door to the carport, as if judging the time it would take to skedaddle. Zeke looked at Milo sharply.

"Hey, man," said Milo in defense, "she came on to me."

"Shut up, Milo!" Zeke barked as he moved toward the door, shoving his cheesy-orange hand into the pocket of his fatigues and wiping it off before pulling it back out.

Brandon opened the door and Barrington entered without waiting to be asked. He ignored Zeke's proffered, slightly less cheesy-orange hand, and looked him directly in the sternum.

"Damn environment is ruining my sex life . . ." was all the star said by way of greeting.

"Did you get exposed to some DDT or PCBs or something?" asked Brandon, attempting, as always to solve the problem. But Barrington ignored him and just kept talking to Zeke's chest.

". . . and I expect you to do something about it."

Milo looked at Barrington and Zeke, then at Brandon. "Maybe he already gets good service at fancy restaurants!"

Zeke snapped his head toward Milo for only a microsecond. "Shut up, Milo!" He turned back to their benefactor and looked him in the face. Zeke's expression reverted to the bland, friendly look he used when he was soliciting funds for the group door-to-door or trying to get shoppers to sign an environmental protest petition. "Look, Mr. Barrington," he said in a soft, re-assuring voice, "I'm not sure that chemical contamination . . . or performance anxiety . . . is really our field of expertise. . . ."

Barrington twitched visibly. "I haven't been contaminated," he snarled. "It's global warming. It's ruining my sex life!"

"If it's too warm, just turn up the ceiling fan, man," offered Milo.

Zeke didn't even turn around to look at him, but just said evenly, "Shut up, Milo."

"He has one," said Milo defensively. "I saw it when. . . ."

Zeke turned abruptly toward Milo and widened his eyes, tilting his head a smidgen to one side.

". . . I was . . . getting the marker for the signs," finished Milo.

Barrington, however, had apparently not noticed Milo putting his foot in his mouth and almost cramming both feet in. His attention was all on Zeke. The man showed more focused intensity than Brandon had seen in him since the action star had appeared in a David Mamet play, years and years ago. Barrington's eyes focused narrowly as he tilted his head up to fix

Zeke with a steady, almost scary, gaze. His voice took on a preternatural calm as he spoke. "Look, it's very simple. If you can't help me, I'll find someone else who will. I've got to save my house and my sex life."

Brandon watched as the color drained from Zeke's face and his shoulders slumped in surrender. Their leader had nothing . . . nothing at all . . . and he was about to admit it. Brandon stalled for time in an effort to help the guy out. "As you know, Mr. Barrington, sir, global warming is a long-term phenomenon. . . ."

Barrington looked at the dumbstruck Zeke, then over to Brandon. He reached into the vest pocket of his sports coat. Milo flinched slightly, but Barrington only pulled out an eel skin-cased checkbook and a Montblanc fountain pen. He took a few, rapid strides to the kitchen table, swept aside some paperwork and began writing furiously, as he spoke. "One million dollars, but you have to cure global warming now." His eyes flicked at Zeke, who was still frozen in place, so he turned to Brandon. "Comprendé? Now. Not in seven generations, not in two decades, not under the next presidential administration, not next year. Now." He turned to Milo. Apparently, he wanted to make sure they all understood. "And I mean 'cure it.' Not educate the fucking public about it, or lessen it, or stop it from getting any worse. I mean, 'cure it.' Reverse it, so it stops feeding the El Niño or whatever the hell it does." He shifted his intense gaze to Zeke, as he tore off the check and held it out. "If you take this, you have to stop global warming in time to save the beach house—before the winter storms ramp up and the beach disappears completely. Understood?"

Zeke simply stared at Barrington. Brandon jumped into the breach, striding briskly forward and snatching the check out of the hand of their benefactor. "Understood," he said as he glanced at all the zeroes on the check. "Global warming is just a problem that . . . needs to have money thrown at it to be solved in a jiffy."

Suddenly, Zeke was shaken back to life. "Hey," he said, looking at Brandon, "what are you doing?"

Brandon turned to Zeke, his back facing Barrington. "Don't worry," he mouthed, so their crazed sponsor could not hear, "I've got a plan."

Zeke looked at Barrington, then back at Brandon. Brandon could almost see the wheels turning as the group's leader thought through the situation. Give Barrington back his check right now and doom GreensWord to bankruptcy and ignominy as the money flowed instead to a larger, better-known environmental group that had already long-ago proved that millions of dollars solved nothing . . . or . . . trust Brandon and take the money and live to fight the good fight at least one more day. He flinched.

Zeke took a half-step forward and looked past Brandon, straight into the eyes of Matthew Barrington. He smiled broadly, back in fund-raising mode. "Your problem will be taken care of. You have my word on it. You have GreensWord on it."

Barrington relaxed noticeably. He tucked the checkbook back in his jacket, smoothed his hair, and turned on a broad, press-junket-style smile. "I knew you guys were just negotiating the other day," he bantered, "you know, holding out for more money. Have you thought of becoming agents?"

Milo had relaxed visibly, too. He smiled back at Barrington and gestured to his companions. "Dudes, we should consider that. More chicks, more money, and less arduous labor than this gig. I could dig that."

Zeke apparently decided to go with the flow of the overall mood. "We're . . . we're going to use saving the world as a launching pad for publicizing our own agency. Being heroes is good business for everyone." He winked at Barrington. "Everyone."

"Yeah," joined in Brandon. "And we . . . we don't want to lose our status as a 501(c)(3) tax-exempt charity until we're ready for the big move."

Barrington snapped his fingers and pointed at Brandon. "PR savvy and tax smart, too. My manager will give you a call." He grabbed Zeke's hand and shook it, putting his left hand on top in the same way the politicians always did to feign friendship and sincerity with people they barely knew and certainly didn't care about. He headed for the door, turning and giving a casual salute and pointing gesture, just before exiting.

Milo flopped back down into his chair. Brandon gazed at the million-dollar check. Zeke simply stared at the closed door for a few moments. Finally, Zeke spoke. "His manager is going to give us a call when he stops payment on this check tomorrow, that's for sure." He turned toward Brandon, who was still contemplating the check with shock and awe. "This had better be a great idea, Brandon," he said evenly.

Brandon smiled. "Three years as a part-time bank teller to pay my way through school taught me one important lesson. Deposit first. Ask questions later. What time does our bank open?"

Milo picked up the joystick and flipped on the screen to take up his game once again. Then he looked up, grinning, his eyes asparkle. "Dudes, can we get it in cash? It would be totally awesome to get it in cash."

CHAPTER 10

Milo should have been disappointed that they hadn't been able to get the million dollars in cash when they went to the bank the next morning. Brandon had mumbled on and on about cash float protocols for window tellers and funds availability and clearance delays imposed by the Federal Reserve as they drove to the bank. Milo must have been so bored he fell asleep, because when he woke up Brandon was explaining how L. Frank Baum originally wrote *The Wizard of Oz* as an allegory about monetary policy. At least Milo hoped he was awake—if he was going to start dreaming about crap like William Jennings Bryan and the gold standard, life would no longer be worth living.

"Dude," he finally said, one eye half-opened, "where do you get this shit?"

Brandon looked perturbed. "It's as clear as day. 'Oz' is an abbreviation for ounces, as in ounces of gold—the yellow bricks in the yellow brick road. Why is that so hard to believe?"

Milo closed his eye and tried to let the rhythmic sway of the van rock him back to sleep. "What's hard to believe is that you say you didn't do drugs when you were in college. What does Toto represent in this hallucination of yours?"

Brandon's voice took on its customary professorial tone, as he continued his explanation. "Well, actually, 'Toto' is short for 'teetotaler', representing the alliance of the Prohibition Party. . . ."

Milo didn't remember anything more of Brandon's explanation, thank God. He fell asleep and dreamed of *The Wizard of Oz* playing over Pink Floyd's *The Dark Side of the Moon*. The next thing he knew, they had arrived at the bank and Zeke had endorsed Barrington's check for deposit.

The teller, a good-looking, twenty-something-year-old woman dressed in a fashionable skirt and silk blouse that no doubt came from one of the stores in the high-end suburban mall across the street from the bank, involuntarily gaped when she saw the size of the check. Her eyebrows shot up and her mouth opened long enough for Milo to notice that her tongue was pierced, although she wasn't currently wearing any jewelry in it.

The girl needs a stud, Milo thought to himself as he gave her a wink. Flustered by the check or the wink, Megan—he saw from the slide-in nameplate at the teller window that her name was Megan Parker—called for her supervisor. The supervisor gave the trio the once-over, then initialed the deposit slip and explained the bank's funds-availability policies in even more detail than had Brandon.

While they couldn't access Barrington's money yet, Zeke did get the several thousand dollars of cash that represented the remainder of GreensWord's funds. The procedure gave Milo time to tell Megan about GreensWord's mission to save the world from the soulless corporations that seek to pollute the environment and enslave the masses in mind-numbing, meaningless jobs.

By the time they left with the cash, Milo had Megan's phone number and plans for Saturday night. Errand accomplished, the trio stopped at the grocery store to stock up and headed back to headquarters. Everyone was in a good mood for a change, so they decided to splurge.

Almost two hours later, Milo surveyed the kitchen table at GreensWord's office, overflowing with expensive food: steaks, lobsters, imported beer, European chocolates, and all that tofu, bean curd, and other inedible, but expensive, organic, vegan crap that Brandon always ate. Milo smiled at Zeke, who was chowing down on a half-gallon of ice cream, but his smile turned to a sneer when he saw the Häagen-Dazs brand name on the carton.

"We should have gotten Ben & Jerry's, dude. How can you call yourself an environmentalist and not buy Ben & Jerry's?" Zeke stopped stuffing his face with the creamy, high-fat chocolate delight only long enough to reply. "Chill out, Milo. It's just another company. Ben and Jerry don't even run it anymore."

"Yeah, but the average consumer doesn't know that—it's about appearances, man. You just can't trust an environmentalist that doesn't buy Ben & Jerry's. It's like an environmentalist that smokes. Duh!"

Brandon interjected. "You smoke, Milo. Does that make you a moron or a hypocrite?"

Milo shook his shaggy head. "Weed doesn't count, man. It's medicinal."

Brandon didn't look convinced. He bobbed his head toward the ancient Quompat. "You get glaucoma from staring at your computer games, or something?"

"Medicinal for the earth, man," Milo replied, cutting off a piece of his steak and stuffing the juicy, medium rare morsel into his mouth just to pimp his vegan adversary. "It mellows out the planet," he mumbled with his mouth full.

Zeke again stopped spooning ice cream into his face just long enough to attempt to quell any argument. "Could you two just possibly be quiet long enough for me to enjoy my ice cream? I didn't complain about what you bought to eat."

They ate in silence for a moment, but Milo just couldn't let it go.

"You know, it's a totally made-up name. The guy wasn't even Danish."

"What guy?" asked Brandon.

"The guy that started Häagen-Dazs. He was from the Bronx. The name doesn't even mean anything."

"So what?" said Zeke matter-of-factly as he scraped the bottom of the carton for a few last spoonfuls of half-melted ice cream.

"Don't the systematic falsehoods of our society bother you, dude? What do you think it teaches children? Do you think there's a Sara Lee and, if so, that there's nobody out there that doesn't like her?"

Brandon egged on the rant. "Yeah, what about Betty Crocker or Mr. Goodwrench?"

Zeke scrunched up his nose slightly. "Colonel Sanders is real."

Brandon was on a roll. "Yeah, but he's dead. And what about the Keebler elves?"

Milo took up Brandon's reference. "You know, I saw a news story about Keebler employees once. They don't like being called elves."

Zeke tossed the empty confectionary carton into the trash container next to the sink. "That's nice to know, Milo. There'll be no elf-calling or . . . dwarf-tossing coming from me, but let me tell you what bothers me. Now that we've started spending our benefactor's money—or at least what was left of our money because we're depending on his—I really need to hear that there is a plan."

Milo jumped up and started waving his hand in the air, like he imagined Brandon did all through high school social studies class. "Ooh, ooh. I got one."

Zeke leaned back in his kitchen chair. "This I gotta hear," he said warily.

Brandon stopped eating his organically grown plantain and looked over to Milo. "Fortunately, I still have two ears, so I'm willing to listen, too."

Milo leapt up onto his chair for dramatic effect. "It came to me when I was looking at the boxes of sugar cubes in the store."

Brandon snorted. "This isn't going to be some drug thing, is it?"

Milo waved him off. "Nah, man. Nothing like that. But, look, a million bucks would buy. . . ." He looked heavenward and then shut his eyes as he tried to do the math . . . any math . . . in his head. Finally he gave up. ". . . I dunno, a whole bunch of boxes of sugar cubes. Brandon can figure out how many."

Brandon made no attempt to run the calculation. "Let's just say for now that it would be enough to give even you a sugar rush."

Milo bobbed his head vigorously. "Yeah, sure. No need for details now. We're talking big picture, really big picture."

"Wide screen, high-definition picture," said Zeke, with a hint of sarcasm.

"Here's the thing," said Milo, leaning down toward them from his precarious perch on the chrome and vinyl kitchen chair, "y'see, the three of us, we split up with boxes and boxes of sugar cubes. . . ."

Dressed in muted colors to avoid standing out or catching anyone's attention, we stroll casually through parking lots and large parking garages. We wear backpacks filled with boxes of sugar cubes and we wear baggy trousers, with, like, specially sewn-in deep pockets. We act like we can't find our car or we're admiring the new vehicle model or we dropped some change or we're checking for parking stickers or whatever we need to do to look inconspicuous. Then, then we drop sugar cubes in everyone's gas tank. It's simple, just pop open the little door, unscrew the cap, and drop three or four cubes down into the tank. Screw the cap back on, close things up and move on to the next car.

At the end of the day, the overpaid vice-presidents, the mindless bureaucrats, the middling managers, and the harried workers all stream out of their offices or tiny cubicles or noisy factory floors into the parking facilities. Our prototypical worker gets into his vehicle to head to his heavily-mortgaged home and loveless marriage forty-five minutes away. He drives seven or twelve miles, listening to traffic reports every four minutes on the radio. Then, whammo! The car slows in a sudden lurch, smoke pours out of the hood. The sugar has reached his German-engineered engine. It caramelizes, freezing the pistons. The engine seizes like the cardiac artery of an overweight executive. Rods fly everywhere. He gets out of his car and sees the same thing happening to other cars on other streets and highways all around him.

Throughout the city, stopped cars block the roadways, backing up highways, snarling traffic into a gridlock of Olympic proportions. The Auto Club and AAA are flooded with calls for tow trucks. People swear at their cars until they are as blue as the smoke that still trails from the hood of the car. Repair shops are flooded with damaged vehicles, but the repair job is huge, expensive, and unusual, requiring a massive influx of parts from suppliers all over the world. The cars are off the streets until the repairs can be made. People have no choice . . . no choice at all . . . but to take public transportation or carpool 'til their cars are fixed. They enjoy the relaxing bus ride down practically vacant streets, where they can unwind and read a paper . . . or, imagine this, a book . . . on their way to and from work.

At least twelve days goes by. Presto! New habits are formed. GreensWord saves the day. Peace and love flourish. Everyone names their kids Milo. Milo! Milo! Milo!

Brandon looked at Milo, jumping up and down on the kitchen

chair, shouting his own name in ecstasy. He probably did the same thing when he was having sex . . . er . . . celebrating in pirate fashion.

Brandon couldn't stand it. "You know," he shouted loud enough to be heard over Milo's ranting, his volume dialing down as Milo stopped jumping and looked at him with disgust. "Sugar cubes don't dissolve all that well. I'm not sure they dissolve in gasoline at all. Any particulates would just get caught in the gas filter."

Milo stared at him, one side of his lip quivering as if he were going to break into a snarl. "So we'll use honey. That's already a liquid. We'll just get some squeeze bottles and squirt some in."

Brandon tried to reply, but Milo continued. "But none of that organic honey you get. It's freakin' expensive and, I don't care what they say, the beekeeper has no way of really knowing whether the bees go to wildflowers or Miracle-Gro potted marigolds to get the nectar."

Brandon was about to defend the organic farmers (and beekeepers) of America when Zeke took command of the situation.

"I hate to burst your bubble," said their leader without ecstasy, or even much in the way of emotion at all, "but haven't most gas-cap doors been locked since . . . I dunno . . . the gas lines in the seventies . . . you know, before we all were born?"

Milo stopped jumping and simply stood on the chair, towering above his two compatriots. He tilted his head to the side and thought for a moment, then shrugged. "We could have crowbars with us or something."

Brandon noticed that Zeke was tapping his foot beneath the table, a sure sign that he was not pleased.

"And how long," continued Zeke, "before the three of us are in the pokey for malicious mischief?"

Milo clambered down from atop the chair and sat. "It worked

91

in a role-playing game I played once."

Zeke looked at Milo sharply. "This isn't a game. This is life." He turned toward Brandon. "Please, Brandon. Tell me you have a real idea. A practical idea. An idea that doesn't come from role-playing games or *James Bond* movies or *Scooby-Doo* cartoons. Tell me that GreensWord isn't staking its future on sugar cubes and white paint."

Brandon relaxed his usually perfect posture and leaned back in his chair. It all depended on him. He relished the sense of power, the thrill of everyone looking at him for solutions. He had finally come into his own. He had the power. But he decided to be gracious in his exercise of that power.

"You said it yourself, Zeke. All we need to create a cooler earth is a bunch of volcanic eruptions or a large-scale thermonuclear war. Voila! Nuclear winter."

Milo was picking at the remains of his food. "I dunno, man. Nuclear winter sounds pretty harsh. I need my rays—they help the body produce Vitamin D, you know."

"Not to mention skin cancer," said Zeke with a slight edge of irritation to his voice. "But since we're talking about cancer-inducing agents, let's get back to the nukes. You, Brandon, can control the forces of nature and/or arrange a full-scale nuclear war for a million bucks?"

"After this month's fixed expenditures for rent, etc., more like nine hundred ninety-eight thousand, eight hundred and four dollars and change. . . ."

"Whatever!" snapped Zeke.

Brandon ignored the put-down. He was clearly still the one with the answers. "Don't you watch the news, guys? The army in Russia doesn't even know where all the old Soviet nukes are. I'm sure we could buy one for less than what we have. Maybe two."

Zeke shook his head. "I can't believe that I'm even saying

this . . . that I'm having a conversation about acquisition costs of nuclear warheads . . . but two is not enough. They took out Hiroshima and Nagasaki, not to mention the Bikini atoll and pieces of Nevada, without creating nuclear winter."

Brandon tried not to look smug. They never would've figured it out without him.

"That why we use the nuke to set off a volcano or a series of volcanoes. Like John F. Kennedy said, 'a bigger bang for a buck.' Plenty of particulate matter shot straight up into the ionosphere."

Milo tossed an organic orange to him. "Dude, I own a sphere, too."

Brandon flinched from habit, making no attempt to catch the orange, which thumped to the floor and rolled under the couch, where it would undoubtedly be discovered sometime next summer when Milo was scrounging for pocket change. It was time for Brandon to assert his leadership.

"Be serious, man! We're talking about saving the earth here."

Zeke grimaced. "Well, that and killing a gazillion or so people."

Milo quickly moved into one of his standard rants. "Man is a blight on the planet. Totally multiplying without control or respect for nature." He looked at Zeke, then at Brandon. "Mankind needs to be taken down a notch."

Brandon smiled. He was drawing Milo in. Now, to work on Zeke. "Besides, we could warn the people or something. Those that listen and leave will live."

"And those who don't or can't will die," said Zeke simply.

Milo grinned broadly. "Evolution in action, man. Evolution in action."

Zeke still did not seem convinced. "I don't know, Brandon. What about the animals? You can't warn the animals. What're you going to do, herd them into an ark or something?"

Brandon knew that Zeke had a soft spot for animals. He could watch the evening news reports about fires and muggings and murders with relative aplomb, but a story about a horse being put down or a fire in an animal shelter would make their leader tear up. He decided to tread lightly.

"Killing people for the cause, especially people too stupid to heed our warning, doesn't bother me so much, but, you're right, killing helpless animals, that does give me pause."

Milo ruined the mood. "Maybe the radiation will give everyone paws," he said, grinning goofily once more.

The response was automatic.

"Shut up, Milo!" grumbled Brandon and Zeke in unison.

Zeke seemed to ponder for a few moments. "Let's not put the cart before the horse . . . or, in this case, the horses before the people. Look, just because *Dateline* says things are screwed up in Russia doesn't mean we could score a nuke."

Brandon sighed. "Anybody can score a nuke. North Korea's got 'em and nobody likes them."

Milo rubbed the stubble on his chin. "Hey, man, I know a chick in the Russian disarmament program."

Brandon looked at Milo with genuine interest for a change. "Those guys that witness decommissioning of the big intercontinental ballistic missiles as part of a verification program under SALT?"

Zeke even looked interested. "The Strategic Arms Limitation Talks?"

Milo nodded. "Yeah, her name's Svetlana. She was a speaker at the Earth Day rally last year."

Brandon thought back to the rally, but no one came to mind.

"Smart," continued Milo, pausing before continuing. "Committed." Pause. "A great speaker." Pause. "A true believer in the environment."

Brandon concentrated furiously. Still nothing.

A twinkle came into Milo's eye and a sly smile appeared on his face.

"Bodacious jugs."

Brandon found himself blushing and nodding in unison with Zeke.

"Yeah, I know her," he said warmly.

Zeke shared Brandon's reverie for only a moment. He got up and started pacing the room, taking charge of the situation.

"Look," he said, stopping in mid-pace to turn toward Brandon and Milo, "this isn't something we can do off the cuff. We need to think it through, to plan it all out. This is serious business."

Zeke looked at Milo. "Serious." Milo rolled his eyes slightly, but tilted his head almost imperceptibly in agreement.

Zeke turned to Brandon. "Business." Brandon bristled inwardly. He had come up with the idea, but Zeke was lecturing him, even if it was with one-word sentences. Still, he tilted his chin at their supposed leader with an almost military acknowledgment.

Zeke continued. "Brandon, you focus on the tactical details. How we get it, what we do with it. I'll work out where we put it to accomplish our objectives."

Brandon started to get up to head for the library, when he was interrupted by Milo.

"What do I do?"

"You give Brandon Svetlana's phone number," Zeke said breezily and then thought for a moment before continuing. "And . . . figure out how to make sure we don't get caught."

Milo grimaced. He looked at Brandon, then back to Zeke. "But you heard what Brandon said before. You can't help but leave some evidence behind. They always catch guys that way on the cop shows."

Brandon pursed his lips and inclined his head slowly in agreement. "Nobody gets away with it on TV."

Milo piped up again. "Nobody, dude, nobody. And I watch a lot of TV, man."

Zeke looked at them both with a deadly serious expression. "This isn't TV. It's not even reality TV. It's reality. Whatever we do, whether we get the nuke or not, whether we place it successfully or not, whether we set it off or not, whether it works or not . . . we can't get caught. It would be the end of Greens-Word."

"Not to mention our lives," said Brandon quietly.

Milo gave Brandon a wry half-smile. "You call what you got a life?"

CHAPTER 11

Zeke had never trusted the government. It was powerful. It was secretive. And it didn't do anything useful, as far as he was concerned. So it troubled him that he was depending so much on the government to find out the best way to research Greens-Word's nuclear winter project. He took mass transit to get where he needed to go. He did a lot of research at the public library, including reading books by survivalists who thought they could live through World War III. He got pamphlets from FEMA, the Federal Emergency Management Agency, showing evacuation routes. He even snuck in at a public university and audited a couple classes in a course titled "Nuclear and Classical War." He heard a lecture there on optimal burst heights for maximum overpressure and minimal fallout from an old coot of a professor who couldn't button his own vest straight, but that wasn't really helpful. They didn't have the capacity to do anything but a ground burst. Besides, maximum depth of penetration at ground zero and corollary shock wave impact through the ground was much more important to their desired effect than maximum overpressure at ground level or minimizing fallout.

There was even a book put out by the U.S. Office of Technology Assessment called *The Effects of Nuclear War*. It was scary enough that the pre-Soviet-collapse volume not only had maps showing the location of ICBM fields, airfields for SAC bombers, and submarine support bases, but scarier still that it actually showed the blast radius for bombs of different sizes centered on Detroit. Oddly, it also noted that one of the effects of nuclear war was that vacation patterns would shift to locations closer to home. Jesus! The government studied everything.

He was careful, of course, not to leave a trail, just in case the government was studying him. No requests to the library staff to help him research Soviet nuclear systems or anything. He had, after all, seen *Star Trek IV.* He just tracked down what he needed himself, then went to the local Rand McNally store to get maps of the geological areas that were of interest to him, then to Target for a grade-school compass so he could draw concentric rings on the maps. He didn't hang around the school supply aisle any longer than he needed to, that's for sure. He didn't need someone thinking that he was a pedophile on the prowl. A suburban mom with a can of pepper spray could be more dangerous than the FBI. And the FBI was plenty dangerous.

Zeke didn't trust the government—he didn't trust anyone at all.

Brandon loved the government, at least the bureaucratic part of the government. It provided more free information than the Internet, and with considerably greater accuracy. Want historical data on prevailing wind patterns? Check with the National Weather Service. Need information about geological features? Chat with a ranger with the National Park Service. Need forms to run an export/import service? Drop by the Customs Bureau. You could get passport forms at the local Post Office and demographic statistics from the Census Bureau. And it was all free. Free, free, free.

Everything was coming together. Barrington's check cleared. They had a workable idea. GreensWord would save the world. He patted his clipboard affectionately and dropped it into his knapsack as he completed the last of his information gathering and headed off to prepare his presentation.

A little planning, a bit of legwork, and a bunch of someone else's money and you could actually score a nuclear weapon or two. Heck, it was less work than his Eagle Scout community service project had been. And this time, somebody besides his mom might notice his public service.

Milo had no use for government libraries, government bureaucrats, or government-sponsored information. His world was self-contained. With Brandon and Zeke off doing God knows what, he had the GreensWord headquarters all to himself. He worked hard, watching TV for hours and hours on end, including classic reruns on TV Land. *CSI, NCIS, L&O-SVU,* even *The Man from U.N.C.L.E.* He listened to Jay Leno kvetch about stupid criminals and watched Monk and Matlock and Barnaby Jones catch 'em. He tuned into Court TV and the Discovery Channel. He read popular mystery novels and true-crime books and he surfed the Web for sites used by writers to check their forensic facts. And when he needed a break, he played *Terrorist Threat* or dropped by Matty's beach house, to play with Mitzi when Matty wasn't around. Fortunately, Barrington was enough of a has-been that Milo didn't have to worry about paparazzi lurking around the beach house snapping a shot that would give him away to their benefactor. Which was good, 'cause he hated to think about problems like that.

All he wanted to do was blow things up and get laid. Who needed the government for that?

The fact was that even though the government went to war and screwed people all the time, it actively discouraged its citizens from engaging in either activity.

CHAPTER 12

Zeke was keyed up. This evening would be a defining point in his life, GreensWord's life, the history of the fucking planet . . . and he was in charge. He'd done his homework. If Brandon and Milo had carried their weight, this would be the night that it would all come together.

He swore under his breath when he walked into the living room of GreensWord's tract house. Fucking Milo was sitting at the computer playing the same damn computer shoot-'em-up he had been playing when they'd last gathered. He could tell from the incessantly annoying background music and the constant static-riddled explosions.

Worse yet, Brandon was setting up an easel on which to display a stack of poster-sized visual aids. He wanted to snap both their heads off, but he counted to ten, then to twenty, in an effort to calm his tone. When he did talk, his tone was more plaintive than angry.

"Please," he said to Brandon, "please, tell me that you didn't go to Kinko's to make visual aids for our plan to set off a thermonuclear bomb."

Brandon stopped in the middle of grabbing the first piece of poster board, with a sheepish look on his face.

"Well, I couldn't figure out how to make a spreadsheet on the computer."

Milo spoke without bothering to look up from his game, his fingers twitching the controls rapidly. "Freakin' Nakajami. All that Macrosurf crap is too complicated for the average user. We should just ditch this conformist hunk of junk. . . ."

"Hey!" interjected Brandon.

". . . and get a Macintosh. It would up my score on *Terrorist Threat* by at least twenty percent."

Zeke desperately wanted to avoid this argument, at least tonight. "Look," he said, "if we have any money left over after buying the nuclear weapon, you can get yourself some new toys to play with out of Barrington's money. Okay?"

Milo actually looked up from the computer screen in astonishment. "Awesome, dude! Awesome! Who says that actors are money-grubbing, no-talent, worthless slime?"

"Everybody," said Brandon.

"Yeah, pretty much," agreed Zeke. He turned back toward Brandon's easel, grimacing as he did so. "But that solves the problem for the future. It doesn't help with the current . . . lapse."

Brandon bristled. "I didn't breach security. It's not a lapse. So stop worrying. It's just a few spreadsheets of shipping costs and ports."

That was a relief. "Great. No problem. We're fine then." Zeke sat down. "Let's start."

Brandon consulted a list on his clipboard. "First thing, Svetlana's on board."

Zeke was surprised. Brandon could barely talk to women in most situations. "What did you tell her?"

Brandon flipped back several pages, apparently consulting some sort of crib sheet he had used for the call. Zeke was impressed with the forethought the boy had displayed, but less impressed with him as a man, once he realized Brandon had actually used a script.

Brandon scanned his papers and answered in a veritable monotone. "I told her: Quote, we need the radioactive material to plant at a power facility so that it can be discovered in a non-secure area and provoke a public-relations crisis. The resulting controversy will help make sure the asshole politicians don't go back to nuclear power plants just because electricity costs too much, unquote."

Zeke couldn't believe Brandon had actually scripted out a phrase like "asshole politicians." He guessed it was an effort to make him sound tough and uninhibited, instead of uptight and geeky. He guessed it hadn't worked. But before he could say anything in response to Brandon, Milo chimed in, still without looking up from his computer game.

"That's right, dude. The only way to cure energy dependence is to stop using it."

Zeke's foot tapped lightly. "That would be so much more credible," he said, "if you could put your joystick down."

Milo's hands never wavered at the controls. "Hey, computers are different." He pressed a button furiously and another tinny explosion rocked the crappy speakers. "They're a production enhancer. . . ."

"I can see that," murmured Zeke to himself.

". . . as well as the future residence of the human race."

"Huh?" said Brandon, before Zeke had the chance.

Milo apparently maneuvered his commando to lay down suppressing fire, so he could turn away from the screen for a few moments to talk. "Look, we got super fast computers. . . ." He hesitated for a moment, before gesturing at the Quompat. ". . . well, not here, but mankind has super fast computers—getting faster all the time when they're not bogged down with Naka-jami's god-awful software."

Brandon still looked confused. "Yeah?"

"We also got. . . ."

"Mail?" interjected Brandon.

Milo gave Brandon a disgusted look. "No, doofus, we got

memory out the wazoo."

Zeke narrowed his eyes to mere slits. "Your mastery of technical terminology has always amazed me," he said sarcastically.

Milo flipped him off with casual nonchalance before continuing. "On the medical front, you got CAT scans, MRIs, gene sequencing, the whole shebang."

This wasn't moving things along. Zeke was losing his patience. "And your point is?"

Milo looked at them both as if his point was obvious, but Zeke sure didn't know what he was getting at. Finally, Milo threw up his hands and apparently decided to explain, with just a touch of a patronizing tone in his voice.

"Dude, it's just a matter of time before they can scan our brains down to the molecular level, drop us into a virtual reality world in one big mother of a computer, and let us live our lives there forever 'til the end of time." He paused for a moment before continuing, the patronizing tone increasing just a bit. "Once we're uploaded, they can *Soylent Green* our bodies to . . . feed the whales or something. We won't care. We'll have a consciousness in the computer."

Brandon looked at Milo incredulously. "Milo, my man, you have got to stop reading so much science fiction."

Zeke was genuinely disturbed by Milo's explanation. He stalled for time as he took it all in. "And you believe this is a real possibility?"

Milo acted as if he was amazed that this was news to anyone. "It's inevitable. Dude, why do you think we haven't located any other intelligent life in the universe?"

"You mean, aside from dolphins," interjected Brandon.

"And whales," said Zeke. "Don't forget about whales."

"Pigs are pretty smart, too, they say," mused Brandon.

"I had a dog as a kid that knew how to play hide-and-seek," said Zeke.

"I mean," interrupted Milo, "on other planets. Why haven't we located any other intelligent life elsewhere in the universe?"

Zeke looked at Milo in bewilderment, then at Brandon. Brandon stared blankly back.

Milo grabbed the sides of his shaggy head in apparent frustration, then held his hands out toward them as if he were holding the solution out for them to see and feel.

"Because any intelligent life advanced enough to be capable of interstellar space flight rapidly figures out that it can exist in a virtual reality environment much more safely and much more pleasantly than in the real world, so it bags the real world for a better one."

It almost, just almost, made some twisted sense to Zeke on a logical level, but he couldn't quite fit it into his world view. "So why," he said, his voice betraying both confusion and frustration, "why exactly are you an environmentalist?"

"I think he said it was for the chicks," quipped Brandon.

Zeke ignored Brandon and enunciated his question with more clarity. "Why, if you are inevitably going to live in a virtual world, do you care what happens to the planet?"

Milo leaned back in his chair and began pivoting it back and forth by pushing off with one foot. "Jeez, Zeke, I gotta live here 'til they perfect the technology and if Nakajami keeps his stranglehold on software applications, that could take a while."

Zeke's head hurt. This wasn't the way the evening was supposed to be going.

"I'm glad we've established," he said, "that the world is worth saving until the triumphant and inevitable dominance of Apple Computer. Can we get back to the point?"

Now Brandon seemed confused. "Which was?"

Zeke sighed in frustration. "Svetlana."

Milo sighed in lust. "Yeah, Svetlana."

Zeke turned to Brandon. "I'm not criticizing; I'm just asking.

Why in the world would Svetlana give us a working nuclear weapon just so we can get our hands on some radioactive material?"

Now Brandon's tone became patronizing. "Think it through. That's the easiest way. If she just takes the radioactive payload, there's still an empty warhead, and the bean counters will check to see if the nuclear material is still intact. But, if she dismantles the whole missile and puts the pieces we don't take into the spare-parts inventory, there's no weapon to check. She bypasses the decommissioning process completely; there's no one else involved. They don't notice an ICBM is missing until the count comes up one short at the end of the whole task. In addition, she doesn't risk contamination by removing the nuclear payload from the warhead—not to mention it ships better in its intact state."

Zeke nodded. It made more sense than Milo's plan to live out his retirement years in a computer.

"Sorry to say, though, that she isn't exactly giving us anything. A six-hundred-thousand-dollar contribution to her cause is, however, within our budget for a nuke." Brandon's hand fluttered in apology. "I tried to get her to go two for nine hundred fifty thousand dollars, but I guess I'm not that good at haggling, or maybe she just figured that two was much more likely to get her caught." He brightened up. "But I did get her to give us one of the big ones. Fifty megatons."

Zeke whistled a low note between his teeth.

Milo chimed in with a soft "Boom, there it is."

"When and where do we get it?" asked Zeke.

Brandon flipped to yet another page on his clipboard. "The Novgorod Wastewater Treatment Conference next week provides a perfect cover for going over there."

Thank goodness Zeke could actually count on Brandon to do what he was asked. This just might come together, despite

Milo's lack of any meaningful contribution besides Svetlana's phone number. He got up and began to pace as the discussions continued.

"Let's talk about where we would detonate then. That's the big question, isn't it?"

Brandon flipped through some more pages, but didn't really seem to find anything. Finally, he simply said, "Gotta be northern hemisphere, right? Not enough particulate matter will make it up here to affect weather patterns in Malibu if we do it south of the equator."

Zeke pivoted slowly at one end of his pacing. "Agreed. It also seems best to do it on U.S. soil—we don't want to set off a war or anything."

Milo thumbed the pause button on his game. He seemed to be getting interested in the conversation. He scratched his stubble with a languid caress of his chin. "It's a Russian nuke. Won't they be able to . . . I dunno . . . fingerprint the payload with a spectrometer or something?"

Zeke stopped pacing for a moment and scratched an itch behind his right ear. "Maybe all that science fiction is paying off after all, Milo. Yeah, we gotta assume that there's some kind of science stuff that will let them identify the radioactive material as coming from a Russian warhead. But we can keep them from blaming Russia. We'll take care of that when we give the warning."

Brandon looked relieved. "Yeah, there definitely has to be a warning."

Milo seemed more skeptical. "Just understand, dudes, that's a major . . . major . . . complicating factor in not getting caught. You have to make the warning credible enough to be believed without revealing so much information that we get busted or the bomb gets found." He tilted his head left, then right, and cricked his neck. "It could be tricky."

Zeke smiled lightly. Maybe even Milo was taking his task seriously. He decided to lead by encouragement. "You're a gamer . . . and a pretty smart fellow all around. I'm sure you can figure something out."

Milo started playing with a rubber band. "Enough time to evacuate means enough time to search, which means there is a possibility . . . a definite possibility . . . that they stop the bomb and investigate the crime scene." He crinkled up his nose.

Zeke pushed ahead. "Next purchase at Target, a box of disposable plastic gloves."

"As a starter," mused Milo as he rotated and stretched his rubber band and continued to rotate his chair back and forth. "Don't worry. I think I can cover it. In fact, I'm sure I can. It's a piece of cake."

Brandon looked up from his clipboard at Milo's last statement. "Speaking of which," he said, with an embarrassed tone to his voice, "could we, maybe, take a break and eat?"

Zeke looked at Brandon in confusion. Was he serious? They were finally on topic and making progress. But then Milo jumped on the bandwagon.

"Brandon's right. Let's nuke some popcorn or something before we decide what else we're going to nuke. I don't want to obliterate the wrong place just because I've got low blood sugar."

A great leader, thought Zeke, knows when to follow. Besides, everyone has to eat, even people planning nuclear attacks. He wondered if there was a take-out menu in the briefcase of nuclear codes that followed the President wherever he went. He remembered back when the first Gulf War had started. His dad had called home to his mom and suggested she order a pizza, so they could sit in the living room and watch the war without interruption. From that day forward he had always associated the green peppers on the pizza with the green flares of antiaircraft fire broadcast by CNN through their night-vision lens that first night of the attack.

Whenever his dad ordered pizza, he called it the Baghdad Blitz special.

Zeke didn't go home much anymore.

And he never got green peppers on his pizza.

CHAPTER 13

They ended up getting three pizzas. They could agree to create nuclear winter by blowing up a volcano somewhere, but there was no way the three of them could agree on pizza toppings. Milo, of course, wanted everything on his pizza. Zeke wouldn't eat anything with green peppers. Brandon, the vegan of the group, wanted almost nothing except mushrooms and veggies on his macrobiotic-crust pizza—not even cheese.

"Dude," said Milo. "I've got some packets of ketchup and some saltines in the paperclip drawer of the computer desk. Why bother ordering a pizza if you don't put any cheese on it?"

Brandon sighed wearily. "Milo, we've been through this a zillion times. I'm vegan. I'm not eating cheese. It exploits cows."

Milo was in a good mood, so he refused to let up. "How exactly does it exploit cows to milk them? If the farmer didn't milk the cows, they'd like explode or something."

"Only because they've been bred and engineered to have huge udders and produce enormous amounts of milk," Brandon retorted.

Milo smirked. "I like huge udders. Truth told, cows never had it so good. They get fed regularly, get put up in a barn when it gets cold, and their shit gets carried away by conveyor belts and processed into odorless bedding. Doesn't sound like exploitation to me."

Brandon harrumphed. "I'll remember that the next time you are talking about employees as serfs. Besides, it's not natural."

Now Milo really got into it. "It's completely natural, dude. It's evolutionarily sound. If cows had never been domesticated, there wouldn't be huge freakin' herds of them all over the Midwest, the plains states, and large parts of South America, Australia, California and even Hawaii. They would have been wiped out like the Bison or those weirdly-named, spindly-legged antelopes in Africa. By allowing themselves to be milked and raised, there are millions of them, breeding like crazy and living the good life."

Brandon looked truly disgusted. "Until we slaughter them and eat their bloody carcasses and process their hide into belts and leather upholstery for overpowered and overpriced cars."

Milo was unperturbed by Brandon's argument. "The wolves would eat 'em if we didn't."

"That's your standard of moral conduct? Wolves would do it, so why don't we? No wonder you sleep around so much."

Milo wagged his head, smiling. "Don't press me, dude, or I'll pee on everything to mark my territory, chew up the couch cushions, and hump your mate, if you ever have one. Wolves would."

"Yeah," said Brandon, "but we've evolved beyond carnivorous, primal instincts. Some of us have evolved sufficiently that we don't eat our fellow animals—we stick to plants. Eating sentient creatures is just barbaric."

Milo raised his eyebrows. Brandon was so easy to set up that there almost wasn't any sport in it. "How do you know what is sentient and what isn't?" he said, as innocently as he could.

Brandon was so clearly flabbergasted by the question that Zeke came to his defense. "C'mon, Milo. It's obvious. Cows may not be bright, but they're sentient. They react to their surroundings, they have social structure, they all face the same way when they stand around in a pasture. . . ."

Milo waved Zeke off. "Not cows, dude, or even wolves.

Everyone knows mammals are sentient. The thing is, how do you know plants aren't?" Zeke closed his eyes and sighed, but Brandon looked positively forlorn, so Milo pressed on. "Take sunflowers, man. They react to the environment around them and they all face the same direction when they're in a field together. Did'ya ever think that they might always be facing the sun, not because of a need to get the extra tiny bit of sunlight in order to live, but because they are sun worshippers and are merely trying to show their obeisance to their god?"

Zeke snorted loudly. Brandon's face relaxed and he gave Milo a slit-eyed look. He had obviously figured out he was being had.

Milo held his hands up in concession. "Just a thought, dude. It doesn't make any difference to me. All I know is, whenever I hear someone mowing the lawn, there's this high-pitched whine that I never hear when the mower is just idling on the driveway—like a gazillion blades of grass screaming in agony as they are sliced apart by a mysterious force they can never know or understand. They tend their wounds and struggle to grow again when all of a sudden . . . *BANG!*"—he slammed both hands palm down on top of the kitchen table—"the same thing happens to them the next week. No wonder they scream. I would if someone cut a piece off of me every week."

Dinner arrived in thirty minutes or less. They ate in relative silence. Brandon picked at his pizza, concentrating on the mushrooms.

Finally it was time to get back to business. Milo smirked slightly as Zeke tried yet again to assert his leadership skills by framing the discussion.

"So," he said, "U.S. territory."

"Let's take out west Texas, man," volunteered Milo with enthusiasm. "Nobody but George W. Bush. . . ."

111

They all spat exaggeratedly in unison.

". . . cares about west Texas."

Zeke, of course, had to be practical. "Not exactly a lot of volcanoes there. Basically, our choices are Hawaii or the Pacific Northwest."

Brandon, in Milo's mind clearly still smarting from having lost the cattle battle earlier, shifted into his usual smarty-pants, problem-solving, pain-in-the-ass mode.

"What about Alaska? Aren't there volcanoes in Alaska?"

Zeke had an answer ready, though. "Pretty far north. Not to mention that there are more animals than people in Alaska. It hardly seems fair—people can be warned, but critters can't." Milo hated when people mentioned things by saying "not to mention" before reciting them, but he didn't interrupt their leader. It would bust his already low self-esteem. "Besides," continued Zeke, "you'd wreck a huge percentage of total national forest acreage."

Brandon conceded the point. "It does seem counterproductive to protest drilling in the Arctic National Refuge just so we can blow it up."

Milo thumbed towards the window. "What about L.A., dudes?"

Zeke sighed. "There aren't any volcanoes in L.A., Milo."

Milo couldn't believe it. Didn't these guys pay any attention to popular culture? "Duh. Maybe not now, but the La Brea Tar Pits mean there could be. Didn't you see the movie, man? *Volcano: The coast is toast.*"

Brandon huffed. "Jeez, Milo. Don't believe everything you see in a movie. Where's your critical objectivity? You're not going to let what some yahoo in a movie says dictate policy are you?"

Zeke interjected before Milo could respond. "Besides, brainiacs, Barrington's house is in Malibu. If we nuke L.A., I don't think it's going to improve his property values."

Milo slumped back in his chair. "Oh, yeah, man. Right."

Brandon leaned forward. "Yellowstone. There's a lot of geologic activity there. Steam vents, geysers, boiling mud."

Zeke thought for a moment. "Same thing as Alaska, except more populated. You hate to go out of your way to target a treasured National Park, especially one where a lot of people actually go to teach their kids about the wonders of nature. It hardly seems fair. I'm willing to hit a park—it's hard to find an acceptable target outside of one—but only if there is actually a real, live volcano there. I don't want to nuke a geyser."

When no one objected, he continued. "I'm thinking Hawaii."

Milo tried to think about Hawaii: surf, sand, hula girls, and getting lei'd. But Brandon didn't reflect for even a moment.

"Gee, I don't know, Zeke. Aren't there some bird species which aren't found anywhere else? Like the O'o and the O'u? We don't want to be hasty. Species extinction is an important environmental issue."

Milo saw Zeke's eyes narrow. "Uh-oh," he whispered.

Zeke quivered for a moment, then seemed to lose it. He sat forward on the recliner in an abrupt motion and slammed his open palm down on a TV tray that held the box of uneaten crusts from his pizza, sending a shower of crumbs up into the air and back down. His voice cracked with tension as he spoke: "Planetary extinction is the critical environmental issue! We're talking about setting off a goddamn nuke here, not because it's fun, but because it has to be done to save the fucking planet." His volume and his tempo increased as his diatribe continued. "Somebody has to make the hard decisions that the politicians are afraid to make. Somebody has to take action before it's too late. Somebody has to lead!"

Milo stared at Zeke. He hated this rah-rah, patriotic, "go team" crap. He turned calmly to Brandon, who was looking a trifle chagrinned for having set off Zeke.

"I think," said Milo softly, "Zeke is saying that when you set off a nuke, some eggs . . . and birds . . . are going to get fried."

Brandon looked from Zeke to Milo and back again. Zeke shook his head and leaned back in his chair, interlacing his fingers atop his head and massaging his temples with the heels of his palms. Finally, Brandon looked back to Milo.

"Scrambled."

"What?" said Milo.

"Some eggs . . . and birds . . . are going to get scrambled. That's the expression for what happens when big plans are put in place."

Milo's hand fluttered in dismissal. "Scrambled, fried, then vaporized in a heat flash hotter than the surface of the sun in July. . . ."

Brandon interrupted, raising his hand as if in class as he spoke. "Ah, Milo, the sun's not any hotter in July than any other time of year. . . ."

Zeke sat back up, removing his hands from the sides of his head, palms outward in a motion to stop. "Can we please . . . please . . . not have a discussion about the temperature of the sun and what causes the seasons right now? We were talking about whether Hawaii is an acceptable target. Can we go back there? Please?"

Brandon started to speak, then stopped. Finally, he started again, but did not make eye contact with Zeke. Instead, he stared at the empty kitchen table. His unfinished pizza had been neatly boxed up and put away before the discussion began. "There is a bigger problem with Hawaii than species destruction."

"Okay," said Zeke, his tone businesslike. "Like what?"

"It's an island . . . well, eight major islands." Zeke glowered at Brandon. Brandon rushed on. "Evacuation would be a nightmare on an island. People smart enough to leave might not be able to."

Milo nodded amiably. "It flunks from my perspective, too. Too little egress, too closely monitored. We either have to leave the thing armed and ticking for too long or we have to take a plane out of there just before we give the warning."

Zeke's eyebrows furrowed in thought for a moment, but then relaxed in apparent frustration. "So?"

"If the nuke doesn't go off and they get a lead on us, they have a tape from some airport security cam which proves we were there," said Milo. He shook his shaggy head slowly. "You gotta stick with a car, camping, and cash for gas, man."

For once, Brandon looked at him with respect. "Yeah, that would work."

Milo pointed at Brandon and shook his finger in warning. "Don't get too cocky, man. Look at McVeigh." He turned toward Zeke, to make sure their leader felt included in the discussion. "After the Oklahoma City bombing, they got every security video in the city—ATMs, fast-food joints, the works. They synced 'em up and followed his whole journey to the parking space."

"So, we have to leave the . . . device . . . someplace remote," said Brandon.

"Yep," said Milo, "and hope the electromagnetic pulse blows out the few videos we might have been caught on outside the actual blast zone."

Zeke joined in again, finally. "That brings us back to the Pacific Northwest. Somewhere in Oregon or Washington."

Milo snorted in laughter. "Dude, I could never figure out why those fascist survivalists live in Oregon, man. The Cascades, that's a powder keg they're sitting on, even without our help."

Zeke fumbled briefly with a map. "The farther north in the range, the more volatile the volcanic possibilities and the less impact any fallout will have on the major population centers eastward."

"I've been to east Washington," chimed Brandon. "It looks like it's already been nuked."

Zeke frowned for a moment and scratched his cheek as he studied the map on his tray. "That does put us near Seattle."

Seattle! Milo practically jumped for joy. "Two for the price of one!" he shouted with delight.

Both Brandon and Zeke looked up at him with confusion on their faces. Brandon spoke for them both: "Huh?"

Didn't they see? Wasn't it obvious? Milo turned from one to the other of them in quick succession, his face alight with joy. "We save the world from global warming and. . . ." He paused for dramatic effect. ". . . and we save the world from Macrosurf in one fell swoop! We gotta put the nuke on Rainier."

Zeke pored over his map and his information sheets. Milo quivered in anticipation. Finally, their leader spoke: "The rift lines between Mount Rainier and Mount St. Helens would have a favorable chance of rupturing."

Milo licked his lips as he looked over Zeke's shoulder.

"And the rock on the north and west flanks is altered . . . ," Zeke murmured, reading from a sheet, ". . . uh . . . that means weakened by sulfuric acid percolating since the last really major explosion almost five thousand years ago, so the blast is more likely to trigger an eruption."

He looked up. "It could do the trick."

If Milo got any more excited, he was going to have to pee. "And, even if it doesn't, we've made the world a better place by taking out Nakajami and his cyber goons."

"I don't know," temporized Zeke. "Lots of people, including African-American leaders, for sure, would say that causing a disaster in an urban area, even with a warning, is inherently racist because the poor have less chance of escaping."

"You're saying it's racist to nuke the Pacific Northwest?" exclaimed Milo. His fingers flew over the keyboard of the computer. Charts and numbers flowed over the screen. "Blacks are barely over three percent of the population in Washington State." He played with the cursor, pointing and clicking in a blur of motion. "Highest fallout incident areas are even less: Oregon, one point six; Idaho, point four; Montana, point three; the Dakotas, point six apiece. I'll bet Saskatchewan is even less. We couldn't pick a less racist place to nuke, except maybe Sweden."

That seemed to satisfy Zeke.

Brandon scrunched up his face in thought. "Maybe we should take the leftover money and short some Macrosurf stock."

Milo cut off Brandon. "No way! Classic mistake. The Securities and Exchange Commission will track you down electronically. Never . . . never inside trade on a terrorist act. It just makes you look like some money-grabbing capitalist."

Brandon looked baffled. "Let me get this straight. You're willing to be a mass murderer, but not a capitalist?"

"Duh, yeah!"

Zeke smiled. They had a plan. They had a deal to acquire the means and the money to pay for it. They had a place. "Okay, let's get to work."

CHAPTER 14

"Just squeeze rhythmically," said the young nurse to Milo. Even though she was wearing a blue smock instead of the white uniform he often fantasized about, Milo was getting a hard-on as Angie—her nametag read Angie—leaned in toward him. He was about to say something witty and charming about swapping bodily fluids when he remembered he was supposed to be doing this incognito. Before he could work his way around that, the moment passed. Instead of exchanging fluids or even clever banter, Nurse Angie simply released the rubber tourniquet on Milo's arm with a snap and removed the needle from his arm as she leaned back.

She handed him a small square of white gauze and quickly turned back to her supply counter of testing vials, collected specimens, empty plasma bags, and other medical sundries. "Hold the gauze firmly against your arm," she said in an amiable, but professional, monotone. He obeyed meekly, his organ deflating with his ego.

She turned back to him with a Band-Aid in one hand and a slip of paper in the other. "Put that on your arm," she said as she handed him the first item. "Take that to the front desk and they'll give you a 'I Saved a Life' sticker and get your info to send you a donor card listing your blood type," she said as she handed him the second, punctuating her instruction with a smile.

Milo got up from the chair, his arm crooked to maintain

pressure on the puncture site where Nurse Angie had taken his blood. He flushed slightly. "I know the routine."

Nurse Angie headed out the examination room door to the next room, the next donor. "Don't forget to grab a cookie and some juice on the way out."

Milo started to follow her, but as soon as she turned down the hallway and out of sight, he stopped, dashed back to the counter holding the specimens of blood for testing, grabbed two handfuls of the small vials (avoiding his own) and shoved them into his pocket. He rushed down the hallway, past the receptionist, and out the door into an unfamiliar neighborhood.

Brandon started to stow his carry-on luggage in the bin above their seats when a perky flight attendant rushed over to do it for him. He thanked her and sank into his wide, leather seat, next to Zeke. A flute of champagne appeared almost instantly on his tray table, which was so far from his seat that he actually had to lean forward to reach it. He had never traveled like this before. Never. He took a sip of the champagne. It was better than the Asti Spumante his parents served on New Year's Eve.

He looked over at Zeke sitting sullenly in the roomy window seat, his champagne untouched.

Brandon took another sip of the champagne and ogled the flight attendant as she assisted stowing another passenger's bag. Finally, he looked back over at Zeke.

"What's wrong?"

Zeke leaned over, speaking in low tones. "I still think it's unethical to be spending so much GreensWord money to fly to Russia first class."

"It's the only seats I could get on short notice," whispered Brandon. "Besides, nuking Seattle is okay, but flying first class bothers you?"

"Yeah," said Zeke.

"Boy, would my therapist like to meet you."

Milo parked the van in the first space he could find after he saw the "Help Wanted" sign in the front window of Barber Anne's Surfside Hair Salon. He banded his unruly hair into a ponytail and opened the door, receiving a blast of cold air and Beach Boys' music as he stepped inside. He winced, wondering if he would freeze to death first or go insane from the looping repetition of "Barbara Ann" over the cheap stereo system, but he gritted his teeth and grabbed the sign out of the window.

Ten minutes later, he had been assigned a broom and a dustpan. The rest of the day was spent sweeping and nodding politely when the Korean manicurist said something to him which he didn't understand. He only made two dollars in tips by the end of the day, but he got what he came for. As Anne was closing up, he dumped the hairy contents of his dustpan into a plastic bag he had hidden in his pocket, then quickly seized the tray of nail clippings off the manicurist's tray and emptied it into a smaller Baggie. He wiped the broom handle off with a hand towel and headed back out to the van. He vowed never to listen to surf music again.

Zeke looked over at Brandon. The boy was fidgety, stamping his feet and looking around with frightened eyes as Svetlana expertly maneuvered the heavy forklift carrying their purchase. Finally, Svetlana laid the crate gingerly into the back of a large, panel truck and began to back the forklift away, the beeping of the forklift keeping time with the jiggle of her ample bosom from the vibration of the equipment. Brandon, however, seemed not to notice. Despite the pleasant weather on the Russian steppes, his collar was turned up and his head tucked down into his jacket. He shifted his weight, dancing from one foot to the other, as if he needed a restroom. The boy would make a lousy spy.

"Relax," hissed Zeke. "Even if she'd dropped it, it wouldn't have gone off."

Brandon looked up toward the truck. "Huh?" He spied the empty forklift heading back toward the maintenance shed. "Oh, it's loaded."

"Yeah. Are you all right?"

Brandon looked around yet again. "So, exactly how far away is Chernobyl from here?"

Zeke smiled. "A hundred kilometers. About sixty miles."

Brandon coughed. "Is that enough?"

"It was a long time ago."

"Yeah," said Brandon, scanning the area again, as if his eyes could detect the invisible death that was high-level radiation, "but not in a galaxy far, far away."

Zeke smiled at the reference. "We're upwind. It's enough."

Brandon squeezed his eyes and scrunched up his face, looking decidedly unconvinced.

Zeke touched his friend's elbow in an effort to reassure the kid. "They even give tours there these days. Not all the way to the reactor, of course, but to the evacuated town."

"They do?"

"Humanity always delights in celebrating its mistakes. Besides, for the locals, it may not be a life, but it's at least a half-life." Zeke chuckled at this own joke.

Brandon looked like he was making an effort to relax, but it just came off as forced nonchalance. "Nuclear stuff just makes me nervous, especially when it's not properly contained."

Zeke knew that Brandon's worries were silly, but was still proud of him. Brandon's being here despite his fears just made him seem more courageous in Zeke's eyes. Zeke put his arm around his colleague and clapped him on the back. "Hey, it's safer than mimicking a stunt on *Jackass.*"

Milo pulled the van onto the shoulder of the interstate and killed the engine. He quickly donned a pair of mittens and slid out the passenger side door, away from the screaming traffic, grabbing a half-empty, black plastic garbage bag on his way. He hurriedly began to collect beer bottles, soda cans, cigarette butts, and assorted debris, including two mismatched shoes, from the weeds along the side of the road. He even found a combination lug-nut wrench and crowbar someone had left on the shoulder when they had changed a flat tire. After a few minutes, he returned to the van and eased it back into the flow of traffic.

Three empty trash bags waited their turn on the backseat. The road was long and Milo hadn't gotten laid and hadn't blown anything up for many days.

Brandon was trying his best not to stare at Svetlana's chest as she walked back toward them from the maintenance shed. He wasn't succeeding. But, then, she didn't seem to notice or, perhaps, mind. She sidled up to him, as if flirting or speaking to a co-conspirator. She was, of course, doing the latter, but the only other person within a kilometer was Zeke and he was in on the conspiracy.

"You know, Brandon," she purred, her accent husky and rich, "I wouldn't do this for just anybody."

His heart raced. "I know, just for us."

Her full lips formed a pout as she leaned into him further, her breast pressing against his arm. "Just for the cause."

"Y-y-yeah, sure," Brandon stammered. "I understand. You don't do anything for me . . . I mean . . . you do plenty for me . . . for us . . . for the cause." Zeke looked as if he were going to burst out laughing. Brandon swallowed hard. "I'll just shut up now."

Svetlana turned to Zeke, her teasing over, her manner businesslike. "I put the instruction manual in the crate. It's not something you want to be carrying in your hand luggage when you go through customs. Now, what do you want me to put on the packing slip and customs forms? I stripped out all the guidance components and, of course, the nose cone, but the basic warhead is still bulky and heavy—not the size of something the average tourist or businessman would be shipping home."

Zeke's mirth faded quickly. "I don't know. It's got to be something heavy and eight feet long, but something Russia has plenty of and no one cares we're taking."

"But," interjected Brandon, "something that a bunch of students from UCLA would want and could afford."

Svetlana screwed up her face in determination. Brandon could do nothing but wait, as did Zeke, and try not to look at her breasts. Finally, her face brightened and she ran over and pulled out a clipboard and a sheaf of forms from the front seat of the panel truck. She scribbled on them and handed them to Zeke.

Zeke looked down at the forms and looked back at Svetlana. She grinned and gestured at the Cyrillic lettering. "One statue of Comrade Lenin for export, coming up."

"How can I help you, sir?"

Milo looked up to see a sales clerk striding toward him. The earnest fellow wore blue slacks and a short-sleeved, white shirt with a clip-on tie. His nametag identified him as "Frederick."

"Well, Fred, I want to get new carpeting for my apartment."

"That's what we're here for, Mr. . . . ."

"Banner, but you can call me 'Dave.' "

"All right, Dave. What color are you interested in?"

Milo shook his shaggy head and pursed his lips. "I'm just not sure."

"Let's talk texture . . . style. What did you have in mind there?"

"I haven't the foggiest idea, Fred. I really don't know much about carpets. I guess we're going to have to look at them all." Fred's professional smile sagged momentarily, but he soldiered on. "Right this way, Dave."

Truth be told, Milo felt sorry for the guy. He was going to spend hours here and not make a purchase and he was pretty sure that Fred worked on commission. Oh well. Maybe it would help spur Frederick into doing something else with his life, something worthwhile, something he could be proud of. Nobody grew up wanting to be a carpet salesman. The world wouldn't miss another carpet salesman, but it would embrace another committed environmentalist. Of course, Milo wasn't here to recruit, so he put his mind back on his task.

As Fred started showing him samples, Milo plucked at the carpet with an aluminum comb, pulling strands loose and collecting them in a pile on the countertop. Fred looked perturbed, but only said, "Sir?"

Milo kept plucking at the different carpets as he glanced up at the salesman. "I've got a cat at home, a Siamese. I need to know whether the rug can stand up to her sharpening her claws." Fred smiled weakly as Milo continued. "Don't worry, I won't leave a mess on the counter."

"To saving the world," murmured Zeke as he clinked his champagne flute against Brandon's in the first-class cabin of their return flight.

"To saving the world," responded Brandon.

Zeke drank up and waved over the flight attendant for a refill. He was beginning to have a good feeling about the plan, about

GreensWord, about saving the planet from the curse of global warming. True, his leadership role would probably, hopefully, never be known to the general public, but he would know, and that would be enough for him.

Making a difference, making the difference between survival and extinction of the planet, would nourish his soul forever. Not just serving the cause, but fulfilling it, would fuel a life of contentment and satisfaction.

He was in a very good mood.

He leaned over to Brandon. "You know, you missed your chance with Svetlana."

Brandon was wary. "What do you mean?"

"She was into you. You must've noticed."

"She was just teasing me. You're just teasing me."

Zeke shrugged and sipped more champagne. "All I know is the last thing she told me was how disappointed she was you didn't come by her room last night."

"Yeah, right."

"Scout's honor." Zeke had never been a Boy Scout, but he knew Brandon took the phrase seriously.

"Scout's honor?"

"Yep," said Zeke.

Brandon tilted his head to one side and seemed to reflect a moment. "She did practically throw herself at me after she loaded the cargo." He swigged down the rest of his drink. "Maybe I'll call her up and we can get together when she is in the States."

"No can do," said Zeke, as seriously as he possibly could. "I couldn't take the chance that she'd feel scorned and, you know, get mad or something. It could've jeopardized the project."

Brandon stared at Zeke, confused, as Zeke continued. "So I told her you were gay."

It was a long, quiet trip back to the States.

"Would you like fries with that?" said Milo in a weary monotone to the beefy customer at the counter.

"Fries?"

"They come in medium, which is our small size, large, which is our regular size, and mega, which is our large size. Or you can order a mega-combo and add a medium drink, which is our small size, for only fifty cents more." Milo adjusted his paper hat, which perched forward precipitously over his forehead because it didn't fit over the stump of his ponytail in back.

"I ordered breakfast. Who gets fries with breakfast? Or are you implying something?" The large man was growing red in the face and his ample belly and double chin were quivering in time to the throbbing of a large vein in his neck.

"I'm not implying. You must be inferring."

"Calvin," yelled the manager from the egg station, "why don't you take out the garbage while I help this gentleman?"

"Yes, sir," replied Milo in meek submission, as he shuffled over to the bins without removing his plastic serving gloves and pulled out two large bags to haul to the Dumpster. He dragged the garbage out the back door, which had a height marker on the side to help identify escaping robbers. The marker was also useful in pegging members of the local high school basketball team, who were actually getting work-study course credit for sneaking their friends free food at the drive-thru window. The Dumpster, which was not very well hidden behind a shabby decorative fence enclosure in the back, was unlocked and unmarked, leaving it open to thieves of any height.

Once in the back of the parking lot, Milo took a sharp left at the entrance to the trash shack, as his trainer had called it, and quickly opened the Minibus and tossed the two bags inside. The van, sitting in the morning sun, was already an oven, meaning the garbage would percolate in the heat all day. He'd have to drive with his head hanging out the window like Ace Ventura just to breathe when he completed his shift and left . . . in just six more hours.

It was going to be a long day on the front lines of the fast-food wars and an even longer drive through the twilight of America.

Brandon shifted uneasily as the stevedores loaded their crate onto the bed of a pickup truck. Zeke had borrowed the transport from a friend for a few days so they could collect their shipment in Phoenix. They had purposely come to the warehouse to retrieve their cargo right near closing time. That way, the crew would be in a hurry to get them on their way and would take less time to inspect their paperwork. Of course, the rush work also meant that the burly men were not handling the cargo with too much care.

Still, Brandon grinned, and tried not to fuss. The last thing they needed was to piss off the air freight workers or, worse yet, do something memorable. He turned his back on the truck to talk with Zeke.

"It's a heckuva long drive from here back to our office and an even longer drive once we switch it into the Minibus for the trek to Seattle."

Zeke didn't even look at him, but simply said softly: "Harder to trace, my friend. Harder to trace."

Milo wandered the aisles of the Wal-Mart without hurrying, as if window-shopping. In the clothing department, he pulled loose threads from cheap clothing. In the shoe department, he grabbed several random boxes of shoes of various styles and sizes, without opening them to even look inside. At check-out, he paid cash. This was the tenth discount store he had hit in the last six days.

Later that night, he parked the Minibus in Al's Sleepytime Campground and Fun Center. After the kids around the camp had all settled in for the night, he headed for the rustic, communal showers. He carried a towel, but he didn't get wet. Instead, he pried open the drain and used a screwdriver to haul out a soapy, slimy, hair clog that looked disgustingly like a dead rat, dropped it into a plastic bag and returned to the crowded, smelly Minibus.

At dawn, he was on the road again.

Zeke watched nervously as Brandon adjusted the mirrors in the truck for the third time. Finally, Brandon turned on the engine and reached for the gearshift.

"Take it easy, Brandon."

"Huh?"

Zeke counted off the points on his fingers as he made them. "No speeding. Full stops at all stop signs. Use you blinker changing lanes. Yield to pedestrians. Don't follow too closely."

"Zeke, it's me, Brandon. I'm a careful driver; you know that, despite the three traffic tickets from Milo's fiasco."

"I'm serious, Brandon. Are you going to follow my instructions or do I need to drive?"

Brandon furrowed his brow. "Milo was right. You are way too uptight."

Zeke sighed. "Look, there's three things you need to know if you're going to be a professional agitator."

Brandon simply blinked in astonishment.

"Number one," Zeke continued. "Don't throw rocks at people carrying automatic weapons."

Brandon nodded.

"Number two. Don't stand next to people who are throwing rocks at people carrying automatic weapons."

"That makes sense," said Brandon. "Who says the left hasn't learned the lessons of Vietnam?"

Zeke didn't smile. "And number three. Don't get stopped by a highway patrolman in a borrowed pickup while carrying a live thermonuclear weapon through the hood."

Brandon chuckled, but Zeke was still dead serious.

"We now have more weapons of mass destruction than Saddam Hussein did," Zeke reminded Brandon, "and the government started a war to try and find those. Let's make sure they don't find this one."

The music was pounding, the babes were gyrating, the drinks were flowing, and Milo was back in his element, weaving his way through a trendy club, sipping an overpriced and heavily-watered drink mixed from house brands, and making eye contact and occasional hip contact with members of the opposite sex. He felt like a sailor on leave, a convict just released from the slammer. He badly wanted, needed, to get laid.

He watched a vixen in a sexy, blue number for a bit. She noticed and didn't seem to mind. In another world, he knew what he would be doing with her tonight, but not in this world. Instead, he broke off eye contact and wound his way to the bar. He took out a paper lunch bag and started emptying ashtrays into it.

Unfortunately, the bag began to smolder. He patted the burgeoning flame out with a bar towel, but his veritable-sitcom antics attracted attention he didn't want for a variety of reasons. The bimbo in the blue silk was giggling as she whispered to a girlfriend and pointed his way. He gave up any pretense of coolness and ran for the door, grabbing another full ashtray on the way out.

He still badly needed to get laid.

CHAPTER 15

Zeke might be the ostensible leader of GreensWord, but Brandon knew that he, not Zeke, was the one who had stepped up to save the organization. While Zeke was dumbstruck in front of their raving benefactor, Brandon was the one that had taken the check. While Milo had slathered white paint on the Minibus and rambled on about sugar cubes and fake kidnappings, Brandon was the one who had pressed the only viable solution. He was the one who realized that the nuclear winter approach was not only the one solution that was fast enough to meet their mandate, it was within their budget and their means.

Now, it was all coming together. He and Zeke had secured the fifty-megaton solution to the world's problems. In the meantime, Milo had been left to make sure their tracks were covered in case anything went wrong. But when he and Zeke arrived back at GreensWord's office, there was Milo, in the same place they had left him, playing on the computer, without a briefing book, flip chart, or map in sight.

Brandon huffed audibly as he turned to scan the room, his eyes wide.

"It's like we never even left! Did you do anything while we were gone except play your stupid games?"

Milo barely looked up from the screen. "Fifteen cities in ten states."

Brandon gave him a dubious look. Zeke just stared at Milo, as if expecting him to continue his inadequate explanation.

"Doing exactly what?" prompted Zeke at last.

Milo thumbed the button to pause his game. "Not getting laid. This incognito spy stuff sucks."

"You could not get laid right here in L.A.," noted Zeke.

Milo worked the computer mouse, minimizing his game and calling up another program. "No, that would be Brandon."

Brandon was in no mood to be made fun of. "Some of us have standards," he retorted.

Milo glanced at him languidly. "Some of us don't print them up on a laminated checklist."

Brandon felt the blood rush to his face. He was searching for a clever response when Zeke interrupted.

"Look," said their supposed leader, setting down his bag and flopping onto the couch. "Can we avoid the squabbling until after we nuke Seattle? How's your assignment going, Milo?"

Screens of geeker gobbledygook flashed across the computer as Milo maneuvered the mouse. "Just a sec," said the tech whiz as he clicked and scrolled away with abandon. He pointed at the screen as if the arcane symbols and text meant anything to the rest of them. "You see here? I'm all set to hack into a variety of systems in order to create rumors about a domestic terrorist organization. Those rumors will make our eventual warning credible, so, you know, we'll be taken seriously. All I need is a name for the phony organization."

Brandon set aside his irritation. They were working on the plan now, and that is where he excelled. "How about 'Nuke the Whales'?" he volunteered.

Milo screwed up his face and shook his head lightly. "A little obvious. We don't want these early rumors to tip our hand on the weapon and trigger a search for a missing nuke. We'll save that tidbit 'til the last minute, when the warning goes out."

"Makes sense," Brandon admitted.

"Saviors of the World," said Zeke in a low voice.

"Huh?" Brandon stared at their leader. The guy could be a little grandiose at times. Fortunately, Milo cut him down to size.

"SOW?" said Milo, waggling his straggly hair at Zeke. "You want every news organization in the country . . . in the world . . . to abbreviate the sinister organization that nuked Seattle as SOW?"

Time for Brandon to show off his education. "Maybe we could use something historical," he volunteered. "The Know-Nothings or Fifty-Four-Forty-or-Fight or something. We could say we were protesting the current border with Canada."

Zeke waved a hand in dismissal. "We're supposed to be avoiding starting a war, not resurrecting old battle slogans. Besides, I don't think it makes much sense to blow up the current border in order to claim the land surrounding it."

"Jeez," whispered Milo, "you haven't read up much on the history of Eastern Europe, have you?"

Zeke glared. Milo stared. Brandon thought.

Finally, Brandon started to speak up, but Milo cut him off. "Dude, don't even think of suggesting 'Slytherin.' "

Brandon shut his mouth and thought some more.

"Hey," he eventually said, "when I was in Chicago, there was this street gang or whatever, that called themselves the 'Insane Unknowns.' They left graffiti all over the place. I always thought it was pretty creepy."

Nobody objected right away. They seemed to be mulling it over.

After a few moments, Zeke spoke. "It is spooky. The news media would lap it up. I can almost hear Griffin Gantry saying it—a deep baritone rendition, with just a hint of disgust."

They all savored the sound in their imaginations for a moment.

"But," continued Zeke, "we don't want to make it sound like

our project is anything but perfectly rational."

"To hell with that," blurted Milo. "I don't want to piss off a street gang by stealing its name."

Brandon saw yet another of his suggestions belittled into nothingness by his less-imaginative companions. He tried desperately to save it. "Then, what about the 'Sane Unknowns'?"

Milo snorted. "SU? You want the world to take seriously a terrorist organization named SU? Sounds like an old Johnny Cash song."

"Maybe," interjected Zeke, "it could be the Sane Unknown Volunteers. It makes it clear that we get nothing out of our actions personally."

A smile crept over Milo's face, until the ends touched his scraggly hair. "SUVs destroy the Pacific Northwest. Now, that's a headline I could get behind."

Zeke grinned back and Brandon gave a small whoop. It was all coming together. They were actually going to do it.

Zeke was cranky by the time that they had gotten the Minibus loaded and were headed for Mount Rainier. The uncrated bomb, itself, had been a bitch to fit into the van. A tarp covering it, the cylindrical device of mass destruction was shoved over the middle of the front seat at a slight angle, blocking the rearview mirror and crowding the passenger side of the compartment. On top of that, Milo had loaded the van with four mounted tires and eight or nine large, black plastic bags full of God knows what, so that there was barely a place to sit. Worse yet, the ride was terrible—rough and wobbly. He didn't know if it was from the weight of their cargo, the awkward distribution of items in the van, or if Milo had wrecked the thing in some way on his travels while he and Brandon were gone.

All he knew was that it was going to be a long, uncomfortable ride to Washington State. He knew he should just suffer in silence, but he couldn't help himself.

"Jesus, Milo. What is all this crap?"

Milo waggled his head from the driver's seat. "You'll see."

Brandon took up Zeke's cause, thumping a tire that was intruding into his personal space. "Worried about flats?"

Milo grinned, as he shifted the Minibus into third gear with some effort. "You don't need to worry about that. Just focus on learning how to arm the bomb on time. You've only got twenty-some hours 'til we get there."

Brandon looked more concerned about the cramped quarters than about his task. "Don't worry. Svetlana sent along an instruction manual, so we could, uh, you know, take out the radioactive material safely."

The van swayed heavily as Milo took a slight curve onto an expressway ramp.

"You might want to get at it," said Milo. "The light's crappy in the van after it gets dark."

Brandon looked at Zeke expectantly.

Zeke stared back. "Yeah?"

"Give me the instruction manual," said Brandon.

"I thought you had the instruction manual," replied Zeke.

Zeke fumbled around in his backpack. Brandon opened his briefcase and looked underneath his clipboard.

A half hour later, after Milo had taken the next exit and circled back to headquarters, they were once again on their way. This time Zeke had the instruction manual in hand. He flipped through it idly before handing it to Brandon. Zeke's eyes went wide and he frantically flipped to the back, then opened it to random pages.

His mood went from aggravation to despair. "Fuck! This is all in Russian!"

Brandon turned white. "Shit! I haven't read any Russian

since college."

Milo laughed. "You took Russian in college? No wonder you never got laid. Any other useless skills?"

Zeke glared at Milo. "Shut up, Milo." He turned to Brandon. "Can you do it? You were okay with the road signs in Russian when we were headed to meet Svetlana."

"Yeah. . . ." Brandon pondered for a moment, his arm resting on a spare tire. "In school they teach you conversational Russian, not technical stuff. I don't know."

"Look," Zeke said, in an effort to reassure his colleague, "the average grunt in the Russian Army can't be that well-educated. It's probably pretty simple language."

Brandon winced. "I'll try."

"That's the old college spirit, dude," said Milo from the driver's seat. "What's the worst that could happen?"

Brandon gave Milo an icy stare. "We could be vaporized in a microsecond."

"At least that doesn't leave any time for regrets, man."

Zeke patted Brandon on the shoulder, then turned to Milo. "Stop at a Waldenbooks, will you? We'd better pick up a Russian dictionary."

"All right," said Milo, "but remember to pay cash and keep your baseball cap tugged down low over your eyes, just in case."

Zeke sighed. It was going to be a long, long trip.

CHAPTER 16

The sun was shining again by the time they reached Mount Rainier National Park. The day was crisp and clear, the dazzling white of the mountain's glaciers was sharp against the blue sky. The dark green of the forest in the lower reaches of the mountain promised cooling shade from the glare of the bright sun.

If Milo wasn't so bleary-eyed from having driven all night, he might have enjoyed the scenery. But he was too tired for that. Not counting their aborted start, going back to get the instruction manual, they were twenty-three hours into their trip. Driving under the speed limit sucked.

Milo had made no stops except to gas up, piss, and buy fast food. They'd talked very little during the ride. Brandon had been muttering to himself in Russian a good part of the way for one thing. The only excitement had occurred when Milo had to stop his idiot companions from using one of his trash bags to dispose of their fast-food wrappers. Other than that, it had just been the uneven hum of the tires and the wind shrieking through the various rust holes on the Minibus for the last day and night.

Of course, Brandon and Zeke had dozed a bit during the night, so they were relatively perky. Especially Brandon, who seemed to have gotten a bit of an adrenaline rush from their proximity to accomplishing their mission. His energy manifested itself in its usual, professorial way; he was attempting to teach

Zeke Russian, or something.

"Yeah, it is a different alphabet, but you can write it cursively using our letters, if you want. It's just that the same letters don't mean the same thing."

"Huh?" muttered Zeke, who was attempting to look at some maps.

Brandon apparently ignored the fact that he was being ignored.

"Take the word 'student.' It's spelled the same way and pronounced basically the same way in Russian, but if you write it out cursively using our version of their alphabet, it comes out 'c . . . m . . . y . . . g . . . e . . . h . . . m.' "

"Smygem?" said Zeke, looking up from his maps.

"No," replied Brandon. "Studyent. See the c is an s, the m is a t, the y is a u, the g is a d. . . ."

Milo decided to show Zeke some mercy by interrupting.

"We're almost there. Which way do I go, boss?"

Zeke's eyes flicked back to his map. "Follow the signs towards Sunrise. The info you got me says the caves are a mile off the road on the way to a campground up that direction."

"There are caves at Rainier?" asked Brandon.

Zeke talked without taking his eyes from his cumbersome, folding map. "It's mostly known for its ice caves, you know, up in the glaciers near the summit. But like most volcanoes, it has some caves caused by earthquakes and partially collapsed lava tubes. There's a big one outside of the park, near Cliffdell. Called Boulder Cave. Goes a mile or so back from the entrance and has some huge western bats living in it. But we're not going there. Too far from the mountain."

"And much too public," added Milo from the front seat. "People going in and out all the time. You couldn't hide anything there, even if you took it way in."

"I asked Milo for some help and he found some references

on the Internet to smaller caves inside the park that aren't that well known," continued Zeke.

"Whaddya do? Hack into the Park Service computers?" asked Brandon.

Milo grinned ear to ear, despite his weariness. "Actually it was on a website for the BFRO." He waited for Brandon to try to guess.

"I give up," said Brandon after only a few moments. "My brain is fried. What is the BFRO?"

"The Bigfoot Research Organization, dude. They search the caves looking for Sasquatch, or at least his footprints."

Brandon reacted just as Milo thought he would. "You mean my . . . our . . . plan depends on a bunch of lunatics?"

Zeke looked up sharply. "Don't get started, guys. I'll verify the cave location as soon as we get there."

Milo shut up. He had had his fun. Brandon fell silent after only a few grumblings.

Zeke continued. "Once I've scouted out a suitable location, I'll come back to the van. Then, we'll park somewhere unobtrusive and nap a bit. We'll wait 'til after dark, unload the bomb, then leave it behind in one of the caves. We can cover the entrance with some tree branches."

Milo mocked Zeke with false outrage. "Cutting live branches is against park regulations, dude!"

His companions were weary, but not too weary to muster up their traditional response. "Shut up, Milo," they said in languid unison.

Brandon sat in the Minibus, twiddling his thumbs, while Zeke and Milo slept. No one, of course, had thought to bring an alarm clock, so Brandon was elected to sit awake in the van, while his companions slept, to make sure they got underway at the appointed time. Milo had suggested that they could use the timer on the nuclear trigger for a wake-up call, but no one had laughed. Things were getting serious.

So Brandon sat in the stuffy, increasingly rank van and thought about what they were about to do. Seattle gleamed through the haze in the distance.

At sunset, he woke the others. "Time to go."

He was about to wander off into the woods to take a piss when Milo stopped him.

"Dude, where are you going?"

He looked at Milo wearily. "Mother Nature calls," he said. He could feel himself blushing slightly.

Milo reached into the back of the van and pulled out an empty, plastic, milk jug.

Brandon raised his eyebrows. "You have got to be kidding."

"Evidence, dude. Evidence. It's like Boy Scouts. Leave nothing behind but your footprints, man."

Brandon wandered into the bushes and pissed into the milk carton. A slight waft of sour milk assaulted him as he opened the jug. You'd think Milo could have rinsed the jug out at least. It didn't smell any better once he'd pissed into it.

The things you'll do to save the world.

Zeke took his turn with the milk carton, then returned back to the van. He reached into the back of the Minibus and grabbed a small box, tossing it to Milo. "Here's the rubber gloves you asked me to get. Guess it's time to put them on."

Milo stared at the box. "Dude, I told you to get plastic gloves. These are latex."

Zeke simply stopped and looked at Milo. "So?"

"Man, I just hope I don't have an allergy to latex."

"Don't you know?" asked Brandon.

Milo tilted his head down just a tad. "How would I know?"

Brandon tapped his foot on the gravel roadway. "Condoms

are latex, man. Do you have a reaction when you use a condom?"

Milo smiled broadly. "Well, it does swell up. . . ."

"Shut up, Milo," said Brandon and Zeke, automatically.

Brandon and Zeke took the tarp-swaddled bomb, which was heavy and awkward. Milo followed behind, laden with his many garbage bags. Milo made them all wear paper hospital gowns and hair nets. They looked like a bunch of orderlies maneuvering a body bag and the day's trash up a hill.

Zeke had reconnoitered before they slept, so he took the lead. He still seemed to be having a tough time figuring out where he was going, though.

"It sure is dark," he said in irritation at one point, after stumbling over a rock.

"New moon, Zeke," said Brandon. "That's why I picked tonight. All elective military operations occur during the new moon. Ask Saddam Hussein."

Zeke merely grunted in response. They struggled on for a while before Zeke spoke again.

"Do you think there are any bears out here?"

Brandon would have shrugged his shoulders, if the bomb wasn't so damn heavy. Instead, he simply said, "Black bears, not to mention the endangered Northern Spotted Owl."

"Don't worry, man," Milo hissed from behind them. "I'm the one carrying the bags of trash. You'll be relatively safe."

Zeke harrumphed. "Sure, we all know that bears are such masters of subtlety that they'll only go for the guy actually carrying the food."

Milo began to chant, slow and low: "Lions and tigers and bears. Oh my! Lions. . . ."

Zeke interrupted in kind. "If you only had a brain. . . ."

Brandon could take the silliness no longer. "Jesus! I am never taking you guys on a covert mission again. What a lame-ass group of spies!"

"We're not spies," Milo giggled.

Now Brandon was getting really pissed. "What a lame-ass group of terrorists!"

Zeke stopped moving forward, almost causing Brandon to stumble. "We're not terrorists," he said firmly. "We're . . . we're concerned citizens."

"Sane Unknown Volunteers, man," chimed in Milo from behind. "Sane Unknown Volunteers. Saving the world from global warming."

Brandon let it go. They were quiet for a while as they continued their slow progress uphill toward the cave. Finally, Brandon spoke up.

"Do you think they'll bring back aerosol cans?"

He heard a grunt from way in back. "Damn, I hope not," said Milo. "I don't want to have to nuke the Cascades every twenty years just because chicks can't be bothered to pump their own hair spray."

This time, Zeke was the one not in the mood to talk.

"Can we please stop talking about hair care and focus on the thermonuclear weapon?" He gestured with his head, though Brandon could barely see it in the starlight. "Look, I can see the cave."

Milo set up a few flashlights along the floor and walls of the cave at odd angles to illuminate the scene. Now that they were in the cave, he figured it was safe to use the lights. Brandon and Zeke sat the device down atop a couple of boulders and unwrapped it gingerly, cutting the ropes with the sharp edge of the crowbar Milo had found on the highway. Then, Brandon started working on the bomb with a set of tools and the Russian-language instruction manual. Zeke took up a lookout station at the cave entrance.

They had done their bit; now it was Milo's turn to show his stuff.

Milo opened a small plastic bag first and started flinging fingernail clippings around the room. Next, he pulled out a larger bag, filled with clumps of hair, and began distributing the contents around the room. In the midst of that task, he sat down and opened one of the large garbage bags, producing a mismatched pair of shoes, and put them on. Then he stomped around the cave for a bit, sat down, and repeated the task with another, different set of mismatched shoes, none of which seemed to fit.

Zeke glanced over at him from his lookout perch.

"What the hell are you doing?"

Milo simply grabbed another mismatched pair of shoes and continued. "Don't you watch Court TV, man?"

Zeke's face suddenly lit up in understanding. "Ahhh. That explains the tires."

Zeke continued to glance over from time to time in amusement as Milo continued with his tasks. Opening another bag, Milo began tossing cigarette butts about the cave, along with burnt matches. After changing shoes yet again, he opened several vials of blood and splattered them one after the other about the room. Then he changed shoes and stomped some more before opening several of the large bags and dumping their contents—everything from fast-food wrappers to clothes and license plates—about the place.

Milo kept at it. More shoes, then carpet fibers. More shoes, then more blood spatters. More shoes, then a bunch of used condoms. Zeke didn't even want to know how or why Milo had gotten them. More shoes, then more cigarettes and a clump of intertwined hair that Milo tore apart and deposited in the nooks and crannies that seemed to have been missed by his earlier mayhem.

After a while, Brandon looked up from his work on the timer. "You know all this stuff will be vaporized in the blast, don't you? What's the point?"

Milo stopped flinging sand about the room for a moment and looked at Brandon. Although he was the mastermind of their plot, he could be exceedingly simple about some things.

"Dude, that's why criminals are so stupid. They never think about what happens if they get caught." He looked at each of them in turn. "Say the bomb doesn't go off. . . ."

"The bomb doesn't go off," recited Zeke and Brandon in a monotone.

"Cute," said Milo, with a chuckle. "What happens then?"

Brandon straightened up from his work on the timer. "Global warming continues. The coasts flood. Weather worsens. Massive hurricanes take out all the major cities remaining in the South, not to mention coastal Mexico and the Caribbean. Crops wither in the fields. Massive starvation. The end of life. . . ."

". . . as we know it," intoned Milo and Zeke.

Milo continued on. "No, dude, what happens to us?"

Brandon furrowed his brow. "Well, let me think."

Milo shook his head. His hair would have waggled about his face but for the incongruous hair net. "I'll explain it to you later. How about it, Brandon? Are we armed and dangerous yet?"

Brandon looked back down at the timer. "Just about. I've switched over from the altitude trigger and verified the default detonation time. I just have to input the hours and minutes into the countdown timer. How about forty hours? Enough?"

Zeke looked over. "Yeah, that should be plenty of time."

Milo stopped tossing food wrappers about the room and looked at Brandon. Could they be so stupid?

"Dude, you're not going to have it go off at zero, are you?"

Brandon's eyes darted over to Milo in surprise. "It's the

default setting. What's wrong with that?"

Milo reached into a plastic bag and started flinging different matchbooks around the place. "Haven't you ever watched a *Bond* movie? Even to jerk off during the credits? The bomb always goes off at zero and the person trying to deactivate it always knows exactly how much time they have left to work on it. That way they can pull the wire with eight seconds to go and get the girl."

"I don't think there's much chance of Brandon getting the girl," quipped Zeke. He gave Brandon a sheepish look. "Sorry."

Brandon let it slide. "So?" he said, his eyes on Milo.

"So," said Milo, "don't do that."

Brandon sighed. "Okay, secret agent man. How much before zero should it go off?"

"Six hours or so," interjected Zeke, after cocking his head to one side. "Short enough that the warning will have gone out and the smart people will be far away. Long enough that the authorities probably won't be working to remove the bomb yet."

Milo started jumping up and down. He'd just had a totally cool idea.

"Dude, you gotta do it! Six hours, six minutes, and six seconds. They'll figure that out later and spend weeks, months even, tracking down all the apocalyptic devil-worshippers."

Brandon just stared at him with amazement. Finally, he scratched his head through the hair net and capitulated, "Fine, but it will mean resetting the default on the timer. That'll take a few minutes." He grabbed the instruction manual, flipped several pages and studied it for a few minutes. Then he picked up one of his jeweler's screwdrivers and fussed with the mechanism, referring back to the manual two more times as he went. Finally, he shut the door on the timing mechanism and looked up, with a wink. "There. I'm ready to go."

Milo filled one of his empty plastic bags with all of the other empties. Finally, he reached under his paper gown into the pocket of his coveralls and pulled out a can of spray paint.

"One last touch, man."

He walked over to the far wall of the cave and, using his left hand, sprayed the word "CROATOAN" in semi-glossy enamel.

Zeke simply stared. "What's that mean?"

Brandon gave Milo a thumbs-up. "The only clue as to what happened to the abandoned Roanoke Island settlement in 1590. Brilliant! Nobody's ever figured it out."

Milo was pleased that Brandon appreciated both his intelligence and his humor. "Somebody's got to give Oliver Stone a new conspiracy to whine about."

Zeke, however, had a worried look on his face. "Yeah, Milo, but what about handwriting? You just manufactured a permanent, semi-glossy piece of evidence that can finger you . . . can finger all of us."

Milo hobbled over to Zeke on his mismatched shoes and patted him on the back. "Not to worry, dude. Did it southpaw. Besides, I've been practicing. Best I can do it, that handwriting looks exactly like Patsy Ramsey's."

Brandon beamed again. "They never figured out JonBenet's murder, either. It'll be a mystery for the ages . . . or at least for the cable news networks."

Zeke wrinkled his nose. "Didn't they finally arrest somebody for that?"

Milo snorted. "They let 'im go. Besides, facts never get in the way of a good conspiracy theory, dude."

They gathered up everything they were taking with them and prepared to exit the cave.

"Okay," said Milo. "One last thing. Everybody changes into a different set of foot gear. Be sure to make plenty of tracks while we're leaving and covering the entrance with branches."

Brandon and Zeke looked at each other, but did not protest, at least until Brandon tried to put on his mismatched shoes: a low-heeled women's pump and a similarly-sized women's sandal.

"These don't fit!"

Zeke looked over from where he was stuffing one foot into a kid's rain-boot while the other swam in an oversized hiking shoe. "I think that's part of the plan."

Milo shook a finger at them as he did his best Johnny Cochrane imitation: "If it doesn't fit, you must acquit."

Finally, they gathered up and extinguished the flashlights, left the cave, and arranged the branches to cover the entrance. Milo stomped heavily with his right foot, but treaded lightly with his left the whole time. Suddenly, as they were walking away, a new thought occurred to him.

"Dudes!"

"What now?" came the weary responses.

"If we walk backwards, they won't find any prints leaving. It'll totally fake 'em out!"

"Court TV again?" said Brandon wearily.

"Uh . . . Road Runner cartoon, actually."

Zeke threw up his hands and turned, so he would be walking backwards, his neck strained over his shoulder in an attempt to see where he was going in the dark.

"Okay, but if I break my leg walking through the woods at night, you have thirty-three hours and fifty-some minutes to get me the hell out of here."

Zeke and Brandon clumsily made their way back toward the van, grumbling the whole time. Milo followed, walking backward and using a branch to obscure their tracks. They were almost to the van before Zeke realized what Milo was doing.

"What the fuck!" he exploded. "Why the hell are we risking our necks making these moronic, backwards tracks in other people's shoes if you are just brushing them away?"

Milo turned to face his accuser. For smart guys, his companions didn't really think things through before they got upset.

"Well," he finally said, "you don't want them to think we're amateurs, do you?"

Now Brandon was riled. "Yeah, I can tell by your impeccable personal appearance that you're all about projecting a professional image."

Milo rubbed the stubble on his chin. "The branch will wipe out most of the tracks," he explained, "but convince them the ones that they do find are important."

Brandon limped on toward the van. "You watch way too much TV, man."

CHAPTER 17

Brandon awoke from his nap in the van to the sound of gravel ricocheting off the interior of the van's walls. Sunlight streamed through the windshield, but a dusty haze filled the Minibus. Zeke was driving and the ride was smooth.

"What the. . . ." Brandon turned to see Milo flinging sand and stones around the cargo area.

Milo stopped his odd antics for a moment. "You don't want to get caught. I'm making sure we don't get caught." Then the flinging began anew.

Zeke cracked his window in an apparent attempt to clear the growing dust cloud. "Hell, Milo," he said in an exasperated tone. "We've already changed the mismatched tires, dumped them into four different Dumpsters fifty miles away from each other, and tossed our clothes and dozens of shoes, including our own, out onto the road at various places."

"Explaining, at least for this stretch of backcountry interstate, where all the clothes you see on the highway come from," interjected Brandon.

"We've washed the van inside and out at some crappy self-serve carwash that ate more quarters than most arcade games. We're heading southeast, instead of straight south towards home, and we've got to get the warning out soon."

Milo seemed to ignore Zeke's tone. "Yeah, but if they check the van really carefully, they might find some incriminating dirt from the site, so we have to mix in other dirt, don't you see. I've been scooping up sand and dirt from plants, parks, and beaches for weeks, dude. I even got a bunch of weird rocks from one of those nature stores and crushed them up."

Brandon just shook his head wearily and tried to go back to sleep.

When he awoke, the Minibus was pulling into a rest stop someplace in Oregon. Milo hauled out a beat-up and obviously antiquated laptop and headed over to a pay phone. He was wearing a pair of latex gloves.

Milo inspected the phone and bobbed his head vigorously. "I told you Oregon was progressive, man. Data ports on the public phones."

Zeke leaned over to look, without touching anything. "Even better, if they trace it. . . ."

Milo shot him a wounded look. "They can't trace it. I already told you."

"Even if," said Zeke in a conciliatory tone, "they miraculously could trace it . . . it will be coming from nowhere near home."

Brandon got out of the van and sauntered over, stretching the kinks out of his legs and shoulders on the way. "Not to mention," he added, "that Oregon's got almost as many kooks per capita as Montana. . . ."

He continued stretching as Milo fussed with the connection and called up an e-mail account on the screen. The laptop was even slower than the Quompat back at headquarters.

"Not exactly the setup I thought you would have, Milo," Brandon mocked gently.

Milo flashed him a severe look. "It's not mine, numb-nuts. I fished it out of the garbage someplace in New Mexico, I think. Harder to track, that way. Sensible people throw out their crappy computers, you know."

After a few keystrokes and a brief wait, Milo called up a

saved message on the screen. He scrolled through the address list for the message. "One warning. Copies to the Seattle police, the governor of Washington, the local television stations, the Red Cross, FEMA, sixty random e-mail addresses located in Washington State, and West Coast Caffeinators."

Zeke had been looking around, apparently on guard against being observed, but his head whipped back around to look at Milo. "West Coast Caffeinators?"

Milo winked. "I figure if West Coast Caffeinators shuts down, everyone in the state will leave in a quest for caffeine."

He scrolled down to reveal the message. Brandon leaned in and began reading it aloud.

"Imperialist technophobes, be forewarned that a nuclear device will detonate on the morrow, the true millennium." He looked up at Milo in confusion, only to see that Zeke was doing the same.

"Dude," said Zeke to Milo, his tone modulated as if he was talking to a child, "the millennium occurred years ago. You remember, don't you? Lots of hoopla about Y2K, but nothing happened."

Milo snorted. "As if that was the real millennium. . . ."

Brandon winced. "Please, let's not bring up the whole year zero thing again. . . ." But he couldn't stop Milo.

"Not only," intoned Milo, "was there no year zero, but the calendar doesn't match the historical indicators of the actual date of Christ's birth, there have been several adjustments between the Augustinian and Gregorian calendars, leap years weren't properly taken into account in olden days, and. . . ."

Zeke held his hands up in mock surrender. "I give up, Milo. On what theory is tomorrow the millennium?"

Milo laughed. "*None*, dudes. But think, man. They'll spend days . . . weeks . . . trying to figure out what hare-brained cult believes tomorrow really is the millennium. If we're really in luck, there actually is one."

Brandon was irritated. Why wasn't he consulted about this stuff before Milo just ran amok? "Hey, I don't want to get anyone innocent arrested," he said.

Zeke scoffed. "Nuke them, sure. Arrest them? Heaven forbid."

Milo stopped smiling and his voice took on a serious tone. "Focus on the task at hand, man," he said to both Brandon and Zeke, his eyes shifting from one to the other as he pled his case. "We're saving the planet from *homo sapiens americanus,* dudes. We consume a huge percentage of the world's energy and produce a huge percentage of the world's garbage and pollution. No one in America is innocent. Everyone must pay for their crimes . . ."—Milo paused for a moment, before continuing, his top lip curving up into a sneer—". . . except Scooter Libby."

Brandon just shook his head and went back to reading the message aloud. "Your constructs of science will not avail you survival. Your machines of transport will clog the highways of industry. Those who do not leave now will die in torment and suffering for the sins of the elite mechanists. Fire and ice shall rain down and consume the wicked in their wantonness, and, lo, they shall be very awesomely afeared."

"Awesomely afeared?" blurted Zeke. "Elite mechanists? Jeez, Milo, how did you ever pass the freshman writing exam?"

Milo sighed loudly. "It's supposed to sound like the Unabomber, but not exactly like the Unabomber. You know? A credible copycat threat, but based on something besides environmentalism. You don't want to be on some potbellied cop's short list of environmental groups to be investigated, do you?"

Zeke wagged his head "no." Brandon did the same.

"Just do what I say, dudes, and we won't get caught," promised Milo. "Just do it."

Both Zeke and Brandon gave the barest of nods.

Milo grinned goofily. He pressed "send."

There was no turning back now. In a few seconds, the world would know. Action would beget reaction.

CHAPTER 18

Detective Margaret Pulaski surveyed her partner with her usual affectionate disgust. Potbellied and slovenly in appearance, Detective Charles Malbranche (known to the uniformed patrols as What-the-fuck-Chuck) leaned hard on his beat-up laminate-veneer desk, his wooden swivel chair creaking under his scarcely-within-regulations weight. He knocked over two empty Styrofoam coffee cups and dragged his sleeve through his full ashtray reaching over to grab an incoming message off a combination fax machine and printer. The machine rattled noisily when it wasn't blinking a silent notice that, once again, there was a paper jam. She knew Malbranche would have used the reach for the fax to ogle her legs if she hadn't taken to regularly wearing fashionable slacks to work.

Between bites of a day-old, powdered-sugar doughnut, Malbranche read aloud the communication that had been received by the Seattle Police Department. She gathered close to listen with their superior, Captain Bitner. Captain Bitner was well-dressed as usual and stood ramrod straight throughout Chuck's somewhat muffled recitation. But then, of course, Pulaski knew the captain had already been briefed on the message by downtown.

She could sense the irritation growing in her partner as he read the message. "Those who do not leave now will die in torment and suffering for the sins of the elite mechanists." Malbranche interrupted the message with a snort, then continued.

"Fire and ice shall rain down and consume the wicked in their wantonness, and, lo, they shall be very awesomely afeared."

Malbranche threw the fax onto the already cluttered desk. "Fuck this shit!" He looked up and over at the captain. "Where do these pranksters get this drivel? Is this what we're teaching in schools today?"

Bitner remained calm. Margaret had never seen her partner fluster him, even though Chuck pissed off everyone else in the department, including her, on a regular basis. Apparently he wasn't going to get to the captain today, either.

The captain spoke in a cool, professional tone. "Downtown takes the threat very seriously. The Federal Emergency Management Agency also got the message—a strange place to send it unless you actually want to save lives through the warning."

Margaret crinkled her nose. "I don't know, Captain. There are plenty of people who would like to pull a prank, or worse, on FEMA these days."

Malbranche picked the fax back up and scrutinized the address list. "Not to mention that West Coast Caffeinators got the message, too. They want to make sure to save coffee beans, as well as lives?"

Bitner sniffed. "The Psych Division thinks that is the terrorists' way of telling us to 'wake up' and pay attention."

Malbranche rolled his eyes with exaggeration. "They coulda just said 'Wake up and pay attention.' "

Margaret leaned over her partner to look at the fax. "People will pay attention. All the local news networks got a copy. They've probably started preempting soap operas already."

Malbranche pointed a pudgy finger at the address list. "Who are all of these other people who got the e-mail?"

"Uniforms are tracking them all down," said Bitner without emotion. "They'll be questioned extensively until a common denominator can be found."

"What about the millennium reference?" asked Pulaski.

Bitner tilted his head a few degrees to one side as he responded with cool detachment. "The Psych Division is coordinating with Homeland Security's terrorist watch list and the FBI's cult task force to determine which organizations have millennial beliefs that match up."

She scrunched up her face just a bit as she read the end of the message again. "It's signed by the Sane Unknown Volunteers? What about them? Anybody got a file on the membership?"

"The Feds are researching SUVs as we speak. They're not one of regularly-monitored terrorist organizations, although there's apparently been some chatter about them lately on several websites of interest to Homeland Security."

"There's another dead end," growled Malbranche as he searched through the Styrofoam cups on his desk until he found one with some liquid left in it. He threw down the cold coffee without even a grimace.

The right side of Bitner's upper lip twitched once. "Look, Malbranche. Finding the bad guys is not really your focus right now. Finding the bomb is."

Malbranche's face jerked back in astonishment. He blinked twice. "You mean we got a focus? Nukes . . . that's federal stuff all the way. I'm surprised the FBI and Homeland Security are even telling us what *they're* doing."

Bitner's lip twitched again. "It's a manpower thing. They need law enforcement personnel with an intimate knowledge of the area and there are only so many Seattle-savvy Feds to go around. Besides, it's not like we're just going to sit on our hands because the FBI's on the case. It's not their damn city that's been threatened." He fussed with the dimple on his already perfectly double-Windsor knotted tie. "We can help out, as long as we don't get in the way."

Margaret knew the routine. Cooperate, but run the case on your own on the side. "So exactly what are we supposed to do without getting in their way?"

"You two are to join up with an Army demolitions team that'll be here in the morning to search for and disarm the weapon."

Malbranche pushed back from the untidy desk and swiveled to face the captain. "Sounds like Maggie and I are third wheels on that, boss. I don't know nuthin' about disarming no nukes . . . fictional or otherwise." He wiped the wisps of powdered sugar from his stubbled upper lip with the edge of his right hand and sucked the sweetness off his knuckle.

Uncouth he might be, but Malbranche was no dummy. "I gotta agree with the big guy on that, Captain," interjected Margaret, "and you know that doesn't happen that much."

"Disarming the weapon is not your concern," replied the captain. "Finding it is. But you also have an important task they haven't thought about yet. Say the Rangers do find the thing, with or without your helpful knowledge of local geography. Their total focus at that point is going to be on disarming the thing and getting it out of here. And rightfully so. Lives are at risk."

Malbranche harrumphed, but the captain continued. "While they're busy with the bomb, your job is to make sure to get the goods on these terrorists. Somebody with forensics experience has got to be on scene before the site gets any collateral contamination from the disarming and removal effort."

That made sense. Still, Margaret was uneasy. "I hate the thought of getting between an Army demolitions team and a live nuke, boss."

Bitner gave a curt nod of acknowledgement and smoothed his tie with his right hand as he spoke. "Look, no one wants to take chances with public safety. They'll have a rapid evacuation helicopter on hand to whisk that thing out of here if it gets within hours of detonation. And they'll have well-trained officers to disarm it on site if they have to. Just get them to give you a few minutes."

"I guess the mayor must be taking this seriously," volunteered Malbranche. He wasn't ever truly insubordinate, Margaret knew, just congenitally grumpy.

Bitner seemed to appreciate the gesture of concern and obeisance. "His ass is on the line," he said. "He's on the phone with Nakajami now, trying to get Macrosurf to cancel their big software convention that starts tomorrow."

"Ouch! There's a lot money down the tubes." Malbranche made a brief flip of his hand toward the fax. "You sure this whole thing isn't just some Apple freak out to dent the reigning software monopolist?"

Milo fumed at the computer. He was attempting to delete some files, cleaning up the computer while his compatriots were cleaning up the offices, removing all traces of their plot, just to be on the safe side. Notes, receipts, shipping schedules . . . everything was being cleansed.

After what seemed like an eternity, the slow-churning Quompat did something. Unfortunately, an error message popped onto the computer screen: "Error 3.14. Illegal graphics on hard drive."

Milo spewed forth a stream of invectives that would have made a corporate e-mail content filter work overtime. He thumped the keyboard in disgust. "Damn it, not again. I swear Nakajami uses the word illegal in his error messages just to keep people with guilty consciences from complaining. And then he numbers them, as if there's some instruction manual that explains them all if only you take the time to look them up."

Brandon sauntered over to take a gander. He squinted at the

screen. "That's a new one on me. Gee, Milo, what've you been downloading?"

Milo pushed back from the desk hard, the casters on the well-used chair squeaking loudly in protest. He threw up his hands in disbelief. "See what I mean? Macrosurf probably snuck the error message in with the last alleged virus patch to cover up some bug that's letting the Russian mafia steal all of our identities." He looked at Brandon. "Not that they'd want yours, dude."

Zeke called over from the opposite side of the room. "Just delete anything incriminating, okay?"

Like that was easy. Milo leaned back in the swivel chair in exasperation. "Look, Zeke, I can't be sure I'm cleaning everything off the hard drive unless I reformat it. And even then, with Macrosurf software, who really knows? He could have encrypted spyware funneling stuff straight to the NSA for all I know."

Zeke didn't pause in his cleaning. "Yeah, yeah. Apple is superior in every way."

Milo brightened. This was his opportunity. "It is, dude, it really is. With a Macintosh, we could get the new, independent voice recognition software. It's much better than that crap Nakajami puts out. We'd be practically immune from viruses, worms, pop-ups, spyware, Trojan horses, and constant patches to eliminate bugs. We'd be supporting enlightened development and independent shareware. We'd be yet another candle, lighting the world instead of cursing in the Satanic darkness that is Macrosurf. . . ."

Brandon interrupted. "God, please let him get it, Zeke. We've got lots of money left and if I have to listen to him whine about Macrosurf one more time, I'll kill myself, which will disappoint my parents even more than when I took this job."

Zeke stopped tidying things and straightened up to look at

Milo. "I have just one word for you, Milo."

Milo looked at him, wishing, hoping, praying to an unknowing, uncaring, and most likely nonexistent God that that word would be "yes."

"Betamax," said Zeke.

Milo was stunned. "That's two words, I think," he muttered without comprehension.

"One, two. . . . What it *was* was a technically superior video cassette recorder that died because it wasn't the prevailing standard. Compatibility, Milo, compatibility."

Milo was getting irritated. What did Zeke know about anything? Milo was not only the technical wunderkind, but the only member of the misfit GreensWord organization that actually had regular interaction with the rest of the world. "Hey, I'm the one who bagged Mitzi," he sneered. "Don't talk to me about compatibility with society at large."

"Please," pleaded Brandon.

Zeke turned back to his tasks. "Fine," he tossed back over his shoulder. "Buy the damn Apple."

"And the software?" Milo pressed.

"And the voice recognition software. Maybe I'll finally be able to use the thing," said Zeke. "I mean, at least it couldn't be any worse, could it?"

CHAPTER 19

Life at KQZJ couldn't get any worse as far as Dalton was concerned. As soon as some goofball had sent an e-mail threatening Seattle with nuclear destruction, Griffin Gantry had begun needling his superiors to be sent to the "crisis spot" for live reports. Never mind that there wasn't any story going on there that couldn't be covered from here, along with a few live feeds of evacuating citizens and press briefings from the local Seattle affiliate. Never mind that the story would be branded a hoax by the time they got there. Never mind that no one in the nuclear club claimed to be actually missing a nuke or brandishing the ones they had at one another.

An hour later, Dalton and Griffin were at LAX. Griffin read magazines and signed autographs for fans while Dalton struggled to carry the equipment and get it cleared through security. Two and a half hours later, the two of them were on a plane, headed to Sea-Tac. Griffin was rambling on about planned interviews and shots, with no regard for the setup and travel times involved, no regard for the contact coordination that would need to occur, no regard for the fact that every local and several national and international news agencies would be chasing the same interviews and the same backdrops for their live broadcasts, and no regard for the fact that all of this was really Dalton's job as field producer, not Griffin's. Griffin's job was to look earnest and recite his metaphor-mangling copy without too many flubs.

Less than four hours into this field trip and Dalton was convinced that things couldn't get any worse. And that was without taking into consideration that somebody might nuke Seattle while they were there.

Right. Like out of all the coffee bars in all the world, some terrorist would walk into that one. Any terrorist worth his incomprehensible accent would pick some place bigger, someplace showier, someplace the world cared about. Someplace celebrities lived and titans of industry toiled. This, this was just a chance for Griffin to bag some frequent flier miles and be able to ever after declare how he rushed into the danger of a possible nuclear attack in order to report the news.

This was just somebody's idea of a sick joke. All punch line, no punch.

Brandon had never seen the GreensWord offices so clean, at least until Milo returned from the store with several large boxes of computer equipment from Apple. Soon after, the place was once again strewn with clutter. Instead, this time it was cardboard boxes, foam cushion inserts to the boxes, and various plastic bags containing instruction manuals, quick-start diagrams, and assorted cables and peripheral devices.

Given permission to upgrade their computer system, Milo had, of course, run amok. An oversized flat screen sat on the desk, with stylish speakers on either side and a fat subwoofer on the floor, next to an Apple-logoed silver tower to which Milo was attaching cables with glee.

Brandon rapidly grew bored watching Milo ignore the instruction booklets and set up the computer and load software. So, he and Zeke sat on the couch with the television remote. They took turns surfing news channels, seeing what everyone had to say about the nuclear warning from the Sane Unknown Volunteers . . . or, yes, SUVs, as they had already become known. They both agreed that the Seattle reporter, Katie Monsalvy, was doing the best job of actually reporting the story without blathering or endlessly repeating herself. Unfortunately, she was largely replaced when their friend, Griffin Gantry, arrived on the scene.

Brandon wished that meant that Katie Monsalvy was evacuating and relocating to broadcast from somewhere else, someplace safe. The notion of someone he actually knew, or at least knew of and liked, getting killed because of their plan was unsettling. He hadn't put that in the equation when he was calculating things on his clipboard. He put all his intellect into analyzing his feelings. Why was he so concerned about Katie Monsalvy?

Maybe he was just horny. No matter how much he thought about it, he wasn't distressed about the possibility of Griffin getting killed, and he had actually met him. Of course, he didn't like him. Who would? But Katie's imminent demise was wearing on him and it didn't appear that she would escape in time. The network news organizations were reporting the threat as news, but they weren't taking it seriously themselves.

Here she was, introducing Griffin yet again.

Griffin was standing on some bridge over a local highway, with the Seattle skyline in the background. Much more traffic appeared to be leaving the city than going into it.

Zeke thumbed up the volume.

". . . and while the highways are heavy," intoned Griffin, one eyebrow arched even higher than usual, "not everyone is taking the SUV threat seriously. Macrosurf has announced that its software convention will go forward as usual. And this news just in for Lakers fans: the Lakers have announced that they still plan to play tomorrow's scheduled game against the Seattle Netsurfers despite the nuclear threat. The Netsurfers declared today that they would not cancel the game due to 'unconfirmed rumors.' Lakers' management feels that they have no choice but to show up and play, even against a non-division opponent, as they are unwilling to take a forfeit during what is expected to be a competitive season in their own Pacific Division."

Brandon could feel his heart pound harder and faster while they listened to the news. "Jesus, a lot of people are going to die tomorrow," he murmured.

"There's still plenty of time for people to leave if they want to," responded Zeke quickly, though Brandon wasn't sure if their leader was trying to convince him or himself. "You've got to focus on the greater good. Ending global warming will. . . ."

". . . save Barrington's beach house," Brandon whispered.

Zeke heard him. "No," he said, his voice cracking as he tried to use his best leader voice. "It will prevent the polar ice caps from melting. It will prevent low lying areas from flooding as the sea level rises. It will prevent scores of species from going extinct as their habitats change. It will prevent countless deaths caused by El Niño–instigated extreme weather. It will prevent millions . . . millions, Brandon . . . from dying due to high temperatures and drought-induced starvation." Zeke put his hand on Brandon's shoulder. "And, yes, Brandon, it will keep GreensWord alive. There's nothing wrong with doing something good for yourself when you're doing something good for the world." Brandon felt Zeke squeeze his shoulder, as their leader continued. "We're doing a good thing here, a good thing."

"Besides," said Milo as he worked. "Rainier is bound to blow sooner or later. By making it go off before more people move into the area . . . and by giving a warning before it goes off . . . we're actually saving lives here, lots of 'em."

Brandon just stared at his friend. Did he really believe that?

The ensuing silence apparently caused Milo to look up. He stopped fussing with cables and software just long enough to add one more thought. "And nuking Rainier will bring innovation and competition back to the field of software. I think attorneys general for thirty-four states are on our side on this one."

Was that what this was really all about in Milo's mind?

Zeke only had one more thing to say.

"Shut up, Milo."

Hours later, nothing had really changed. Griffin Gantry repeated the same news with unflagging earnestness. Zeke tidied up Milo's unboxing mess. And Milo continued to load software. Brandon stayed glued to the television and munched on air-popped popcorn (margarine, no butter) without really tasting it.

Finally, Milo finished. The new flat-screen computer monitor gleamed in what seemed to be shiny, bourgeois self-satisfaction on the desk.

"See, Zeke," said the computer whiz, "all you have to do is talk and it types for you."

Milo turned the screen toward the couch so that Brandon and Zeke could see the words marching across the screen as Milo talked.

"That's really great, Milo. Time to call it a night, though, I think." Milo jumped up, grabbing a bag of Doritos from the desk as he headed for the door. Zeke gave the motionless Brandon a light pat on the back. "You, too, Brandon."

Brandon didn't get up. "You guys go. I'll lock up in a bit."

Zeke looked Brandon straight in the eyes. "Don't do anything stupid."

Brandon gave a wan smile. "Don't worry."

Milo had just exited the door when he turned back. "Hey, Brandon. Turn off the computer, will you? Last month's electric bill was really high."

"And it's our duty to conserve . . . ," said Zeke as he joined Milo at the door.

"Sure," said Brandon as his companions left. He got up and

went over to the desk. There was a button on the new monitor. He pressed it and the monitor went black, black as his mood.

As he stood at the desk, he found himself face-to-face with the box from Milo's *Terrorist Threat* computer game on the bookshelf to the side of the desk. He picked it up and looked at the front. There was a garish action scene of commandos blowing away several armed thugs as things exploded in the background. Neon-colored starbursts contained reviewer quotes: "Bloody, visceral, and fun!"; "More gore than you could ask for!"; "Kill them. Kill them all!"; and "Nuke 'em til they glow, then shoot 'em in the dark."

He winced, but turned the box over, reading the copy aloud. "Terrorists threaten millions of innocent lives. With no regard for anyone but themselves, they bomb and kill their way across the city. No one can stop them; no one but you."

He dropped the box, as if the glowing sci-fi green text was a shaped-charge of unshielded plutonium. He could feel his own blood pounding through his veins. He felt as if he was being strangled.

"Jesus," he said. He spoke softly, but gained in volume as he continued. "Millions of people could die tomorrow because some egotistical rich guy wants to keep his beach house, Zeke can't fathom not being an environmental leader, and Milo wants to get laid without getting a real job." His voice grew quieter again. "And me, I just tally up the statistics on my clipboard and say it's all for the best."

He looked at his watch, which had once been his granddad's. The luminescent, radioactive glow of the hands mocked him.

"Too late for me to stop it, but maybe not somebody else," he said with growing conviction. "If they find the nuke in the cave at Mount Rainier, they'll at least force an evacuation."

He turned and ran out of the room, flicking off the lights as he rushed out of the door, as was his environmental duty, leaving only a soft, green glow beneath the desk lighting the darkness.

It was hard to find a working pay phone these days. Cell phones had pretty much put pay phones out of business, except in prisons, and the ones that remained were generally not well-maintained. But there would, Brandon knew, be a line of functional pay phones at the beach.

The sun was rising behind the sooty city when he parked at the beach and headed to one of the phones. He reached into his pocket and pulled out a handful of change. Sorting out the pennies—useless for almost anything these days—he counted it up. It should be enough.

He deposited a quarter and pounded out the phone number of a Seattle talk-radio station that Zeke had insisted on listening to for hours over Milo's objections during their roundabout travel home. The chat line number had been repeated endlessly, ingraining itself into Brandon's mind despite his efforts to ignore it. That he knew it now, without effort, he took as a sign of divine providence.

He listened for a moment while the mechanical voice at the phone center demanded more money in clipped, artificial tones. He funneled the coins into the slot.

The phone on the other end rang five times before anyone answered. "This is KPQZ," said the weary voice, "where Seattle talks. What's your comment about tonight?"

"The SUVs are real," Brandon blurted. "The bomb is in a cave in Mount Rainier Park. Leave while you can. Now, before it's too late." His breath was ragged, but the choking sensation lessened just a little as he talked. Maybe, just maybe, fewer people would die.

"Sure, buddy," came the lackadaisical response from the bored producer of KPQZ's morning show. "If you hold, maybe

I can get you on to talk with Gil before the new millennium."

The choking sensation gained strength. Didn't they realize who they were dealing with? Didn't they realize this wasn't a ratings stunt, this wasn't a game? He didn't know what to say, so he responded to the producer's mocking challenge.

"The millennium thing is a hoax, to throw off the police. Leave now. There's not much time."

Then the mechanical operator began to interrupt, asking for more coins, more than he knew he had left. He hung up without waiting for Gil or for a response.

He had gotten all the way back to the car when he realized his mistake. He grabbed a fast-food napkin out of the glove compartment of his mom's car and ran back to the phone. He wiped off the mouthpiece of the phone, then the rest of the handset and the phone. He looked around in terror, but he could see no witness to his actions. He rushed back to the car, shuffling his feet in an effort to avoid leaving footprints.

Milo's forensic paranoia had seized Brandon's soul, however. Thirty miles away, while cruising the Five, he slipped off his shoes and flung them into the weeds. Now he was sole-less.

He drove into the new day, afraid of both what he had done and what he had not done.

CHAPTER 20

Malbranche didn't like helicopters. Truth be told, he didn't like flying that much in any kind of craft. Not only was he forbidden to smoke, but it ruined the illusion that he controlled his fate. Despite the fact that no one would ever accuse him of obsessive-compulsive cleanliness, he was still a control freak. It was why he had had twenty-eight different partners in his twenty-two years on the force, it was why he always insisted on driving, and it was a big reason why Maggie, who had tolerated him for close to three years now, would eventually request a transfer.

He liked being in charge. He hated being told what to do. So the notion of following Captain Bitner's orders and strapping himself alongside Maggie in a huge green machine with no glide capability and a twenty-two-year-old pilot to go on some damn wild-goose chase didn't thrill him.

His discomfort must have shown, because Lieutenant Folberg handed him a barf bag while he was still on the ground strapping in.

"What the hell am I supposed to do with this?" growled Malbranche.

"It could come in handy, sir, should you have any problem once we're airborne," responded the lieutenant without even the hint of a smile.

Malbranche opened the bag and held it up over his head, filling it with air as he brought it back down to his lap with a snap.

"Doesn't seem like much of a parachute if we start plummeting to earth."

The lieutenant looked him square in the eye. "Sir, you're traveling in a modified Chinook MH-47E, air-refuelable, long-range penetration, medium assault helicopter piloted by the best special operations team the United States Army Rangers can provide. It's capable of lifting over twenty thousand pounds, sir. It can get your ass anyplace you want to go. If it starts plummeting to the ground, sir, it will mean that we didn't find the nuke in time and the EMP from the detonation has fried every electrical circuit on board, in which case, sir, you will have a comfortable ride to heaven or you can kiss your ass good-bye, depending on your own personal beliefs."

Malbranche smiled. He liked the guy. "EMP?"

"Electromagnetic pulse, sir. It's a bigger problem with a high-altitude burst than with a ground burst, because of the larger range of effect, but it can get to things that would be outside of the range of the fireball, itself."

So much for his illusion of control.

The twin-rotor behemoth lumbered into the sky and soon they were making rapid time toward Mount Rainier National Park. Six black-clad Army Rangers sat across from him and Maggie, their expressions calm as the helicopter banked and skimmed at a height that Malbranche found unnecessarily close to the treetops. He might need that barf bag after all. Maggie sat next to him with her eyes pressed shut, like she always did in elevators. Maybe that would help.

He was about to try it when he noted that Folberg, on the opposite side of Maggie, was tapping the earpiece to his headset. Malbranche put his own set on as the lieutenant began to talk.

"As you can see, with this light a load, we have a top speed of over 140 knots, that's 160 miles per hour, but even so, we risk being seriously out of position if somebody finds something in the city. The police and the media must have gotten fifty crank calls last night. What makes you think the one about Rainier is worth chasing down with our prime evacuation and disarmament unit?"

Now, here was something that Malbranche could control: plain, old-fashioned detective work. "Fifty crank calls," he shouted into the hands-free microphone, "but only one suggesting the millennium thing is a load of crap. And don't forget the 'fire and ice' reference in the original warning—we're heading straight for a glacier-topped volcano. Everything suggests that this guy knew what he was talking about."

"Maybe he did. But maybe he just wanted to get our team out of the way," replied Folberg. He paused for a moment before adding, "Terrorists plan their missions out with precision, sir. I know I would."

Malbranche snorted, which, given his queasy stomach, was not a pleasant experience. He gripped the airsick bag tighter as he responded, shaking his head "no" exaggeratedly in emphasis. "Terrorists are just criminals with an agenda, Lieutenant. And criminals are stupid. These guys aren't clever enough to distract your nuclear S.W.A.T. team from where they need to be."

Maggie had shown no sign she was following their conversation, but she did have her headset on. Suddenly, she joined in, with a still closed-eyes nod toward where she knew Malbranche was seated. "He's right, Lieutenant. You watch. If we find a bomb at all, there'll be fingerprints and clues galore to pin these maniacs."

The transport banked sharply and started gaining altitude as they got closer to the mountain. It might have made for a nice view if anyone was looking at the scenery. Malbranche looked at his partner. Since she wasn't looking back, it was a long, hard look, without any trace of a leer. She was a tough broad, Maggie Pulaski was. She could put up with a lot, apparently including him.

He decided to give her an atta-girl. "My partner is right," he shouted. He saw a trace of a smile on Maggie's lips as he said it. "No one ever figures on getting caught, so how smart can they be?"

"Would you fucking hurry up?" growled Griffin Gantry as Dalton raced to set up the equipment. "I can hear a helicopter, already. You're going to miss the shot."

"I'll get the shot," snapped Dalton. "I always get the shot." His eyes flicked back to the transmission van and its unfamiliar satellite hookup array that they had purloined from the local affiliate. "It just might not go out live."

Griffin gave him a nasty scowl, but, of course, made no effort to actually help with the technical details of the remote broadcast. Dalton was not looking forward to spending yet another entire day with this egotistical asshole. He flicked a switch and turned up the volume dial in the van, then turned to look over his shoulder at the so-called talent. "You have live audio with the studio, now. We'll have live video in about a minute."

As soon as he told Griffin that the audio was live, Griffin, aggressive as always, started talking. Dalton could hear everything over his own headset.

"This is Griffin Gantry with the Rainier remote. I'll have a live report on breaking news in thirty seconds. Cue the anchor."

"Fuck!" swore Dalton as his fingers flew over the controls. "Fuck, fuck, fuck!"

Suddenly, Dalton heard a click as the studio hooked in the anchor's feed, then the voice of Katie Monsalvy, Seattle's most-watched news anchor: ". . . Hotels, restaurants, and other vendors stand to lose millions of dollars even if the threat proves to be a hoax. All area school districts have cancelled classes and most major employers, including such diverse operations as Boeing, Wizards of the Coast, and West Coast Caffeinators, have closed for the day. Two notable exceptions are Macrosurf and the KeyArena, where the Netsurfers are scheduled to play this evening. Now, to Griffin Gantry, of our sister station KQZJ in Los Angeles, for a late-breaking development at Mount Ranier National Park. Griffin?"

Dalton threw the last switch and cued Griffin with an abbreviated silent three-two-one countdown with his fingers, with the one being an extended middle finger. Gantry's trademark arched eyebrow drooped for just a microsecond toward a burn, before the reporter adopted his usual, bland, reporting expression.

"Thank you, Kathy," he said. Dalton grimaced at the error. The arrogant kid should at least learn the names of the introducing anchors. Katie, polished professional that she was, let the amateurish mistake slide as Griffin continued into the meat of his report.

"Highly placed sources within the Seattle Police Department tell me that authorities are taking seriously a call into KPQZ talk radio early this morning pinpointing the position of the alleged nuclear device here in Mount Rainier National Park. We've seen several Army helicopters pass by in the last few minutes, presumably assisting in the search for this terrorist weapon of mass destruction."

Dalton knew that last bit was a lie. They hadn't seen squat, although they had heard the bass whup of rotor blades in the distance. Griffin got lucky, though, as a huge green transport helicopter came into the shot in the background as Griffin blathered on. "Of course we know from our experience in Iraq that weapons of mass destruction can be very difficult to find, if they exist at all."

Griffin pretended to consult what Dalton knew was a blank reporter's notepad before moving to wrap. "Officials here at the park indicate that they have noticed nothing unusual in the last several days, but they do point out that the detonation of even a large conventional or fertilizer-and-fuel-oil-based weapon—such as the one that was detonated in Oklahoma City—would have a grave impact on the sensitive ecosphere of this pristine alpine environment and could ignite forest fires of devastating import given the recent drought conditions in the Pacific Northwest."

Dalton signaled him to cut.

"This is Griffin Gantry with an exclusive, here at Mount Rainier National Park."

An exclusive? What, that the Army was looking for the nuke? Or that forest fires burn best in drought conditions? Dalton cut the feed and rubbed his temples. He was definitely getting a migraine and he had forgotten his Aleve. The day wasn't going to be getting any better, that's for sure.

Pulaski finally opened her eyes when she felt the Chinook land and its rotor blades start to slow. The six commandos were already long gone, but Lieutenant Folberg was just beginning to help Malbranche from his seat. As they all alighted from the copter, they could see the commandos executing a rapid deployment maneuver. They were moving uphill more rapidly than Maggie thought she could fall down the mountainside. She raised her eyebrows questioningly at the lieutenant.

"Find something?"

"Yes, ma'am. We believe the device may be in a cave about a klick uphill."

"Did you get a radioactive signature from the air or something?"

The lieutenant gave Malbranche an odd look. "No, sir." He hesitated for a moment before continuing. "That may work in the movies, sir, but if you have a nuclear weapon leaking so much radiation that it can be detected through solid rock from the air, that's not a device that you want to spend any time near, sir. The radiation would kill you for sure. Our guys, and the Russkies, well, they handle these weapons on a regular basis and we spend too much time and effort training weapons maintenance personnel to subject them to that kind of hazard, sir."

That made sense to Maggie. Malbranche just crinkled his nose. "How'd you find it then?"

Lieutenant Folberg started moving them away from the helicopter as he spoke. "The park rangers, they found someone had been illegally cutting live branches near one of the trails. They investigated and found the branches covering a small cave entrance." He started walking them uphill.

"Did the park rangers go inside?" asked Maggie.

"No, ma'am. They had been advised to stay clear in the event their suspicions became aroused, just in case of possible booby traps."

Maggie automatically started looking at her feet as she walked on the uneven and unfamiliar terrain, but Malbranche turned to the lieutenant, pleading their case as he walked slowly backwards up the hill. "Look, meaning no disrespect to your men, Lieutenant Folberg, but before you mess up the crime scene, let Pulaski and me in. That's why we came. We want to be able to catch and string up these bastards."

Folberg stopped walking. "I don't know that we have time for that, sir."

Malbranche put his hands on his hips. Maggie had seen the stance before. The old guy was digging in. "Can your men disarm that thing in five minutes, Lieutenant?" Malbranche bristled. " 'Cause if they can't, it doesn't matter. Let us at least do a photo and evidence sweep." Malbranche stared down at

Folberg from the uphill side of the slope, deliberately blocking his path.

Maggie intervened before the testosterone quotient got any higher. "Look, Lieutenant, bring in one guy if you have to while we're doing the sweep. If he says there's no time, we step aside, and your guys do their thing. Otherwise, we do our thing first . . . or at least at the same time."

Lieutenant Folberg was apparently used to making quick decisions. He looked over at Maggie. "I hope you can run in those shoes, ma'am."

CHAPTER 21

Maggie could run faster in her low heels than Malbranche could run in his well-worn, re-soled, wing-tip shoes. By the time they arrived at the cave entrance, Malbranche's wheezing was louder, at least in his ears, than the snapping of the underbrush as they made their way through the evergreens. Maybe he should give the nicotine gum a try again.

The cave entrance had been cleared of its cover of branches before they arrived. Malbranche made note of the stack of illegally cut wood nearby as they approached. He would take it back with them in an evidence bag—actually a large, black plastic garbage bag—when they left.

Three squad members had taken up defensive positions around the cave entrance. One was poking his head into the entrance. His weapon, some sort of automatic assault rifle, led his way into the cave. Two squad members were crouched on either side, behind him, ready to lend support. After a quick scan utilizing a flashlight held along the barrel of his weapon, he barked "Clear" and backed out and turned to report to the lieutenant.

"A bit of a mess in there, sir, but no obvious traps or enemy personnel. It doesn't look as if the cave goes back too far, maybe fifteen meters. I do see what appears to be a Soviet nuclear device on the right-hand side of the cave, resting on some outcroppings."

The lieutenant nodded at the Ranger, who Malbranche could

see from his nametag was named Gutierrez. "Tanner and Hicks will cover you from the entrance. Leave your rifle and move toward the device and assess. Disarm in place only if urgent and necessary. If you need assistance, don't be shy about asking for it. Teams two and three are already inbound."

Gutierrez gave a simple, curt nod, as if he was ordered to disarm nukes every day. Folberg motioned to Malbranche and Pulaski. "These officers are going in with you, soldier. If they cause any trouble or get in your way, tell 'em to leave." Folberg smiled. "If they don't. Shoot 'em with your sidearm."

Maggie's eyebrows shot up, but Malbranche just stifled a guffaw. He really did like this guy.

Folberg spoke louder, to the entire group. "No radios until we confirm they will not trigger the device. This is not a drill, gentlemen. . . ." He tilted his head toward Maggie. ". . . and lady."

Malbranche and Maggie gloved up, then watched from the entrance as Gutierrez made his way through the cave to the device. The soldier moved without sound and without disturbing any of the clutter that covered the floor of the cavern. He stopped several times to shine his high-intensity flashlight at various locations, then finally arrived at a cylindrical mechanical device about seven or eight feet long. He studied it for several minutes, before flashing the light back toward the cave entrance.

"Clear," he shouted back. "No apparent traps. Certainly none hooked to the device." He waved the light, motioning them in. "You can come in, but stay at least six feet from me and the device at all times and if I tell you to do something, you do it. No questions. No arguments. No hesitation."

Malbranche stooped over and stepped into the cave. His heart was pumping hard and he didn't think it was still from the run up here. The prospect of instantaneous nuclear annihilation, a mechanism of death that was more technologically advanced than anything the world has ever seen, somehow evoked the most primal of fear responses. Maybe flying wasn't so bad after all.

He felt kind of stupid wearing a Kevlar vest while heading into a cave with a nuclear weapon. As if Kevlar would do a thing to save him if things went south. Still, you couldn't have paid him enough to take it off.

Maggie followed close by. Once in, they could both stand upright with clearance to spare. Malbranche closed his eyes for a moment to speed their adjustment to the dimmer light of the cave. When he opened them five seconds later, he could make out the detail of the clutter he had only dimly seen from the entrance.

The cave was awash with trash: fast-food wrappers, clumps of hair, used condoms, and spatters of blood or paint were everywhere. There was graffiti on the wall, dominated by "CROATOAN" in large, cursive letters. The dirt revealed a variety of footprints. Both he and Maggie reached into their pockets for their cameras.

"Flash photography," Malbranche warned before he or Maggie started clicking away. The last thing he needed was to startle the guy disarming the bomb.

Gutierrez shielded his eyes. "Take a couple this way now," he ordered. They quickly complied. "No more pointing toward me while I'm working," he said, as he unshielded his eyes and went back to work.

"Roger that," gruffed Malbranche. He took quick photos of the floor and walls before pocketing his camera and pulling out a large garbage bag. "Jesus," he said quietly to Maggie, "how long were these guys here?"

Maggie pursed her lips and crinkled her nose as she surveyed the place between photos. "Maybe kids use this place to smoke pot or hang out or something."

Malbranche reached down with a gloved hand and picked up a fist-sized clump of hair. "If they do, it's making their hair fall out. I haven't seen this much fur since I dated one of those earth-mother types that doesn't shave her legs."

Maggie flicked her gaze over to him. "You don't shave your legs. Why should she?"

Malbranche's lip curled momentarily. "Thank you for your feminist perspective. Shut up and just keep taking pictures."

Gutierrez didn't join in their banter. Special ops soldiers, Malbranche knew, didn't whistle as they passed graveyards and they didn't joke when they were nervous. They were all business when they were in dangerous situations.

"Russian warhead, stripped out of one of the big ICBMs," he reported loudly back toward the entrance, where the information would be relayed on. "Sure as hell looks real. Hooked up to a Stelski timer, bypassing the altitude trigger."

"Whatever," mumbled Malbranche, then louder to Gutierrez: "How much time?"

Gutierrez responded in a crisp, professional monotone. "Timer is counting down from six hours, fifty-four minutes, forty seconds. Repeat. Six hours, fifty-four minutes, forty seconds."

Malbranche knew he should be ignoring the bomb and scooping up evidence, but curiosity got the better of him. "Is it trapped to prevent disarmament?"

"Could be," Gutierrez said as he continued to work. "Don't know for sure. These guys are obviously professionals."

Malbranche stared at the heaps of garbage strewn about the cave. "How do you know that?"

"Didn't you notice they'd tried to brush away their tracks as they left?"

Malbranche hadn't. Quite frankly, his vision had blurred a bit during the sprint uphill, no doubt from lack of oxygen. Seattle

179

was a port city. Here he was probably nine thousand feet above sea level. There was twenty-five percent less oxygen going to his brain even before he started exerting himself. Still, he didn't like being shown up.

"That could mean they're Campfire Girls. Does the hookup to the timer look like a professional did it?"

Gutierrez never looked up from the device. "It will take a bit to check. If it still looks like we are clear of any traps, the l.t. will want to move the device as soon as possible."

"Yeah, sure. But tell Folberg that we need . . . thirty minutes . . . to collect evidence and record the scene. After that, you can bring the entire Army in here if you want."

"Tell him yourself," Gutierrez intoned. "I'm busy here."

Before Malbranche could say anything more, Maggie caught the attention of one of the soldiers at the cave entrance and started to relay the request, but the guards had been listening and already had a response. Hicks or Tanner or whoever spoke up. "The lieutenant says you get twenty minutes, provided you stay out of Gutierrez's way and can the chitchat. There's a police chopper on the way to pick you up. Provided we get the go sign from Gutierrez, he wants the bomb in transit no later than six hours before detonation."

Malbranche looked at Maggie. "Isn't that what I said?"

"Shut up, Chuck," responded his partner, "and start bagging."

Eric Castille knew that the other analysts in the FBI crime lab in Los Angeles called him the "bagman" because of his penchant for accompanying the agents as they collected and bagged evidence. He didn't care. Like many of the meticulous scientific types that gravitated toward forensic analysis, Eric wasn't overly concerned about group socialization. He was, however, very concerned about the particulars of evidence and its collection.

You could prevent a lot of mistakes and foster good evidence technique by simply going to the scene of the crime yourself and making sure that things were done and recorded properly. Temperature, exposure to sunlight, and other environmental factors could affect certain types of evidence. Relative position *in situ* could be a key determinative. Knowing those details could aid in the analysis of the evidence and help put the perpetrators away.

Of course, the agents, like law enforcement officers everywhere, loved a showy entrance, but he was used to it. His seatbelt and shoulder harness were properly positioned and snug as the vehicle in which he was riding and several others came to a screeching halt near a bank of beachside pay phones. So much for any tire tracks.

He alighted with calm deliberation as the agents sprang out, their guns drawn, taking defensive stances around the phone bank. Eric pulled a pair of rubber gloves from the pocket of his white lab coat and approached the third phone from the left, checking the phone number against a list he produced from an inside pocket. He inspected the outside of the phone and frowned. It had clearly been wiped down. Not a good sign. Finally, he took a key out of the pocket that had contained his gloves and unlocked the coin box in slow, careful movements. He gingerly slid out the heavy, metal box until it was clear of the shell containing the phone mechanism. Being sure not to disturb the lie of the coins in the more-than-half-filled box, he backed away.

At a brief motion from him, a fireman came forward with a circular saw most often used to cut people out of their motor vehicle wrecks. As two gloved agents held the pay phone, the fireman leaned down and cut the post holding it clear through. Then he stepped away while the agents dropped the entire pay phone into a large, plastic bag and loaded it into an unmarked van.

He returned to his vehicle and gingerly wedged the coin box between his legs as he buckled up. When his driver climbed in, he coughed twice to attract his attention.

"Drive back to the lab like you are my grandmother," he said without emotion. "If these coins spill, it's your job. Take your time."

"Time's up," said Folberg as he entered the cave.

Malbranche was still stuffing debris into garbage bags. He was sweating like mad, but trying to make sure he didn't foul the evidence with his perspiration. Sure, his DNA was on file so any personal contamination could be factored out, but running the DNA still took time and money and he didn't want to waste either, even on the biggest case of his or anyone else's career.

He already had five bags of evidence, but there was still more. Maggie had spent most of her time photographing shoeprints of all sizes and descriptions. "Ten more minutes," he begged.

The lieutenant shook his head. "Gutierrez is clear. It'll take ten minutes to get a sling under it and ready to carry. We're moving this thing while there is still plenty of time."

"You've got more than six hours according to Gutierrez. How much time do you need to get it to a base and disarm it?"

Folberg looked at Malbranche with wide eyes. "A base? Are you crazy? We've got our best Russian arms technicians flying to an empty field in the northeastern part of the state. We don't take live nuclear weapons into military bases. At least if they're not ours."

"Let it go, Chuck," said Maggie. "He gave us the time we asked for and then some. Besides he might shoot us."

Malbranche sighed and acquiesced. He picked up his evidence bags and started passing them through the cave entrance, then took a few moments to bag the cut branches stacked nearby. As he and Maggie headed downhill toward their new transport, a police chopper that was undoubtedly even more dangerous than the Chinook they had arrived in, Malbranche relaxed a bit. "I shoulda known you wouldn't talk back to Folberg," he teased. "You always were a sucker for a guy in uniform, Maggie."

Maggie gave him the kind of warm smile he rarely saw in his partners and he almost never saw in women. "More than you know, Chuck. Maybe someday you'll get busted back to uniform and we could be friends."

"Hmmmppphh," was all Malbranche grunted in response. Anything else would get him in trouble and might lose him the best partner he had ever had.

Their pilot looked at his watch not once, but several times, as they approached the police chopper with their awkward burden of proof. Malbranche didn't take it as a good sign.

"Don't worry, Officer . . ."—Malbranche squinted to read the name insignia, despite the dust and sweat in his eyes—". . . Grady. The timer's got almost six and a half hours left on it. You'll be home with the missus long before then."

Grady nodded, but still rushed them into their seats as soon as the bags had been stowed. They took off for Spokane and headed away from Rainier at top speed.

Malbranche kinda wished he had a barf bag.

CHAPTER 22

Zeke stared at the television screen as Griffin Gantry's visage disappeared and the station cut back to Katie Monsalvy at the studio. He thought for sure he was going to be sick. But the moment of nausea passed and an overwhelming feeling of panic fell into the pit of his stomach instead. He leapt up from the couch and turned on his companions, his arms waving wildly as he screamed at them.

"What the fucking hell did you do? Are you insane? Is that it? Or are you just the stupidest fucking moron the world has ever known? There's cops and Army all over Rainier. They'll find the bomb. They'll find us!" He wanted to say more. He wanted to interrogate them under hot lights with a maniacal partner who would beat the crap out of them if they didn't answer his questions. But no more words came. He just quivered in anger, his rational mind blanked out by his primal rage.

Milo immediately raised his hands in surrender and submission. "It wasn't me, dude. Swear to God, it wasn't me." Milo looked over at Brandon as he finished his denial. Zeke's smoldering gaze went with Milo's.

Brandon hesitated so long in responding to Zeke's accusations and his stern glower that Zeke was sure he was going to have to strangle an answer out of the boy. His hands quivered to do it, but he managed to control himself until the pipsqueak finally answered.

"They weren't t-t-taking the warning s-s-seriously," Brandon choked out.

"Jesus, Brandon!" Zeke finally knew that it could be literally true that people could want to pull their own hair out. "You didn't call from here, did you? God, please tell me you didn't call from here."

Brandon seemed to firm up a bit. He sat forward on the couch. "I'm concerned, not stupid. Don't worry. I used a pay phone."

"A pay phone?" interjected Milo from the kitchen, where he had lowered his hands and started fixing a snack.

Brandon turned away from Zeke, apparently seeking support from Milo. "I didn't use my calling card or anything. I'm not an idiot. I used coins."

Milo dropped his food and made no effort to recover it. "Zeke, we gotta get outta here and fast."

Zeke stopped waving his hands above his head and, instead, pressed them to it. He had to think, but they had to act.

"Yeah," he said to Milo, "but we can't make it look like we're on the run." He gestured broadly about the room. "Only take what you need and . . . and we'll take a little run into the desert." He turned to face the traitor on the couch. "Brandon, call your mom and tell her we're on vacation . . . camping . . . or birding . . . or something. Yeah, that could work. If no one is looking for us, we come back in a couple weeks. If they are, we go underground."

Milo flopped into one of the kitchen dinette chairs. It scraped rudely across the linoleum floor as it accepted his momentum. "Man, I'm never gonna get laid again if we go underground. Chicks always think that's a line."

Brandon started grabbing things and stuffing them into a duffel bag. "We'll have to make a pit stop for the rest of the cash."

Zeke nodded agreement as he packed. He looked around

wildly, his adrenaline still racing. "Anything incriminating here?"

"All cleaned out yesterday," replied Brandon. He looked over at the desk. "What about the new computer?"

"It's clean," said Milo as he moved out of the kitchen toward the desk. "I just barely got the new software loaded."

Zeke cut him off. "Good. Then leave it."

"Leave it?" protested Milo.

Zeke gave a curt nod. He was the leader. It was a crisis. It was up to him to make these critical decisions. He shouldn't have to explain himself, but he did. It would avoid a fight they didn't have time for. "It'll look suspicious if we take it."

"Man," whined Milo, "I just got it and you want me to leave it?"

Zeke grabbed his friend by the shoulders. "Look, you're the Court TV guy. What do you think it will look like if we take it?"

Milo slumped in the chair. "I hate it when you're right. It offends my sense of superiority."

Zeke gave a wry smile as he looked at his friend. "Shut up, Milo," he teased. Milo smiled back and jumped up to grab his knapsack and stuff it with snack foods.

Zeke forced himself to take a deep breath as the others rushed for the door. He was in charge. It could all still be all right.

"Guys," he said, with deliberate calm. "Slow down. Look casual." He looked at his friend, Brandon. He wasn't really a traitor. Just a confused, simple kid, who meant well but didn't see the larger picture. Zeke needed to lead. "Be calm. In your case, Brandon, look as uptight as normal, if possible. We don't want to draw any attention. Pretend it's a fire drill in grade school. Move efficiently, but don't run."

They departed the GreensWord headquarters single-file, without talking. A few minutes later their fugitive flight had begun.

★ ★ ★ ★ ★

Pulaski opened her eyes for just a moment and tried to look back at Rainier from the helicopter, but it was straight behind them and out of sight. She gave up and glanced over at her partner, Chuck. He had sweated through his shirt and, frankly, looked a little green around the gills. She motioned with her head back toward the mountain.

"Do you think they'll make it?"

Malbranche grunted. A typical response. His right eye twitched twice before he spoke. "Jeez, Maggie, keep your maternal instincts in check. They've got more than six hours. They'll get it transported away from the population centers for sure. Then, it's just a question of disarming it before the timer counts down. And, if they mess that up, at least there's nothing much to lose in eastern Washington."

She closed her eyes and tried, as usual, to quell her fear of flying.

Milo's hands were fidgeting. He wished he had grabbed a large rubber band before they left the house. There was one thing he hadn't thought through before they had gone forward. Now it was eating at him. Finally, he could stand it no longer. He blurted out his concern.

"Dudes, we're toast. Svetlana's going to know what happened. She could give us all away."

Brandon spread his hands in a calming gesture. "Don't worry, Milo. Svetlana's cool."

Milo looked at his friend with shock. "Don't worry? 'Don't worry,' says the guy who probably gave us away? 'Don't worry,' says the asshole that turned us into fleeing felons, undoubtedly at the wrong end of a 'shoot to kill' order? I'm supposed to stake my life on . . . on a professional virgin's assessment of what a *woman* will do? A virgin who's already proven by ratting out the location of the bomb that he has no balls whatsoever?"

Brandon responded as Zeke just kept on driving. "Look, I know you're pissed, but Svetlana's covered. Really. Actually, she's been in on the whole thing since Zeke and I met her in Russia."

Milo's eyebrows shot up. "That was risky, wasn't it?"

Zeke glanced at Milo through the rearview mirror. "It was necessary. It was inevitable that she would figure things out if we went forward. We had to make sure she was okay with it."

"And she was?"

"Sure," said Zeke. "I mean, think about it. Europeans care more about global warming than we do."

Milo scrunched up his face for a moment in thought. "Because their political parties are numerous enough that a true liberal wing can survive?" he guessed.

"Well, no," said Zeke, without taking his eyes from the road. "Because global warming causes glacial run-off, which dilutes the salinity of the water near Greenland and Iceland, where cold, salty water sinks and heads south, creating a return loop for the warm North Atlantic Current."

"If the water isn't really salty," Brandon interjected to explain, "it doesn't sink and the North Atlantic Current slows or is even disrupted completely."

Zeke picked back up on the explanation. "Bad news for Europe, which is mostly as far north as Canada, but much more temperate and arable. It's kept warm by the waters of the Gulf Stream, which turns into the North Atlantic Current."

Milo scratched his nose.

Zeke continued. "So, while the planet is warming up as a whole, Europe goes into the deep freeze for a few years."

Brandon joined in again. "Food riots on top of the flooding of the Netherlands . . . they're going to need more than one finger in the dike."

Milo shook his head, his unruly hair flapping about his concerned face. "Man, environmentalism is complicated."

CHAPTER 23

Gutierrez watched with frustration as his squad tenderly lifted the nuclear device onto the sling for airlift east for disarming. It wasn't that he feared a booby trap; he was dead certain that the weapon wasn't wired to trip, except by way of the time. And it wasn't that the bomb wouldn't be handled properly. He knew his squad; he knew the device would be handled with more care than a donor heart in an operating room with the President opened up on the table. But he wished to God they had let him disarm the nuke in place. It wasn't that he wanted the notoriety of being the soldier who saved Seattle and it wasn't that he didn't trust the disarmament team that would, no doubt, take over at the other end of the helicopter transport. It was just that he wanted to do his job. This was what he had studied for, trained for, drilled for. He could do his job and the risk would be gone.

Besides, something could happen in transport. Although he didn't fear helicopters, he knew that transport crashes were a significant factor in Army casualties in times of war and in times of peace. Sure, the device wouldn't likely be triggered by a crash, but he hated the prospect of his fellow soldiers trying to locate a downed bird in a hurry and search through the wreckage for the nuke so that it could be disarmed in a rush amidst the smoke and flames of the scene. Why not do it here? Why not let him do his job?

A soldier questions, but he never asks. It wasn't his call. It wasn't his place to argue. He'd just baby-sit the thing during transport, then go to work on it himself or turn it over to his superiors, most likely his trainers, when they landed in eastern Washington.

As the squad manning the sling cleared the cave and began the trek down-slope to the waiting Chinook, he glanced at the timer. Six hours, six minutes, and twelve seconds, still counting down.

There was plenty of time.

It was time. Dalton had it timed down to the second.

After a few tense conversations, the local news station had finally put Griffin on a regular update cycle, undoubtedly to stop him from interjecting into the stories of his fellow journalists with blather that really could have waited. Now, they just allocated him ninety seconds every half hour. Of course, that meant that Dalton's routine had become ninety seconds of filming, followed by thirty seconds of Griffin fishing for compliments, followed by twenty-seven minutes of Griffin bitching about how he needed more air time and how he needed it now, followed by one minute of Griffin fussing over his hair as Dalton cued him over for the next ninety-second broadcast.

He cued Griffin, then turned to watch the monitor as the newsman began his spiel.

"About twenty-five minutes ago," intoned Griffin at an acceptable sound level, "a police helicopter headed at full speed toward Spokane, where the state patrol's regional crime laboratory is located. None of the Army helicopters have. . . ."

There was a loud burst of static and the monitor screen went blank.

High on the side of Mount Rainier, Gutierrez's eyes registered a minute dimming of the readout from the Stelski timer as it ticked down to six hours, six minutes, and six seconds.

Oh, shit, thought Gutierrez with an uncharacteristic lack of professionalism.

But even before he could discipline his own thoughts, even before he could verbalize either those words or a fruitless warning to his fellow soldiers, even before he possibly could have heard the soft click of a relay closing, Gutierrez's thoughts, his body, his companions, and most of the mass of the northwest side of Mount Rainier were vaporized by the conversion of a small amount of nuclear material into pure energy.

Katie Monsalvy was too much of a professional to smirk when Griffin Gantry's broadcast was cut off by an apparent technical glitch, even though he was a pompous asshole. Her pupils widened, however, as the station's power crashed and the emergency backups failed to switch on. In the blackness of the windowless studio, she heard one of the cameramen begin to count out loud, his voice clear amidst the mild hubbub of the other personnel.

"One thousand one. One thousand two. One thousand three." He had started strong, but a quaver began to creep into his voice as he continued. "One thousand four. One thousand five."

Suddenly, she realized what he was doing. He was counting down the seconds until the shockwave hit, until they all died.

It was a complex equation: burst location, critical mass, local topography, and more, but blast yield was the only meaningful variable. $E=MC^2$. The laws of physics mandated the time. Death came on cue.

In the instant of the explosion, Rainier ceased to be a mountain. Much of the rock and vegetation vaporized or was pulverized and thrown high into the atmosphere, creating a tower of super-heated ash more than fifteen miles high. What remained of the mountain shaped the radius of the blast, elongating it from a simple circle to an oval, extending it north and west toward the southern reaches of Seattle. But even the glaciers on the far side of the mountain liquidated in a brilliant flash of light and thundered down-slope, sliding along the remains of the mountain, boiling and vaporizing during their rapid descent. The water, released from millennia of captivity in the sharp blue confines of the crystalline mass of Rainier's ice fields, mixed with the dirt and debris from the mountain's showy destruction to form a slurry of rushing mud, a lahar forty feet high that picked up ice and boulder and trees, gaining in size and speed as it roared down the six river valleys emanating from the mountain. Following close on the heels of the shockwave of compressed air that expanded from the source of the destruction, the liquid torrent raced ahead of the firestorm that consumed everything it touched; a trifecta of death.

Mere moments after a flash of light etched the shadow of Nakajami's lakefront mansion upon the rocky ledge to its west, the shockwave reduced the massive stone and timber structure to its component parts, intertwined with strands of cable and filaments of optic fiber. Then the wall of churning, hot mud pounded tumultuously upon the detritus, sweeping the scattered remnants of the billionaire's residence aside like Macrosurf destroyed start-up competitors. Finally, hellfire breathed upon the scene, boiling off the water, baking the muck into rock, and seeking and setting aflame everything that could combust.

Find. Rip. Burn.

Air, earth, water, and fire—all the elements of the ancient world—came together to touch the home of the reigning king of the Internet and bring it down.

The conventioneers at Macrosurf's software extravaganza never saw the flash, never felt the electromagnetic pulse that fried their PDAs in their holsters, never knew that the software that powered their laptops had been stripped clean away, never saw the mushroom cloud towering miles above the location where Rainier had once played peekaboo with the residents of greater Seattle. Instead, the lights merely flickered off, generating a cacophony of hoots and whistles of derision that were soon drowned out by an earth-shattering roar as the shockwave destroyed, and then the fireball consumed, the convention center and all their precious gadgets.

In the end, it didn't matter who had the most toys. They all died.

Irvin Duke was just happy to have made it into the NBA. Picked in the sixth round of the draft by the Seattle Netsurfers, he had excellent hustle, great passing and defensive skills, and a deft touch at three-pointers, at least when someone eight inches taller wasn't towering over him as he attempted to shoot. Sure, he didn't get to play many minutes coming off the bench, but if the Netsurfers could get past the Lakers in the Western Conference finals this season, he could get a championship ring—a gaudy hunk of gold and diamonds so massive it actually weighed down your hand—just like everybody else on the team. And he would know he earned it from skill and heart, not just by being an inordinately tall freak of nature.

He was just dropping one in from downtown, nothing but net, when the back-glass spontaneously shattered. The nuggets of safety glass had barely hit the hardwood floor when the lights went out. Then, there was a roar and the roof of the KeyArena collapsed, tons of steel showering down upon the practicing players like the glass had mere seconds before.

Irvin had a short career, but he made his last shot. He went out a pro, along with the rest of the team. They didn't make the playoffs, but, then, neither did the Lakers.

The waterfront markets were closed for the day. Few tourists were about. The street cafes of the local purveyors of caffeine were empty and silent. No espresso burbled, no steam hissed, at least at first.

More distant from ground zero, downtown Seattle was not touched by the initial fireball, but the firestorm generated by the blast and boosted by the magma released from beneath the mountain doomed it just the same. The residents of Seattle—those, at least, who had not heeded the warning—had a chance to witness the flash of the thermonuclear blast, to see the swirl of colors radiating through the cap of the mushroom cloud amidst strikes of lightning as it ascended heavenward, to see death coming for them in the form of an unstoppable wall of fire, and to panic or pray. While expletives led the early count, most residents of Seattle died within seconds of saying "I love you" to someone near and dear and soon to be dead.

Those who were trying to leave by car, but had not departed soon enough, were seared across the face with the nuke's flash reflected by their rearview mirrors as their cars lost power in the tight traffic. Some watched as the cars behind them were thrown about by the shockwave and incinerated by the firestorm. Some made a scramble to flee their cars and outrun the nuclear blast, like the throngs of Tokyo in one of the myriad cheesy *Godzilla* movies. It didn't matter which. Armageddon didn't yield the right of way to cars or pedestrians.

Next time, they vowed, they wouldn't wait. They wouldn't make the mistake too many residents of New Orleans had made as Katrina thundered across the Gulf. They would heed the official warnings and leave earlier. Of course, they knew there would be no next time. They had made their last bad decision.

Inaction became evolution in action.

The experienced seamen in and around Puget Sound saw the flash of nuclear detonation and turned for open sea, throttle wide open. Then they flung their survival suits down onto the deck, straddled them and sat down hard, thrusting both legs into the suit at once, then arching back to shove their arms down the open sleeves before reaching forward to zip the rubbery gear shut. Tsunamis could be almost imperceptible far enough out to sea, but they were death-on-a-stick close to shore. You couldn't outrun them and you couldn't surf them, no matter what the movies said. You just had to be ready to go into the water and hope you weren't bashed against something hard at more than five hundred miles an hour or held away from air for more than a minute at a time.

So they roared for open water without bothering to steer as they donned their suits, besting their quickest drill times by seconds in almost every case. It wasn't that distance could save you, but deep water might. Without that, a survival suit gave them the only faint glimmer of hope that remained in their lives.

As they surged seaward with reckless abandon, lava began gushing up from the gash that was once Rainier, hidden by dark clouds of ash surging higher and higher into the atmosphere. Pressure released and tensions shifted in the earth's crust and fault lines began to shift. While all eyes were riveted upon the expanding plume above Rainier, small puffs of sulfurous steam erupted in the craters of twelve other volcanoes, south and east.

The police helicopter was barely above the treetops when the power failed. There would be no time to recover, Malbranche knew. They were going down.

He wanted to swear. He wanted to have a final epiphany—

maybe not his life flashing before his eyes, but something event-ful, meaningful. For a wild, panicked moment, he wanted to blurt out "I love you" to Maggie or at least look soulfully into her eyes. But, as always, her eyes were shut as she rode the cop-ter. She probably didn't even realize what was happening as the bird dipped toward the trees, veering somewhat off to the left. He popped his seatbelt and threw himself over her just as the trees and the helicopter started to tear each other apart.

They hit down hard, but not so hard he didn't feel it. It was like taking a round in your Kevlar vest from a thirty-eight-caliber Saturday night special. It hurt like a son of a bitch as you felt yourself going down from the impact and you weren't sure you would ever get back up from it.

CHAPTER 24

The usual rule of cross-country drives in the Minibus was that nobody touched the radio but the driver. He was the one in control, the one who knew whether he needed traffic or weather info and whether the current radio play list was putting him to sleep as the monotonous miles droned by. If you forgot and reached for the dials, it wasn't uncommon for the driver to slap your hand away. The same rules applied to fussing with the vent, heater, and fan knobs.

Today, the usual rules did not apply.

Zeke drove forward across the flat wastelands of the Southwest at sixty-four miles an hour, one mile an hour under the legal limit. His hands were strangling the steering wheel in the ten and two positions and his eyes were narrow slits, intent on the straight, featureless road ahead. But his mind was clicking along at a million miles an hour, playing out permutations, considering alternative courses of action, and rejecting them one after another, as quickly as the white stripes on the highway flew by. His inexpensive, yet sturdy, digital watch was beeping softly, but he made no move to release his death grip on the wheel and quiet it.

Brandon was working the radio dial feverishly, searching for a station with enough signal strength to reach into the most barren stretches of the high desert. Milo was sitting in the backseat, as usual, but the ear buds of his iPod dangled around his neck. He was leaning forward over the middle of the front street, straining to assist Brandon in locating a fresh FM broadcast.

Finally, there was the blorp of the tuner being dialed across voices talking over the radio. "There, dude. Go back," said Milo impatiently and unnecessarily as Brandon reversed his twisting of the dial to center in on the strong feed.

". . . rupt this broadcast for a special news bulletin."

They all listened with a red-hot focus more intense than the sun blazing on the roof of the aging van as they traversed the desert. They all listened like they never had to their parents, teachers, or lovers. This was important. Their world hung in the balance.

"This just in," intoned the announcer, continuing to delay with blather the sentence they knew was coming. "A nuclear explosion has just engulfed the city of Seattle. I repeat: A nuclear explosion has just engulfed the city of Seattle."

"Turn it up, dude," said Milo, as he started to reach for the controls.

Brandon's deft hands beat Milo's to the dial. "Shhhh!" he hissed as the radio announcer's next words reverberated from the cracked speakers, drowning out the murmur of the tires on the road.

"Preliminary reports indicate that the blast was well in excess of forty megatons, thousands of times the size of the blast that leveled Hiroshima, and was centered south and east of the city in the general vicinity of Mount Rainier. Despite the distance, the resulting shock wave, mudflows, and firestorm have obliterated Tacoma, Seattle, and surrounding communities. Great loss of life is feared. A tsunami warning has been issued for the Pacific basin, north from Alaska, as well as west and south to the Hawaiian islands and beyond. Falling ash is blanketing the area. Stay tuned for further developments."

Brandon's hand, still resting on the volume control, quieted the announcer for a moment. "Jesus, guys, what do we do now?"

Zeke gripped the wheel tighter and said nothing. His right foot edged forward and the Minibus strained to top the speed limit. They had probably just saved the world with a nuclear explosion. Now they had to outrun a world that would never understand or forgive them for what they had done. Simple, shaggy Milo had been right the other night. Environmentalism *was* complicated.

Eric Castille moved with slow precision, carrying in his gloved hands with tender concern the coin box from the beachfront pay phone. He moved across the room in small, even steps and, finally, set down the coin box at the forensic fingerprinting station. As he did, he heard some commotion outside the lab, in the hall, but he paid it no mind. Emotional anguish, no doubt.

Sure, like many others in California and the rest of the nation, he had loved ones in Seattle: two nieces and a coterie of friends. He could be jamming the cell phone circuits with everyone else, trying to call into the area of devastation, but he didn't see the point. The call systems were overwhelmed. And, of course, the EMP that undoubtedly accompanied the blast would have fried anything even remotely near the areas of greatest damage, even though it, of course, had no effect down here in California. Besides, the survivors had better, more critical things to do than answer the phone. But most important, he preferred to direct his full attention to catching the bastards that did this. That was his job.

He donned a hands-free microphone and inserted his personal earplugs. It wasn't that the sounds of his coworkers in the hallway or the generator outside the shaded window were that loud—the power grid had crashed in L.A. and, he ventured, most of the rest of the Western states when the nuclear device had detonated—he just liked to block out background noise while he worked. It helped his concentration.

He adjusted his work lamp and positioned a spiral notebook on the counter, well to the right of the coin box, and placed a Uni-Ball pen next to it. Then he opened a drawer in the counter and removed a pair of tweezers. He gently reached with the tweezers into the coin box, talking softly while he worked.

"Coin number one. Top of the pile, center. One of five coins with no initial overlap from any other coin."

He withdrew the quarter from the coin box and laid it on the clean countertop. He put down the tweezers and assembled the equipment to dust the coin for prints, first heads, then tails. It was a tedious, but familiar, process. He did not hurry. Several minutes later, he had finished and entered the partial prints lifted into the nearby computer terminal. He slid coin number one into a small, paper envelope, labeled the envelope, and set it far to his left.

He picked up the tweezers and reached into the box once more.

"Coin number two. Top of the pile, right. Second of five coins with no initial overlap from any other coin."

He continued the process long into the night, when his colleagues had returned to their homes to listen to the news on old, transistor radios and console their families.

The coins at the bottom of the pile, he knew, were unlikely to be relevant to the pending investigation, but he did not hurry them. Each one got the same painstaking treatment, the same respect, as coin number one.

Nothing must go wrong. Nothing must be left to chance. No slip-up could allow a sleazy defense attorney to question his testimony, his procedures. Catching and convicting criminals was a game in which Eric knew the rules and always abided with them.

He took the last coin out of the box and processed it. After he slipped it into its own envelope and labeled it, he reached down to toggle off his hands-free microphone. It was a good day's work and then some on the worst day America had ever known.

He took off his thin, rubber gloves and headed for the lab door, flicking off the light as he left.

"Heads, I win," he said to the darkness as he shut and locked the door. "Tails, you lose."

Brandon clicked the radio off and sat back in the passenger seat for the first time in over a hundred miles. He shifted his eyes, drinking in the stark beauty of the twilight. The setting sun behind them cast a rosy hue over the harsh, desert terrain. Zeke continued to stare forward, his hands rigid on the steering wheel, knuckles white. Milo was leaning back in his seat studying a map, but sat silent, without musical accompaniment from his trendy MP3 player.

Finally, Milo dropped the map and leaned forward again. "We've been making pretty good time. We might as well go all the way to Vegas before we stop for the night."

Zeke's eyes flicked over to Milo. "We're supposed to be birding or camping or something. Why do we want to go to Vegas?"

Brandon scoffed. "Milo is Milo, Zeke. He has an abiding concern for getting laid. That isn't going to happen if we stop at a state park."

Milo looked at Brandon with distaste. "My biggest concern right now, smart ass, is not having sex, at least not in a maximum security facility."

"Huh?" replied Brandon.

"Don't you get it, doofus?" gruffed Milo with genuine vigor. "Due to your boneheaded, *unilateral* maneuver, there is now some chance . . . some real possibility that we will become suspects in this event."

Brandon was taken aback. Sure, they were being careful, but

he didn't see how it could happen, how they could really become fugitives. He leaned toward Milo and lashed back. "Yeah, but you said you had it covered, with all the trash and hair and all. Didn't you?"

Milo gave Brandon a steely stare. "Yeah. I carried my end. But my main focus was to make sure we weren't investigated. Now that's in jeopardy and I think we have a problem if somebody looks at us too closely."

Zeke's eyes flicked over to Milo again. The first time Zeke had looked over, Brandon had been relieved. Their leader had been a car-driving zombie all afternoon. It had at least been a sign that the zombie lived. But now Brandon saw fear in the zombie's eyes.

The zombie spoke, his voice low and cracked. "Deep Throat."

Milo nodded.

Brandon just looked at the two of them in confusion. "What's Watergate got to do with this?"

Milo shook his head, his hair dappling the last light of the day. "The guy was FBI and his advice to Woodward and Bernstein was right on . . . the money."

"Huh?" said Brandon, turning from Milo to Zeke. Zeke usually made more sense than Milo.

"Follow the money. That's what he said to the *Washington Post*. Follow the money. And it worked." Zeke continued to stare ahead as he talked, as if afraid that he would break down in despair if he looked at his companions.

Milo nodded more vigorously. "Follow the money. A paper trail shows clear as spring water that we got a million bucks from Barrington. If we're investigated, it's bound to come out that he gave us the money. We spent close to seven hundred grand on a nuclear device and related incidentals, but when someone asks, we can't exactly tell them that."

Brandon leaned back into his seat for support. His eyes

turned back to the now-gathering darkness surrounding them. "Oh."

Milo pressed ahead with his explanation, an edge to his tone. "Yeah, 'Oh.' So we gotta have a credible story for how we don't have anything to show for seven hundred grand." He paused for a moment. "That's why we need to get to Vegas."

A quarter mile passed beneath the wheels of the aging Minibus before Zeke put the logic puzzle together. When he did, the zombie came to life, gesticulating so abruptly that the Minibus swerved across the center line of the vacant roadway.

"So, you're going to tell them we lost the money in Vegas? Are you out of your mind? We'll go to jail for embezzling!"

Brandon was afraid, truly afraid, and it wasn't just from Zeke's suddenly erratic driving, although the fact that Zeke was staring at Milo instead of at the road began to bother Brandon after a few seconds.

Zeke's eyes returned to the road as Milo sat back in the deepening gloom of the rear seat. Backlit by the last light of the western sky, Brandon could not see his friend in the darkness, but his disembodied voice continued on to finish the explanation he had begun.

"Given a choice between being put in the stir for a few years for embezzling or for eternity and a day for mass murder, I'll take embezzling any day. Might even get minimum security; maybe conjugal visits. You have to do what you can when you can, not put off decisions until they become too drastic, too desperate. That's how mankind got into this whole global warming mess; it put off the tough decisions until something draconian needed to occur to reverse the course of events. We need to be planning for the worst now . . . right now . . . and taking action on that plan."

CHAPTER 25

Malbranche hated crime labs. They were too sterile, too fussy and tidy, and constantly smelled lemony fresh from all the cleaning. Years ago, when he was just another new kid on the force, forensic departments had reeked of alcohol-based disinfectant, a sharp tang associated with the morgue, which was usually right next door. But times had changed and crime labs wanted to be employee and visitor friendly, so they had switched over to citrus-based, scented disinfectants. Now, of course, every time he entered one, the Lemon Pledge jingle jangled through his head endlessly. At one point he had thought that when he retired from the job, he would get a little place in Florida and do a lot of fishing, but if he was going to hum the Lemon Pledge song every time there was a waft of citrus on the breeze, he could never be happy in Florida.

More likely, he would die on the job, he thought as he lit up a cigarette. He had come damn close to that yesterday when the EMP took down the police chopper, but, instead of a tree limb embedding itself in his chest or the bird going up in a fireball of death with him trapped inside when it hit the ground, he had walked, or at least limped, away. The chopper had plowed into a stand of trees which sheared away the blades and mangled the fuselage, but it had burst through to a clearing after only a few seconds. Some kind of marsh or bog or wetland, the type of thing the environmentalists were always suing somebody to save because they harbored rare frogs or provided habitat for migratory fowl or some salamander on the endangered species list.

All he knew was that the muddy ground had cushioned the impact and the shallow water had probably squelched the risk of fire, though the whole place had reeked of fuel as he and Maggie and the pilot, Grady, had run for the relative safety of the nearby tree line. He was grateful that he and Maggie had been wearing their Kevlar vests after all. He had a few bruises and scrapes and Grady, he had a broken arm, but Maggie had come through completely unscathed. Grady had said that it was because she had her eyes closed and never knew the crash was coming, so she hadn't tensed up or attempted to brace herself for impact. Malbranche didn't argue with the guy, especially since Grady hadn't bothered to tell him and Maggie that he had a broken arm before he slogged back to the downed chopper three times to retrieve their bags of evidence.

Only one of the garbage bags had torn open in the impact and Malbranche had quietly transferred the contents into a spare, intact bag. The theoretical contamination of the evidence would never be known by defense counsel, of that Malbranche was sure.

He was just stubbing out his cancer stick and reaching for a paper plate of glazed crullers on the all too sparkling, white desktop, when Maggie entered the room carrying a crime lab folder. Her clothes were clean, but not fresh and pressed, like usual. Otherwise she looked fine, damn fine, in his eyes.

He altered the course of his reach and picked up an FBI bulletin from the desktop. He'd read it earlier. It guesstimated that the nuclear device had detonated when the timer read six hours, six minutes, and six seconds. As he wadded it up and tossed it towards the shiny, aluminum wastebasket at the side of his desk, he rolled his eyes theatrically. "The 'millennium counting' team has more numbers to play with. The numerologists will probably orgasm on the spot when they get wind of this, not to mention all the 'end of the world' religious freaks."

Maggie stopped at the desk, but said nothing, so Malbranche continued. "Please tell me you have something real to go on. A clue, an actual scientific finding, not some speculative voodoo crap last seen on *The X-Files*. Although I gotta admit, that Agent Scully, she was hot."

Maggie harrumphed. "Just because our office is radioactive slag doesn't mean office rules don't apply, big guy. Please spare me your assessments of who is or is not hot."

Malbranche smiled. Yeah, Maggie was none the worse for wear after the crash. He winked at her. "I love it when you call me big guy."

She glanced at the desk and the half-full plate of crullers. "Keep stuffing your face with doughnuts, and everyone will call you big guy."

Malbranche wiped some crumbs of glazing from the corners of his mouth with his fingers, as Maggie flipped open the file folder she was holding.

"One hundred and eighty-six coins," she read aloud. "One hundred and twelve with useable prints according to Castille at the L.A. crime lab." Her eyes tracked down the page, but she was silent for a few moments before going on. "Forty of those are in the California, Washington, Oregon, U.S., or Interpol databases." She looked up, her eyebrows arched slightly in a look of both skepticism and surprise. "Pretty hefty hit ratio."

Malbranche sucked glazing out of his front teeth. "Phone booths," he grunted. "The offices of the underworld." He leaned forward so that the light smell of Maggie's perfume would banish the choruses of the Lemon Pledge song that still bedeviled him. "How many terrorists?"

Now Maggie's eyebrows really shot up. "Zip. Zilch. Nada."

Malbranche wrinkled up his nose in displeasure. "Felons?" he queried, hope fluttering at the edges of the word.

Maggie shrugged and scanned the report, flipping a page to continue her assessment. "Looks like twenty-eight. Drugs, drugs, and more drugs, a couple robberies, and one assault on a police officer, but nothing that comes anywhere close to matching this profile."

Malbranche reached out to take another cruller. He needed the comfort food at times like this. "So, a dead end until we have a suspect. . . ."

Maggie grabbed his hand with gentle firmness, stopping him from taking the doughnut. "Maybe not. The phone wasn't used that much—everybody's got a cell phone these days. Odds are that the caller used one or more of the ten coins nearest the top of the coin box. We'll have the phone records to confirm shortly."

"So?" said Malbranche. She still held his wrist, but he hadn't given up on drowning his woes with a sugar rush.

She smiled. "Coin number three is a hit."

He relaxed his reach and folded his hands on the desk as she let go of his wrist. Now, we were talking.

"Felony?" he asked, the gears in his mind coming up to speed.

Maggie wrinkled her nose just a bit. "He has a few moving violations according to the California DMV and one criminal misdemeanor according to the California state crime database. Trespassing and resisting arrest. Some protest thing about logging or somesuch."

Malbranche was displeased. The wheels in his head were spinning, but nothing was meshing. "That seems pretty far-fetched for this M.O. The nuke took out millions of acres of forested land. The forest fires are still burning and nobody's even trying to stop them. Hell, the smoke from the fires and the ash from the volcano is still visible clear across the country. They say it will circle the goddamn globe. Doesn't sound like a tree-hugger to me."

Maggie's eyes flicked to the wastebasket. "I think you would agree that it shows more promise than the task force's millennium counting project so far."

"Yeah, I guess. What's his name?"

Maggie consulted the folder. "Connoway. Brandon P."

"Check it out."

"You got it, big guy," she said as she turned back toward the door.

Malbranche leaned back in his frightfully clean, ergonomic chair. "There you go again. Go out on a date with me, then say that."

She turned back to him. He wasn't quite sure, but he thought she winked. "Hmmmppphhh. I got close enough when the copter went down in the marsh."

So, she *had* noticed. Malbranche played it cool. "Yeah, that Grady, he's one fine pilot. Saved us and the evidence."

"Yeah, Grady," she said lightly. "He deserves all the credit. I'll have to find a way to thank him."

Malbranche smiled. Two could play this game. And it could be fun. "You do that. And, one more thing, doll-face. Check the grade point averages on the guys on the list."

She tilted her face down slightly and looked up at him, her brow furrowed. "Jeez, Chuck. They obviously bought or stole the bomb. They didn't have to build it. You saw it. They clearly didn't build it. Gutierrez said it was a stripped-down warhead from a Russian ICBM. The Pentagon and the Nuclear Regulatory Commission have a team on likely origins reporting to the FBI later today."

He fluttered his beefy right hand dismissively. "Screw that. Nobody who didn't get an 'A' in high school history would write 'Croatoan' on the wall—unless, maybe they're from Virginia. Check for Virginia connections, too."

"Actually, I think Roanoke Island is off the coast of North Carolina," she replied, then hesitated a moment before continuing. "I . . . took a weekend trip out that way once . . . years ago."

Malbranche harrumphed. "I thought Virginia was for lovers. . . ." He cocked an eyebrow at her.

She ignored his banter. "They could be smart or they could be from . . . the Southeast, or maybe they just don't like our policies in Croatia, if we even have any these days, and don't know how to spell. . . ."

"Lots of possibilities. And the FBI's probably not looking into a single one of them," he said with an easy tone. "You just do the legwork, babe . . . that's what you got them long legs for."

She flushed and looked away, then almost immediately regained her composure, turning back to him with a professional demeanor. "I'll do the work, but I can't imagine the Feds are going to let us have much of a role in the investigation. These terrorists nuked a major American city. Local cops aren't going to hold much sway."

A fire began to burn in Malbranche's chest. He had always hated the whole turf-fight thing, even when it was over crap like whether the department or the D.E.A. got credit for a meth bust. He had no tolerance for it at all anymore, not for this.

"It wasn't their town that got nuked," Malbranche growled, continuing on, his angry tone growing as he went on, even though he knew it was pointless to take out his frustrations on Maggie. He still had to say it. "It wasn't their damn town that got vaporized. It wasn't their department that got wiped off the face of the earth."

"I know," Maggie whispered.

He immediately felt ashamed. She had managed so far to distance herself from the reality of the case, to go on as if it was just another day at the office, but now he had selfishly crashed through the tenuous facade. He could tell that she was trying hard to hold herself together. Her chin quivered ever so slightly and her eyes filled, but he noticed she kept them wide, allowing no tears to be squeezed out and fall. "What do I say if they won't cooperate?" she asked.

Malbranche calmed down. He wasn't the only one having a bad day, a really bad day. Of course some people, too many people, didn't even have days at all anymore. "Tell 'em only girls have the right to say 'No,' " he gruffed amiably, trying to reestablish the earlier mood—official, with jocular overtones. "Better yet," he continued. "Cite precedent. The Feds love precedent; that'll get them. You think the Oklahoma City police weren't all over the bombing there? There was a state murder prosecution of both those guys. Who do you think put that all together? We've got more open murder investigations than we can even count in this case."

"It might work. At least for a while," she said.

He smiled at her. "Besides," he continued, "I was ordered to help out with this bomb threat investigation. So were you. There's nobody around to countermand that order. Let 'em take it up with our superiors."

Maggie gave him a tight smile in return, then turned around and headed out the door. He watched her the whole way.

Maggie was a damn fine woman and a damn fine cop. He couldn't imagine his miserable excuse of a life without her.

He fumbled in his shirt pocket for another cigarette.

Zeke watched with exasperation as Milo circled the big, white cargo van and kicked the steel-belted radials in the parking lot of Crazy Moe's used-car lot. Finally, Zeke just shook his head and walked over to his companion. "We already bought it, so I don't know why you're still kicking the tires, as if that accomplishes anything anyhow."

Milo continued his inspection without looking at Zeke.

"Some deal. I don't believe we only got eight hundred for the bus, man. That van had history."

"Money isn't really an issue at the moment," said Zeke *sotto voce* to his shaggy friend.

Milo waved the comment away. "I also don't know why we couldn't have gotten something a bit more green-friendly than a piece-of-shit, American-made cargo van as a replacement. The mileage sucks!"

Zeke ran his right hand across the top of his head. "We went through this. You can't get a hybrid at a used-car lot, even in Vegas where people lose a lot of money and sell their cars to get a new stake to win it back. They're just too hot. Even at dealerships, the hybrids all have waiting lists, especially the larger models and SUVs. And we need something big enough to carry all our stuff. Something that is nondescript and lacking in windows, so our mugs don't show to everybody we pass by."

Brandon piped up as he headed over to the van with a suitcase. "Zeke's right. No way we could score a hybrid big enough for all three of us and our gear. They're a big fad these days, at least while gas prices are high." He gestured at the van with his unburdened hand. "Besides, we did what we could. At least it's white. We're helping out the cause, reflecting solar energy back out into space."

Milo halted his inspection with a shrug. "Yeah, that part's going better than expected." He glanced around before continuing. "Did you see the news on the television in the car dealer's office? Two more volcanoes in the Cascades blew overnight. Baker, Adams, who knows which one will go next."

Zeke shot Milo a stern look. "Shut up, Milo," he hissed.

Another shrug. "I'm only sorry Nakajami jumped on his Learjet two hours beforehand and got away."

Zeke's face flushed. He pointed a finger at Milo, the tip twitching, bouncing in time to the artery in his neck. "Cut that out. I mean it, Milo. Just shut your yap about that. This wasn't personal. This was political. I'm not a murderer." His eyes swept over both of his companions. He dropped down his hand, but the artery continued to throb. He could almost hear the blood rushing to his brain. "We're not murderers."

Brandon, at least, looked chagrinned. "Yeah," he said with quiet resignation, ". . . political." He put the suitcase in the back of the van and pressed the door shut, then looked about. "So, now what?"

Milo started working a rubber band with his hands. He must have lifted it from the car dealer's office. After a minute of stretching and twirling it, he finally spoke. "Look," he said, then lifted his head and glanced about them again, "we got about three hundred fifty thousand dollars left, right?"

Brandon pulled a small, spiral-bound pad from his hip pocket and flipped through a couple of pages. "Three hundred fifty eight thousand, five hundred sixteen and change."

Milo slapped his hand against his forehead. "Whatever. First thing. Get rid of any notes you have tracking the money." He walked over to Brandon and held out his hand for the notepad.

Brandon looked at the notepad, then at Milo's hand. Finally, reluctantly, he started to hand the pad over. Milo snatched it away.

"That's poor bookkeeping," Brandon complained.

Milo glared at him. "No, dude," he chided, waggling the notepad at Brandon. "It's evidence." He ripped out a bunch of pages and started tearing them up, continuing to talk as he shredded them and dropped them into a nearby Dumpster. "Maintaining our charitable status is kind of the least of our problems right now." He headed back toward the van. "Right now, we need to be seen losing large sums of money."

Brandon shook his head in apparent disbelief. "So, we're just going to go in and lose the rest of our money? That could take a while."

Milo shot a look toward the Strip, where neon lights beckoned not far away. "Not as long as you think. We're going to put almost all of it on the roulette wheel at a no-limit table—something that pays three to one odds."

Brandon looked skeptical. "I don't think anything on a roulette table pays three to one. Six to one, yeah, or two to one, unless maybe there is some combination of numbers. . . ."

Milo waved off the digression. "Six to one, then. Even better. We place our money and we take our chances."

"You watch way too many *Bond* movies, Milo," Zeke chimed in. It wasn't that he disagreed with Milo's plan. It was just that he never would have believed in a million years that he would be having a discussion like this. How to lose more money than he'd ever imagined having and how to do it in one easy step.

Thank God it wasn't twelve steps, or losing money could become a habit.

"Look," continued Milo. "If we lose, we lose, but it's a big enough loss that it sure as hell gets noticed and we can say we gambled a bunch away in smaller amounts and tried to make back our losses on one spin of the wheel."

Brandon looked forlorn. Zeke was sure that he was upset enough to wring his hands, but nobody did that kind of thing anymore. He also probably felt naked without his notepad. "Couldn't we," Brandon finally blurted out, ". . . couldn't we, like, give the money to help the victims in Washington?" He hesitated for a moment, before continuing in a softer voice. "It would . . . I dunno, I guess . . . I would just feel better about it if we gave the money to the victims."

Milo shook his head firmly before Zeke could even answer. "No way, dude. This isn't about feeling better. It's about saving the freakin' world and not getting caught doing it."

Brandon looked at his shoes. Zeke wondered if he was crying, but didn't want to ask, so he changed the subject. "What if we win?"

Milo flashed a brief smile. "If we win, we pay taxes on the gain, but have enough cash left over to deposit back in the bank so that maybe, just maybe, nobody looks too hard at Barrington's donation. We could even return it or at least offer to. That way nobody gets suspicious. No conviction for embezzling. No jail. Maybe we save the world and get away with it. And no one ever knows we did it."

Zeke's mood had been lifted, but only for a second. He looked at his two friends and the white van. Then he spoke softly to himself: "And no one ever knows we did it."

CHAPTER 26

Pulaski could scarcely believe how quickly Chuck could mess up a workspace. This was only their second day in Spokane and already Chuck's desk was filled to overflowing with reports, empty Styrofoam coffee cups, crusty containers of take-out Chinese food, and an overflowing ashtray (the latter despite the crime lab's no smoking policy). To top it off, his clothes were wrinkled and spotted with coffee stains and at least one desiccated Chinese noodle. Sure, she was still in the same clothes as yesterday—her wardrobe had been vaporized with the rest of Seattle—but she had at least rinsed things out in the sink last night.

She walked toward him, but stopped a few feet short of the desk. "God Almighty, Chuck. Did you pull an all-nighter? You gotta get some sleep."

Chuck rubbed his stubble, then pushed the graying wisps of hair that were dangling over his eyes back, sliding both of his hammy hands over his balding head. "Yeah," he murmured. He leaned back in his chair and glanced over his stomach toward the desk. He discovered the Chinese noodle and worked to dislodge it while he spoke. "You know, when I was a rookie detective, I would keep my old cigarette stubs." He pinched the noodle between fat fingers and dropped it into the ashtray. "Then, when I wanted to impress the captain, I would leave after everyone else, grab a few beers, hook up with a lady if I was lucky, or a woman who wasn't so much of a lady if I was luckier still, then come in the next morning. Same clothes . . ."—he gestured at his rumpled outfit with a wry smile—". . . same coffee stains. Unshaven. I'd drop the old butts I'd saved up into the ashtray and put my head on the desk and go to sleep. Everybody else shows up, I'm snoring away."

He smiled at her. "But you know what? The captain fell for it every time. Thought I'd worked all night."

Pulaski didn't know what to say, so she just gave him an encouraging nod. "Hmmmpphhh."

"Now I work all night and I don't care if anybody's impressed. I just want to get these bastards."

The FBI, the CIA, all of Homeland Security, and the Army, Navy, Air Force, and Marines were looking for these bastards, but Pulaski knew that, somehow, Chuck had the edge on all of them. She smiled. "You want to catch 'em? Then grab your coat. It's cold outside and we need to take a trip to California."

Malbranche sprang up with amazing alacrity for an old guy who had been up for more than forty hours. "Something break?" he said. She could hear the rising excitement in his voice, like a kid hearing the ice cream truck two blocks away.

"It's Connoway," she confirmed. "Belongs to a group called GreenSword."

"So?" asked Malbranche. "We knew he was a green freak."

"Passport office says he and another GreenSword member took a trip to Russia a few weeks ago. The Feds confirmed that the nuke was Russian in origin."

Malbranche rushed for the door. "Criminals are so stupid," he said with obvious glee. "Gotta love that."

Even though the logistics and mechanics of the plan to create nuclear winter . . . his plan . . . had worked, Brandon didn't feel any satisfaction. He certainly didn't feel any elation at their success. All he felt was guilt. It pressed down on his soul and it distracted his every thought. He knew what he had done, but the only thought that wanted to surface in his weary mind was "What have I done?"

Still, it wasn't that he wanted to be caught. Sure, he didn't want his friends to be caught either. But, most of all, he couldn't bear the thought that he would be caught. Not because he faced prison, but because then everyone would know—his mom would know—and no one would ever be proud of him again. So he pushed down the guilt that kept trying to surface in his mind, like a million zombies clawing up out of the earth, and put his mind to Milo's efforts to keep them from becoming suspects.

Unfortunately, Brandon just didn't get it. Milo had passed out small piles of cash and told them to scatter throughout the Strip on a two-hour betting spree. It didn't make sense then, and it didn't make any more sense now that they had gathered back at the van to report.

He handed his remaining cash back to Milo. "Jesus, Milo. I thought we were going to just make one big bet."

Milo took the cash without even looking at it, much less counting it. "We are, mostly," he replied, "but it's important to be seen in various casinos and to make some smaller wagers in each. Not only does it make for a lot of witnesses who can come forward in case we ever become undesirably famous and say, 'I saw that guy at the such-and-so casino' or, better yet, 'I played craps with that guy at the such-and-so casino.' It supports our story and makes it hard for anyone to figure exactly how much we won or lost."

Brandon shot Milo a dubious look. "You're the one that was talking about security cams tracking McVeigh. Well, they've got cameras everywhere in casinos. They'll figure out we didn't drop six hundred thousand dollars on the Strip before we made our big bet."

"Yeah," admitted Milo, "if the casinos save the tapes long

enough that they still have 'em when they're asked, we could have a problem. If it comes to that, we just say we dropped the big money in an illegal floating poker game in a South Central warehouse . . . I know . . . the night of our last planning session. We can say that we came to Vegas for an honest chance to recoup the losses we took in a rigged game." He began nodding with enthusiasm as he continued to spin his lies. "When smaller bets didn't look like they were panning out, we got desperate and dropped it all."

Brandon didn't share Milo's enthusiasm, but he had no alternative plan. "Okay, if you say so."

Milo pivoted to catch Zeke's eye. "Then it's settled." When Zeke didn't object, Milo continued. "So? How'd you do?"

Zeke turned in his remaining money, too. "Well," he reported, "I hit six places. Did the blackjack tables and craps in each one, plus a couple of minutes at a roulette wheel. I'm down four thousand three hundred and sixty."

Again, Milo didn't bother to count. "Did you make at least five one-thousand-dollar bets?"

"Yeah," replied Zeke. Then he blushed. "But . . . I won three of 'em."

Milo sighed. "Long odds, dudes. We gotta go with long odds."

Zeke just stared at the ground.

Milo gave him a friendly nudge on the shoulder. "Don't worry about it, man."

Brandon spoke up. He hadn't known he was expected to make a report. "I did the same thing at my places, plus some slot machines."

Milo flinched. "Slot machines? You played slot machines? High rollers don't play slot machines, dude."

Brandon bristled. He was doing his best in what had become a bad, bad situation. "Yeah," he challenged Milo, "what did you play?"

"Baccarat, man, baccarat."

Brandon was almost impressed with his colleague. "You know the rules to baccarat?"

"No," goofed Milo. "That's why I lost so much cash. The dealer. . . ."

"Croupier," interrupted Zeke. "I think they're called croupiers."

"Whatever," breezed Milo. "All I know is that he just kept giving me odd looks as I increased my bets."

Brandon understood, at a logical level, betting Barrington's remaining cash, but he didn't understand trying to lose. You always played a game to win or it just didn't make sense. Maybe it was the stress of what he had done or maybe it was just that the blinking neon lights flashing in the darkness were giving him a migraine, but he just couldn't hold his tongue. "Playing a game you don't know the rules to!" he blurted out. "How stupid can you be?"

Milo remained uncharacteristically calm. "No," he replied in a smooth, even voice. "Smart. The croupier will remember me, if we ever need it. His name was Saul; there can't be that many croupiers named Saul."

Zeke sucked at his front teeth with his tongue and nodded in agreement. He sniffed and hunched his shoulders against the cool of the desert's night air. "Okay. Let's get on with it. I've got the rest of the funds converted into chips at this place down the Strip a bit."

They left the van and walked down the Strip, past the pyramid of the Luxor and its tower of light to the heavens, past the knights of Excalibur, and past the faux geography and small scale reproductions of the landmarks of Paris and of New York, New York. Flashing neon assaulted them wherever they turned. The temporary crash of the Western states' power grid had not darkened Vegas for long.

They arrived at a huge expanse of fountains just as the waters began dancing in choreographed rhythm to classical music. The beats of the music and the leaps of the liquid were syncopated with not only each other, but with the oohs and ahhs they generated in the crowd of tourists mesmerized by the showy display, a mass of middle class Americans who had proved unwilling to give up their two weeks of vacation to wallow in the grief and terror of the destruction and death in the Pacific Northwest. They had fifty weeks a year to be miserable. Right now they were focused on the fantasy that was Vegas. After the water show, they would file into the clanging casinos and gamble away money that they could be giving to aid their fellow man.

People did it every week on the lottery.

Of course, Brandon was doing the same thing. Except he hated himself for doing it. The tourists, they just hated their jobs.

The trio entered into the lobby of a nearby casino and paused beneath a mammoth, colorful glass chandelier/sculpture for a few moments to get their bearings. Nearby tourists turned their digital cameras upwards to take pictures of the fancy glasswork flowers and colors and wavy curtains of fragile excess. Some pointed. Some gasped in delight and awe. But most just commented on how expensive the ceiling fixture was. Nothing excites Americans more than gaudy expense.

Brandon's facile mind churned through the figures. The money spent on this decorative glass feature of one overindulgent casino was more than enough to build a high school, or feed the homeless of Sacramento for a year, or fund Greens-Word indefinitely. It was enough to make a difference; instead it just made a classic spectacle.

He followed his companions to the gaming tables, surrounded by a sea of flashing, clanging, whirling slot machines that could never be described as tasteful, much less classic. Milo ushered the group toward a no-limit roulette table in the most crowded area of the table games.

The croupier raised his eyebrows when he saw the stack of high denomination chips that Milo placed on the table. He counted the chips and called over a pit boss to witness the action.

While this was going on, Milo turned to his companions. "Pick a play with six to one odds and we'll make our bet."

Brandon's brain was going numb. The bomb, the lights, the money. It was overwhelming him. "Shouldn't we watch the table for a while?" he mumbled. Was this really happening? Was it all a bad dream?

"Huh?" responded Zeke. It was the kind of inarticulate reply you never got in dreams.

"To figure out what's hot," explained Brandon.

Milo shook his head, laughing. "Amateur," he chided.

The noise of the crowd, the bells of the slots, and the glint of the lights about him all dimmed. Brandon stood mute and pointed.

Milo pushed the entire stack of chips where Brandon pointed.

An attractive woman in a sequined cocktail dress to Milo's right gasped and pointed. She called back toward a group of friends nearby. "Come quick," she urged, "someone's about to lose three hundred thousand dollars on a single spin."

The only thing tourists liked more than losing their own money, Brandon knew, aside from winning, was watching other people lose money, lots of it. This loss would probably make the woman in sequins orgasm.

Another first for Brandon.

The croupier fingered the ball, then spun the wheel, and launched the ball in the opposite direction, where it glided along the rim, orbiting the numbers, the center of the universe for any roulette player.

"No more bets," he intoned, a slight edge of excitement tinge-
ing the usual monotone. "All bets are final. No more bets."

Milo started to bounce on the balls of his feet and pump his
fists. "C'mon baby. I'm feeling lucky."

Brandon thought he was going to throw up. What happened,
he wondered, if you puked all over a bet in progress?

Eric Castille fidgeted in the front seat of one of the S.W.A.T.
vans belonging to the L.A.P.D. The squad had parked for more
than an hour in the far reaches of the parking lot of a dollar
store while a surveillance team reconnoitered and additional
forces gathered, including a couple of cops from Seattle who
had requested the raid. The pudgy one, an older guy by the
name of Malbranche, had come over to shake his hand and
compliment him on lifting a useful print off of a 1999 quarter.
The guy's partner, a good-looking and more refined woman by
the name of Pulaski, chimed in her thanks, too. Praise was nice,
but catching the bad guy was what he lived for. He hoped the
two of them wouldn't screw anything up.

Finally, the assault team was about to get underway and
Castille was nervous. Not about the firepower or the possibility
of a gun battle or explosion or even the probability that he
would be propelled against his snug shoulder harness as the
police vehicles stopped short after screaming toward the address that was listed as the headquarters of the environmental
organization at which Brandon P. Connoway worked.

No, he was concerned that with all these policemen, all the
adrenaline flowing from the nature of the bust, and the disaster
in Seattle fresh on their minds, that his crime scene would be
mussed, that his evidence would be contaminated. To top
everything else, a cool, light rain was falling. There would be
muddy boot-prints everywhere.

The cars raced up, the S.W.A.T. members took up their positions as a team raced for the door with a battering ram. The ram popped through the cheesy lock on the door, bursting it open with a loud crash. A flash-bang was slid in along the floor a half-second later and everyone shielded their eyes or turned away until it went off. Then a squad in full riot paraphernalia, face-shields down, poured through the door.

A few moments later, shouted calls of "Clear" reverberated all the way out to the street. As Castille alighted from the van, Malbranche and Pulaski, obviously wearing Kevlar vests underneath their light raincoats, entered the house.

Pulaski appeared back at the door as Castille approached it. "I hope you brought a lot of bags, Eric," she said with a smile. "We're going to want to take everything in here."

He tossed her a handful of large, plastic bags. "Way ahead of you." He passed by her to move into the center of the house. A bevy of S.W.A.T. members milled about, keeping an eye out for targets they knew weren't there.

"Thanks for your assistance, boys. But I'll take it from here. Guard the perimeter in case they return."

The brute force filed out, but Pulaski and Malbranche stayed. Malbranche was poking about at what looked to be an office area. A flat-screen monitor sat atop the desk. A computer box sat beneath the desk, a green light gleaming faintly on the front.

"Please don't do that, officer," said Castille in a firm, professional tone.

"Don't worry," replied Malbranche, holding up his hands. "I've got my gloves on."

"That's not what I'm worried about," replied Castille.

Milo, Brandon, and Zeke exited the casino in the company of two burly security guards, their worries banished for the moment.

"I told you I felt lucky," beamed Milo, bouncing with glee

with each long stride. Milo pointed and the group headed down the Strip, past the gleaming waters of the fountains, towards the van. The casino had insisted on an escort to their vehicle when they had determined to turn in their chips for cash.

Zeke grinned back at his shaggy friend. Maybe things were going to work out after all. "Yeah, and the paperwork didn't even take that long." He sidled towards his friends, speaking low so the beefy guards couldn't hear. "I'm not so sure it was a good idea to have Brandon be the one who took the gain and paid the withholding taxes, though. He's a lot more on the grid than either of us."

"Don't look at me," whispered Brandon. "Can I help it I'm the only one who could remember his social security number and present a valid I.D.?"

"Relax," said Milo as he sashayed along the sidewalk, winking at every woman they passed. "I think we're going to make it."

CHAPTER 27

Morris Hartwell slumped on his barstool behind the desk of the Canyon Vistas Motel. He wiped a patina of dust off the countertop with his sleeve and took a sip from his thermos of lukewarm iced tea, no lemon. It was a crummy job at a crummy motel, but at least the work wasn't too demanding. Plenty of time to kill reading magazines or watching TV and no one looking over his shoulder all the time.

Of course, like many of those who had gone to Vegas with visions of boom-town success and poker winnings, he still dreamed of hitting it big, even though he had sworn off going to casinos after Helen left. That's why he had crossed the border back into California to find a job. Helen hadn't come back to him, of course, but he still appreciated the lack of nearby temptation. He worked his job at the sleepy motel in a sleepy town in a scenic area of southeastern California visited mainly by families avoiding the interstate highways on their cross-country trips and assuaged his gambling addiction by putting two dollars on the lottery once a week.

The lottery gave terrible odds, of course. Everyone knew that. But he wasn't playing it with any realistic hope of winning, nor even for the dubious entertainment value of watching his numbers lose week after week after week. He was playing it so his dream of a big score didn't die.

He certainly needed something to keep his spirits up this week. Occupancy was down and he guessed that the nuking of

226

Seattle would have a long-term impact on vacation patterns. The TV, propped up on a nearby chair so as to be visible from the counter, kept up a constant stream of grim news from Seattle. He nudged up the volume with a battered remote as a commercial finished and the news came on.

"Tonight," intoned the announcer without emotion, "day six of the Mount Ranier nuclear aftermath."

The picture faded out to show a grim-faced newsman seated at a desk, with superimposed graphics appearing behind him, over his left shoulder. "Good evening. Now to the news. Government officials attempt to calm fears in metropolitan areas throughout the country, stating that there is no indication that the SUVs pose any further threat to urban areas or that they have in their possession any additional nuclear devices."

Mo smirked to himself. Like they would know.

The newscaster continued. "Meanwhile, rescue workers encountered grisly scenes of burned, smashed, and bloated corpses entangled with the debris in the congealing mudflows that now cover the towns of Orting, Puyallup, Sumner, and Enumclaw. Rescue efforts continue to be hampered as the eruption of the Cascades shows no sign of abating." An aerial shot appeared showing a long view of the range. "Glacier Peak, Mount Washington, and Mount Hood have joined the general eruption along the Cascades, with flowing lava pouring from the caldera of each and ash billowing into the sky."

The graphic changed to a schematic of the country showing the coverage of the ash cloud. "The jet stream has carried ash from the explosion around the globe, with the worst effects along a widening swath arcing into southern Canada and across the upper Midwest and then into the Mid-Atlantic states. The Nuclear Energy Commission indicates that radioactive fallout from the actual nuclear explosion is minimal except in eastern Washington and northern Idaho, but warns that the ash clouds from the volcanic activity are extremely abrasive to human lungs, as well as to mechanical equipment. All individuals in areas of visible ash-fall are advised to stay indoors."

Sometimes it paid to be in the middle of nowhere. Nobody wanted to bomb remote scenic areas of California.

A new picture appeared. "In related business news, the Dow continued to struggle, down four hundred and sixty-two points as recriminations about disaster preparedness haunted the administration. Meanwhile, Energy Secretary Palcow urged conservation of natural gas supplies."

The graphic switched from a bull and bear design to the Macrosurf logo, with "$10,000,000" splashed across it. "Officials field thousands of calls from psychics, citizens, and tipsters of all types eager to claim the ten-million-dollar reward offered by Goro Nakajami for the apprehension of the person or persons responsible for this greatest terrorist act of all time." A clip rolled from the press conference announcing the reward, showing a grim Goro Nakajami saying: "If our government can put a reward of twenty million dollars on the head of Osama bin Laden, I see no reason why it is unreasonable of me to put a reward out to capture those responsible for this despicable and cowardly attack." The hot-line number streamed at the bottom of the screen throughout the story.

Mo yawned. He had seen this same news bit three times already today. The graphic changed yet again, this time showing the face of a young man standing on a beach, a microphone thrust in front of his face. Lit from below, the guy had a crazed, Satanic look. "And police wish to question this man, Brandon P. Connoway, and other members of the extremist GreenSword environmental action group as potential witnesses in their investigation of the nuclear destruction of Seattle. The other members of this organization being sought are Zeke Paulsen and Milo Stanczyk. No photographs of these other individuals are available at this time." The camera zoomed in on the face of Connoway as the film clip from which the still was taken began to run.

". . . mankind will not survive . . . ," warned the earnest young man.

"Stay tuned for all this and local weather. Cooler than normal temperatures. . . ."

But Mo wasn't listening anymore. He grabbed the desk phone, even though he wasn't supposed to use it for personal calls, and dialed the hot-line number established by Macrosurf. "Hello," he said with eager anticipation. "Yeah, how does one go about collecting that reward? 'Cause I got the three guys you're looking for in cabin sixteen."

Zeke lay awake in bed, listening to the chirping of birds, the sounds of nature outside the cabin. It was peaceful and seductive. He almost believed that he could stay here forever, slowly spending the mass of money now stashed in Milo's knapsack and filling his days hiking and communing with the flora and fauna. But the logical part of him knew that was a lie. They needed to keep moving.

He woke Brandon and Milo and the three of them prepared to leave. The only problem was the destination.

Milo was pushing his latest idea: "I'm thinking the Galapagos Islands, man. Everybody in the movement who's been there raves about the Galapagos Islands. Just imagine what it would be like. . . ."

Sitting astride the equator, six hundred miles off the coast of Ecuador, we live as kings in a tropical paradise that is democratically governed and uses the U.S. dollar as its official currency—so no questions about our endless supply of greenbacks. The permanent population of the entire country, spread out over four of the ten major islands, is less than most subdivision-plagued suburbs, so we chat amiably with our Mayberry R.F.D. neighbors, with no fear of crime, crowding, or traffic.

The temperature of our island home never goes below sixty degrees or above ninety, so no one ever wears that much. A short, tropical cloudburst drenches everyone most afternoons during the rainy season, causing the skimpy clothing of both the local señoritas and vacationing coeds to cling to their curvaceous bods until dried by the sunsoaked warmth of playful evening breezes. The sun slowly sets in a mauve and purple haze streaked with orange and red festoons, with a flash of green just as it dips beneath the gentle majestic blue waves of the vast and mysterious ocean.

We visit all of the islands in our catamaran, sipping Margaritas and showing off the exotic bird life to adventurous and comely visitors filled with wonderment and lusty appetites. Storm petrels, frigates, lava gulls, Darwin finches, mockingbirds, and red-footed boobies flutter and roost, flying as free as we are. We take a break after lunch and snorkel, frolicking in clear, cool water with green sea turtles, dolphins, Galapagos penguins, sea lions, and even marine iguanas. The tourist women are enthralled, intoxicated by the ecological grandeur of it all, and entranced by our rugged good looks and easygoing charm. We play the part of wealthy playboys that donate time for species-extinction research by day and make soft, tender, passionate love to them at night, all night, until in the throes of ecstasy, they cry out in shuddering climax, "Milo! Milo! Milo!"

Brandon interrupted Milo as he called out his own name in earthy crescendo, jumping up and down on one of the hotel room's two double beds (Brandon had drawn the short straw and had gotten to sleep on the now folded-away cot): "You tell them your name? Are you insane?"

Milo stopped jumping and bounced slowly to a halt, a confused stare on his face. "Huh? I like my name. I've got a cool name. My name even helps me get laid."

"Right," snorted Brandon in disgust. "Women sleep with guys because of their names."

Milo shrugged. "Whenever I toke up at the university with grad students, I pick out a foxy art history or English lit major and ask her if she wants to join the 'Milo high club.' Dude, it works every time. In the right setting, it's a better line than 'Wanna fuck?'."

Brandon's face screwed up in distaste, like he had just found a piece of bacon on his veggie-burger. "Well, I guess you're going to have to work on your . . . pick-up repertoire . . . , because there's no way in hell that we can keep using our own names."

Milo dropped to a sitting position on the bed. "Spoken like someone named Brandon."

"You saw the news this morning. We're being sought for questioning in the most publicized crime in the history of the world. My name may be pretty mainstream, but how many people have actually met someone named Zeke or Milo? Someone will notice."

Milo scrunched up his nose as he got up to gather his bags. "Maybe the Galapagos doesn't have an extradition treaty with the U.S."

"Oh, yeah. Extradition. That's your only worry."

The rocking of the catamaran on the waves accentuates the rocking of your passionate lovemaking on the aft deck, as the sun sets behind Tiffany, your busty coed plaything du jour, who wears nothing but a thin silver chain, with a tiny blue vial hanging from it, bouncing with the rhythm of your thrusts as she straddles you. She reaches above your head, next to the cooler filled with live lobsters awaiting grilling, as you cuddle in the gloaming. Grabbing a piece of nautical rope, she suggests a little light bondage.

You agree to play along, until suddenly the ropes are too tight, rub-

bing your wrists and ankles raw, your manly passion subsiding as you realize how vulnerable you have left yourself. Tiffany begins to recite how, although she is a cheerleader at USC now, she is originally from Tacoma, where her loving parents, an identical twin and two other sisters, one brother, fourteen cousins, two aunts (with corresponding uncles), and an invalid grandmother still lived and loved and breathed, operating a no-kill animal shelter for unwanted cats, dogs, and an occasional ferret, until that fateful day when a nuclear firestorm incinerated and vaporized them all, leaving nothing behind but gray ash, a tiny bit of which she carries with her in the blue vial.

You watch in both fascination and horror as she leans toward the cooler, her naked breasts brushing your face as she reaches in and grabs one of the still-living gastronomical delights. With an adroit maneuver, she slips off to the side and dangles the red beast above your own. As the large pincers of the lobster seek their revenge for your planned meal, Tiffany produces a razor blade from God knows where and begins to seek her own revenge, naming your victims one by one as she slices off bits of your body. If she takes off an ear for the ferret, what in God's name is she going to slice off to honor the memory of her dead twin?

You smell the sharp iron scent of your own hot blood as it spurts onto you both—definitely not the exchange of bodily fluids you had intended. You begin to scream, a high-pitched wail like the whine you hear above the motor when someone is cutting the grass. As the methodical retribution of your vengeful sex toy continues relentlessly and both your vision and the sky dim toward blackness, you start to vomit, but it's not from the motion of the ocean.

"Jesus," murmured Milo. "We gotta get you laid. You have a lot of pent-up aggression."

"I can't imagine why," said Brandon dryly.

"Enough already," said Zeke. "We're in this together. We'll talk more about how and where to maintain a low profile once we're on the road. For now, play nice and get in the van." He tilted his head toward the door and they all hefted their bags and filed out. Zeke actually thought the Galapagos Islands thing was a pretty good idea, but he had no opportunity to say so.

As soon as all three of them cleared the door of the hotel room, a phalanx of FBI agents, cops, and other menacing-looking types swept in from all sides. Within a few seconds, the three members of GreensWord were down on the ground face-first in the gravel parking lot. A burly cop had a knee in Zeke's back and seemed to be enjoying it. His partner just stood to the side and began the traditional recitation: "You have the right to remain silent. Anything you say can and will be used against you. You have the right to an attorney. If you cannot afford an attorney, one will be appointed for you. . . ."

Zeke looked over at his companions. Milo was clearly pissed, but not making any effort to resist. Brandon was shaking violently. A dark stain and acrid odor made it clear he had peed his pants. "Oh, shit, Zeke," he muttered. "We should've gone with the ear thing."

Milo's head snapped around to glare at Brandon. "*Shut up,* Brandon."

Matthew Barrington awoke with a headache. Once again he had slept with a pillow over his head to dim the noise of the pounding surf that was eating its way across the beach to attack his house. No doubt the buildup of carbon dioxide from re-breathing the same stale air had caused the headache. It would get better quickly with an ibuprofen and a bit of fresh morning air.

He left ever-faithful Mitzi sprawled in soft-core disarray on the bed, as he trundled out to the front door to retrieve the morning paper, which lay neatly folded within easy reach. It paid to be famous or, at least, to tip well. He tucked the paper under his arm while he poured himself some fresh orange juice from the refrigerator and spiked it with a splash of vodka from the freezer. Then he headed back to bed to read the paper and fondle Mitzi while she slept.

As he entered the room, he unfolded the paper. The o.j. slipped from his grasp as he staggered against the door frame.

"Damn!"

Mitzi stirred from the noise as the newspaper also fell to the ground, a light flapping followed by a thump. The four-inch-high, all-caps headline read: "GREEN SWORD NUKED SE-ATTLE."

Mitzi opened her eyes and looked over at Barrington seductively. "Come back to bed, Matty," she purred. "It's cold."

Barrington staggered to the nightstand and grabbed the phone, hitting the speed dial. Mitzi sat up, her nightie falling off her shoulders, exposing her breasts, white against her deep tan elsewhere. Maybe she was looking for action, maybe she was concerned that he was dialing 9-1-1 because he was having a heart attack. He didn't care. She had just become completely unimportant to his life, even more unimportant than she had been when they had fucked last night.

It took long, agonizing seconds for the phone on the other end of the call to begin to ring. It rang three times before it was picked up. But, when it was, Barrington wasted no time. "Harry?" he barked, barely pausing before he continued. "I don't care that it's six o'clock in the morning. You know that bit part shooting in New Zealand? I've changed my mind. I'll take it. I'm leaving on the first plane."

CHAPTER 28

Chuck hated packing. It was why he had stayed in the same dingy little apartment for twelve years. Packing meant organizing, which meant weeding out what was worth moving and what was junk, which meant digging up the past, and he had no desire to dwell on the past. It also meant cleaning and, no surprise to anyone who had ever met him, he couldn't be bothered with that.

Fortunately for him, his dingy little apartment and all of his stuff, junk or not, had been vaporized with the rest of greater Seattle. Not much stuff to move these days; just what he had on his back and the files he had generated since coming to Spokane. Sooner or later, though, he would have to go shopping for some new clothes. He hated that, too. Not only was he pretty sure he could no longer find anything in the style he wore—basically stuff from when he was still dating and had to care about what he looked like if he wanted to get any pillow time—but he no longer remembered what size he wore and he wasn't about to let some frou frou check his inseam.

He maneuvered his wastebasket to the side of his desk and swept his arm across it toward that edge. A torrent of Styrofoam cups, take-out containers, cigarette packs, gum wrappers, crumpled up TPS reports, dried-up pens, and mangled paper clips showered down. Some of them even fell in the receptacle. He would have just let the others miss, but just then Maggie walked her long legs into the room, so he decided to pretend not to be a slob.

She watched him clean up without saying a word. Finally, he decided to start a conversation or she was going to wait until he started vacuuming the place.

"So? Did you find out where the trial is going to be? I can't imagine those assholes are going to be safe anywhere. They probably have more contracts outstanding than all the realtors in all the world."

Maggie eyed a corner of the desk, brushed it off with her fingertips, and perched casually on it while Malbranche dropped back into his groaning, ergonomic chair. He swiveled the chair as she swiveled her hips to face him.

"The plan is to hold it on Kahoolawe," she said. "You know, the Hawaiian island that the Navy used to use for target practice. Limited access. No safe place to hold a mass protest. Easy to avoid mob justice."

Malbranche harrumphed. He'd been doing more and more of that since he had gotten older. He vowed silently to do less of it and, instead, launched into a complete sentence. "I just wish we'd spend more money protecting our citizens and less protecting terrorists once we catch 'em."

Maggie smiled in agreement, her teeth white and straight. "The thing is, I've read up a bit on their organization and seen the transcripts of their early interviews, not that they said much. But it's clear that they never thought of themselves as terrorists."

Malbranche was about to harrumph again, but he managed to stifle it. He wished he could stifle his smoking habit so easily. "Okay," he gruffed instead, "eco-terrorists."

"Not even that. Their pamphlets are a bit polemic, but not exactly rabble-rousing. They just had a hard-on about global warming."

"So?"

Maggie stood up and smoothed her slacks as she did. "Haven't you followed the scientific experts and analysts on all the news shows? They say that there will be years of cooler weather because of the ash blocking the sunlight. Global warming is apparently no longer an immediate threat. If that's what they were trying to do, and nobody really knows that, then it worked."

Malbranche's right eye twitched in consternation. He sat forward in his chair. "You're not sticking up for these jerks, are you?" He stood up and began to pace away from the desk, before turning back to her. "You don't kill hundreds of thousands, maybe millions of people when they tally the collateral consequences all up, to stop global warming. That's not how you accomplish something positive." He wasn't sure if Maggie was serious or was just needling him.

"I'm not sticking up for them. I just think it helps to understand that they probably thought they were saving the planet."

Malbranche pulled a stick of nicotine gum from his pocket and unwrapped it. He crammed the gum in his mouth and wadded up the wrapper, tossing it in the general direction of the wastebasket. It fell well short. He pretended not to have noticed. "You know, I've never understood how a true environmentalist could get cheesed about global warming."

Maggie's head tipped forward in shock, almost as if yet another of the innumerable earthquakes and after-tremors had hit the area. "The planet is . . . was warming up. Six of the ten hottest years ever have occurred since nineteen-ninety."

Malbranche moistened his lips. "Actually, they found a glitch in the numbers. NASA now says six of the ten hottest years on record were in the nineteen-thirties and nineteen-forties."

She gave him a hard stare. "You are not seriously going to argue that it's not getting warmer, are you?"

Malbranche chewed his gum and scratched the side of his face as he thought through his next words. He didn't want to piss her off or make her think he was an idiot. Finally, he just blurted out what he had wanted to say all along. "Compared to what? Hell, when the dinosaurs ruled the earth, the whole Midwest was a giant, tropical swamp. The earth isn't getting any warmer than it was then, just warmer than it's been recently."

Maggie twirled her well-dressed foot in a small circle. "Recently?"

Malbranche didn't hesitate this time. "During most of recorded history. Look, it's like land ownership in the Middle East or the Balkans. Pick your time and you can prove it was any group's land you want. Here, you pick your time of comparison and you can prove anything you want about relative temperature movements. The earth's beginning to warm up from a minor cool spell, that's all."

Maggie's eyes narrowed. "With our help."

Malbranche picked up a paper clip and started to twist it apart. "Maybe. Maybe not. It's gotten warm before without our help."

Maggie folded her arms and shot him a dubious look. "You make it sound as if it's not a problem."

"Oh, sure, it's a problem. Lowland areas, where nobody should have been building in the first place, flood. Weather becomes more severe, crops are wiped out in some places, but helped in others. The thing is, it's a people problem, not a planet problem."

"What's the difference?"

Malbranche smiled. "I thought since the advent of Oprah, you chicks understood men. Mankind is self-centered, even the environmentalists. They only care the earth is warming up because it affects man, not to mention their fund-raising. Ever think that it's just Mother Nature's way of telling us our time is about to expire?"

Maggie unfolded her arms. Her foot stilled. "Some of us aren't quite so near to our allotted time on earth that we think in geologic terms and don't care what happens in the future."

Malbranche's grin widened, even though he knew his teeth were crooked and yellow. "Oh, I care. That's why I vote. I just don't think that you take things into your own hands and kill a bunch of innocent people."

"I'll agree with you there. It really surprises me that anyone in the environmental movement would kill."

Malbranche checked the coffeepot at the far end of the room. Finding it contained only a thick layer of burnt sludge on the bottom, he plunked it back down on the hot burner and headed back for his chair. "People get shot over parking spaces and you're surprised someone would kill over the fate of the planet? People get rabid; they do bad things."

Maggie tilted her head to one side and interlaced her fingers. "You'd think the tree-huggers would have moral issues with killing. Most of them are against the death penalty. Life for the guilty, but death for the innocent? Heck, most of them won't even eat meat."

"Sure," Malbranche drawled out the word. "Most of 'em trend toward the liberal standards, but a lot of environmentalists crossed the moral line on loss of life a long time ago."

Maggie again seemed startled by what he had said. She sat back down on the corner of the desk and her foot started twirling again. "There haven't been that many injuries or deaths connected to environmental groups."

"Maybe not on the police blotter," admitted Malbranche, scratching his right eyebrow as he plopped down in the chair again and continued, ". . . and maybe the simple-minded among them don't realize it, but stopping a hydroelectric dam to help salmon spawn has a cost. More coal-fired electricity, with all the mining accidents and smokestack emissions and lung disease death that causes."

"I'm sure they'd debate the causality. People could always use less power."

Malbranche waved the tangential argument aside. "Fine. So let's talk about scaring people about genetically-improved crops just in case it might affect butterflies. You want people, poor people especially, to just stop eating?" He leaned back to the tipping point on his chair, but held his balance.

"So?" she replied. "They're misguided."

He leaned forward and the chair righted itself with a thud. "And shortsighted. What's the endgame, Maggie? Global warming is slowed so there are twelve billion people instead of seven billion when the crash finally comes and mankind suffers and dies back to a sustainable level?" He gave her a wink as he continued. "Hell, you have a smaller carbon footprint than Al Gore, and not just because of your crappy salary and tiny . . . but fashionable . . . apartment. Why? Because you don't have kids. Warming is a symptom of profligacy. Not just energy waste, but pure overpopulation."

Maggie gave him a hard stare, but said nothing.

"Believe me, I understand the attraction of breeding." He smiled broadly. "Really, I do. But at the end of the day . . . or the day after tomorrow . . . are more people going to die because of the bad guys or the good guys?"

Maggie lowered her chin and gave him a piercing look, her foot twirling rapidly in agitation. "Nobody's perfect and the best intentions admittedly can go awry, but at least environmentalists are trying to do the right thing. These were practically the first guys from the movement who actually meant to hurt someone."

Malbranche knew that wasn't true. "Tell that to the lumber

mill worker who just got impaled when a high-speed saw hit a pike hammered into an old-growth redwood by a tree-hugger to ruin its commercial value."

"Mills and mines and power companies have hurt lots of people, too," Maggie countered.

Malbranche loved it when people resorted to the everybody's-guilty-of-something defense. It proved they didn't really have a leg to stand on, even if Maggie did have two great legs.

"Yeah," he admitted, drawing her in. "But we have a system that's supposed to sort that all out. It's called government."

Maggie laughed. He liked the sound. He wanted to hear it more often. "No wonder nothing works."

"Don't knock civil servants," Malbranche bantered back. "That's what we are."

"Yeah, speaking of which, we'd better pack up. The civil servants from FEMA say Spokane needs to be evacuated because of the ash and quakes and I don't think anyone will ever dismiss an evacuation order again."

They worked at their tasks for a few moments before she spoke up again. "Do you think they'll convict these guys?"

Malbranche was practical. He knew the ways of the world. "If nobody kills 'em first," he responded. "Actions are supposed to have consequences. That's what they pay us for. Who knows? Maybe they'll plead guilty. Maybe they're proud of what they've done."

"C'mon, Chuck. You know personal responsibility is out of style. They'll blame their parents or the President or bad movies or Satanic music or their consumption of junk food. Nobody admits their guilt anymore, not unless they're cutting a deal for a lesser sentence or certifiable."

Malbranche sighed. "I just wish these guys had thought through what they were doing."

"Hey, they almost got away with it. They may still get away

with it if we can't get more on them."

"Not that," replied Malbranche with a flutter of his right hand. "That's for the courts. I mean the consequences, not the logistical plan. Extremists always oversimplify things. It's easier to polarize positions and demonize the other side, than actually work out a consensus, especially one that is both technically and economically feasible."

He swiveled his chair and kicked one of the boxes of packed case files stacked behind him. "These particular bozos were too busy thinking about not getting caught to think about what they were really doing."

The conference room was windowless, just like his cell, and Zeke hated that. He yearned for a glimpse of the outdoors, the sun on his face, a gentle breeze playing with the tips of his hair. But he was denied all that. And for an environmentalist, that was cruel and unusual punishment.

It was funny. They hadn't been tortured in any of the traditional ways. They hadn't even been yelled at, at least not by the guards. Some of the cons had relatives in the Pacific Northwest and had been pretty vocal when they were first brought in, so they were quickly moved to a separate wing, in isolation from the rest of the prison population. And whenever he left his cell, even to go elsewhere in the prison to talk with counsel, like today, he was bundled into a Kevlar vest and surrounded by a squad of guards, their faces and rifles pointed out.

He nodded at Brandon and Milo when he came into the room. They were also wearing vests, as were the lawyers. Jack Gassman, who had made a career out of defending people nobody liked, sat at the end of the conference table. His associate, Randi Schirmer, sat next to him with a yellow legal pad and a stack of files.

Gassman didn't waste time on pleasantries. By all accounts, he wasn't a pleasant guy. Just an effective one.

"You keep telling me they have nothing and they keep telling me they do."

Zeke sat down. "Look, we already explained the money."

"And we were meeting with other environmentalists in Russia," added Brandon.

"Everything is circumstantial," asserted Milo.

"Yeah," Brandon continued, "I could've spent that quarter anywhere. It's legal tender for all debts public and private!"

Gassman didn't blink. He just turned his gaze to Milo. "I'm not talking about that."

"What then?" growled Milo. Prison was obviously hard on the guy. No chicks. No video games. No junk food.

Randi opened up a file folder and handed it to her boss. Gassman glanced at it and set it down in front of him. "How about twenty-three threatening e-mails to Goro Nakajami, famously known as a Seattle resident?"

Milo laughed out loud, a guttural maniacal laugh that scared Zeke. "If you put everybody away who called Nakajami an asshole or a crook or even a Satanic overlord, you'd be putting a whole lot of people in the slammer. And let me tell you, it's pretty empty in there."

"So, I shouldn't worry about Nakajami?"

"Oh, you should worry about Nakajami. Everybody should worry about Nakajami. He's ruining the world. But, I wouldn't worry about the fact that I wanted Nakajami dead. Everybody wants that. Or, at least, they should."

"It still goes toward motive . . . ," responded Gassman.

"I'll tell you what," shouted Milo, with a gleam in his eye. "You get the prosecution to keep their evidence on Macrosurf's document management system and we'll walk away when the thing invariably crashes or gets wiped out by a virus from the

Philippines."

Randi looked a bit frightened, but Gassman just folded his hands on top of the e-mail file. "Let's try not to get too excited. It's not productive."

Milo dialed it down a bit, but there was still an edge to his voice. "You try to not get excited. They got nada. They have no prints, no DNA, no tire tracks, no fibers. They got nothing. The place was incinerated. Nothing survives a temperature hotter than the surface of the sun."

Gassman gave Milo a placid stare. "You might not want to go out of your way demonstrating knowledge about the temperature of thermonuclear explosions when you're on the stand. It might not go over that well."

"Point taken," Milo mumbled.

"The real point is that we have now found out that they did a crime-scene sweep before the nuke went off. Are they going to find any of those things?"

"How would we know?" quipped Brandon. "We weren't there. We're . . . innocent."

Randi spoke up. "Look, guys. They got DNA, hair, and fibers like crazy. The question is, will they get a match?" She turned to look at them one by one. Milo turned away. Brandon stared down at the table. Zeke looked her straight in the eye, though.

"Who knows? Who cares?" he said without emotion. He was as good as dead anyway. Either they convicted him and kept him sequestered from the outside until he took his own life or they gave him the needle. If he got off, someone on the outside would take matters into their own hands. He had no future. He had to content himself that the planet, that mankind, at least, now had a future without him.

He could live . . . or die . . . with that.

CHAPTER 29

Pulaski entered the temporary office space the L.A. FBI had loaned them and found Chuck staring blankly at the computer screen on his desktop. That the desk was still relatively clean showed just how little time they had been here, helping to gather additional evidence to convict the GreensWord/SUV trio. The old-timer poked sporadically with his two index fingers at the keyboard of the computer, but a quick glance revealed nothing was happening on screen.

She knew better than to tell him to hit Control/Alt/Delete to terminate the non-responsive program. Guys hated it when you implied they didn't know how machines work. Instead, she just sat down at her own temporary desk and studied the file she had just brought in.

Chuck pecked and poked some more, then appeared to give up. He leaned back in his chair, laced his hands behind his head, and set his gaze in her direction.

"Please tell me," he said to her finally, "that you've got something useful in that folder. I can't get squat from this program and the damn help-line just has a recording blaming all current software problems on the electromagnetic pulse from the bomb."

Pulaski tapped on the file folder with her pen. "I've got plenty of information—too much, in fact. One hundred and ten different carpet fibers, sixteen or seventeen shoe prints identifiable by brand, seven identifiable only by general style and size, and sixty-seven hair samples so far."

Malbranche scrunched up his face and reached for his cold cup of coffee. "Any from our boys?" he asked, before downing it without a grimace.

"One," she said, "just one." She began to flip through the pages of the report as she continued. "But then, we've got one from a rapist who has been in the stir in Oklahoma for more than a month and supposedly has never been in Washington State. No matches on the rest yet; DNA takes a while, but forty-one brunettes, twenty blondes—only three naturally so—and the rest gray, white, or red. There are at least two blacks and three Asians in the mix."

"Crap!" growled Malbranche as he crushed his now-empty coffee cup and tossed it on the desk, where a few drops dribbled out to stain the wood. He leaned back in his chair again, his hands behind his head, the sweat stains in the armpits of his shirt showing. "What else?"

She flipped through a few more pages. "Seven blood samples. . . ."

"Any. . . ."

"None from our guys," she continued. "Possible DNA on a bunch of the food wrappers, but that will take a couple more weeks. No matches on the shoes. Finally found their old van in Vegas. No tire match."

"What about. . . ."

She preempted him again. She kind of enjoyed it. "The lab is working on the interior, but it was used for hauling recyclables by the new owner for the two weeks before we got to it. Aside from a lot of congealed soda-pop residue, I'm not too hopeful."

Malbranche scrunched up his face. "Sounds like you don't even need me."

She smiled. "I always said you had great deductive reasoning, Chuck."

He gave her a wry smile back and dropped his hands, leaning forward in his chair and putting his elbows on the desk. "Isn't there any good news?"

"Yeah, I saved it just for you."

"Yeah?" There was a playful tone to his weary voice.

"Two out of three of our guys. . . ." She paused just to make him squirm.

He couldn't wait, couldn't hold back. Maybe that was why his wife had left him.

". . . were filmed in Washington State?" he blurted out.

She shook her head. ". . . got an 'A' in high school history."

Malbranche gave a sharp rap on the desk with his knuckles and pushed back on his chair, spinning it clear around once. " 'Croatoan' . . . I always hated those smartass kids in high school."

Milo, of course, still wasn't getting laid, and he missed his video games and his iPod terribly, but he was in a better mood lately. First of all, he had started flirting with Randi when she came by for their legal sessions. It wasn't much, but it was about all he had. Last time she had even taken off her Kevlar vest when she had entered into the conference room. Ostensibly, it was because it was too uncomfortable to wear for hours at a time while they were discussing the details of their case, but Milo decided that she had done it to show off her figure. Whether intentional or not, it had clearly done that.

In addition, Milo had started getting what could only be described as erotic fan mail from a coterie of women. He had heard that high-profile killers often got such mail and that some had even wed while in prison. He found it kind of weird. Most likely the women were psychos with low self-esteem. But it was also kind of kinky and kind of exciting. Besides, it was the only sex life he was likely to have before they were acquitted.

He looked admiringly at Randi, gathering fuel for his fantasies later that night, as she continued to talk about the latest forensic developments in the case.

"One or two matches on the physical evidence, but an overwhelming number that don't match, although there are still some tests out."

"Reasonable doubt," purred Milo. "Any one of those people could have left that bomb . . . wherever it was you said they found it. A cave or something, right?" He glanced over at his co-defendants. "I told you guys we would be in the clear."

Brandon seemed more subdued, more nervous. "But the print on the quarter . . . that applies only to me. . . ."

Milo gave him a friendly elbow nudge. "Completely circum-stantial. Completely coincidental."

Zeke chimed in. "Milo's right. You were right the other day, Brandon. Circumstantial. You could have spent that quarter anywhere."

Jack Gassman, sitting at the end of the conference table as always, cleared his throat, silencing their self-congratulatory banter. "Very smooth, very clever. Except for one thing."

Milo fluttered his eyelashes at the pompous windbag. "I'm sure I don't know what you mean by clever," he said in a mock-ing falsetto.

Gassman shot him a look that said "Cut the crap" clear as day. But his words were much more moderate. "No need to be coy. Privilege applies."

Zeke spoke up, his tone even. "I keep telling you. We've been falsely accused."

Gassman snorted so loudly that Randi jumped at the noise. "Save it for the judge."

Panic filled Brandon's eyes. "You mean they're going to take it to trial?"

Gassman looked at Brandon in astonishment. "Of course

they're going to take it to trial, you morons. They would take it to trial if they had absolutely nothing, because they need to take it to trial for political reasons . . . for humanitarian reasons. They have to sate the bloodlust of the goddamn citizenry. The only thing that could stop a trial is if you all confess and agree to take the needle and waive any appeals so they can set a quick date for execution."

Milo's mood darkened quickly. "They're bluffing. Why would we confess?"

"Yeah," squeaked Brandon, "to a crime we, like, you know, didn't do."

Everyone's attention was now on Gassman. Milo was sure the show-off liked it that way. Now that he had their attention, he took his time answering, dislodging a piece of earwax from his right ear and flicking it into the corner of the room.

Finally, he folded his hands in front of him and looked at them each in turn. Then he spoke.

"They got the computer."

"What computer?" asked Zeke, his voice cracking as he did it.

"From your office," said Gassman, his tone matter-of-fact.

Milo waved his left hand in angry dismissal. "There's nothing on that!" he blurted.

Gassman opened his folder and consulted some notes. "According to the offer of proof forwarded to me there is nothing, except, of course for a terrorist threat message."

Milo guffawed. "Hah! *Terrorist Threat* is just a computer game. I had hardly even loaded it. What they found is an introduction or a file of flavor text or some bullshit like that. Go to Best Buy and get a copy. You'll be able to find the same text on any computer that the game is loaded onto."

Gassman scrunched up his face and he continued to look at the papers in the file folder. He threw up his hands. "This says

Donald J. Bingle

it wasn't in a game file. It was on the word processing system for the voice recognition software. There's a bit about a beach house . . . blah . . . blah. . . ."

Milo closed his eyes and groaned as he dropped his head into his hands.

Gassman continued. "Then something about Zeke needing to be a leader . . . blah . . . blah. . . ."

Zeke shot Brandon a stern look.

Gassman droned on. "Yadda, yadda, Milo wanting to get laid . . . blah . . . blah. . . ."

Randi blushed, but still Gassman went on.

"And then the really interesting part about a clipboard and Mount Rainier . . . blah . . . blah . . . blah."

The pompous lawyer looked up at the trio. "There's more. A lot more."

Milo lifted his head and half-stood as he turned to glare at Brandon. "Dude. I told you to turn off the fucking computer! What have you done?"

Brandon's eyes grew wider still. His hands shook. Perspiration was gathering on his forehead even though the day was uncharacteristically cool.

"I did!" he pleaded. "I hit the button right at the bottom of the screen."

A primal roar erupted from Milo that must have startled the birds outside the prison. "MORON! You turned off the *screen.* The computer was still on. The screen and the computer are not the same thing, idiot." His eyes darted around the room while he searched for an example that even a computer illiterate virgin could understand. Finally, it came to him. "It's not like dial-up Internet. It doesn't turn itself off every few minutes."

Zeke interrupted. "Shut up, Milo. Calm down and shut up."

Milo turned on him. "You shut up, Zeke. Don't you get it? Everything's falling apart. Brandon's killed us all. You're not in

250

charge of anything anymore. You can't lead if no one follows!"

Brandon tugged on Gassman's sleeve. "That voice recognition software isn't reliable, is it? It's probably got enough gibberish in the text that we can attack the whole transcription as inaccurate, right?"

Milo didn't wait for Gassman to respond. "It wasn't Nakajami's crap. I wouldn't count on it not to have gotten everything word for fucking word. Everything you said after we left."

The last breath of air came out of Brandon's sails. "Oh."

Zeke just stared at the table. "And everything we said before we took off for the desert." He closed his eyes and exhaled noisily. "I can't believe we're going to fry because Milo has a Macintosh fetish and Brandon talks to himself."

Brandon spoke again, his voice overwhelmed with despair. It was clear that he was struggling to find any hope . . . any hope at all.

"Maybe we can claim self-defense. Um . . . we were saving the entire planet from imminent harm."

Good idea. Wrong spin. Milo jumped in: "Maybe we can claim temporary insanity induced by toxins in the atmosphere because of Bush's failure to sign the Kyoto Accord."

Zeke stared at Milo, shook his head in sorrow, and turned to Brandon. He put his hand on the boy's shoulder and squeezed, before getting up from his chair and going to the door.

"Guard!" he yelled without emotion. The guard headed for the door, his keys out, jangling like Zeke's frayed nerves.

Zeke turned back to the group at the conference table. "There's no reason for me to be here anymore. There's no point to a defense and, quite frankly, I don't want one. I know what I did and why I did it. I'm not going to turn away from the only thing I ever did that made a real difference."

The door opened and the guard stood to the side.

"Take me back to solitary," murmured Zeke to the guard.

"Put in a request, if you could, for it to be as far from my companions as possible. We're not a group anymore."

"Is that so?" replied the guard, a self-satisfied, mocking tone in his deep voice.

"It is," Zeke affirmed. "The SUVs never even really existed." He walked away from the conference room without looking back. "And GreensWord is extinct."

As the door thrummed shut, Brandon turned to Gassman. "Maybe I should hire my own lawyer. I'm not sure my defenses are compatible with Milo's."

Gassman closed the folder and bent down to drop it into his document bag, sitting open on his left side. "That might be wise. Quite frankly, boys, I think it's all over, except for the inevitable movie-of-the-week."

Brandon wiped his nose with the back of his hand and sat up straight. He seemed to be doing his best to buck up, to go out of the meeting with his head held high. He thought for a moment and spoke to Gassman. His tone had a forced bravado about it.

"They're not going to get somebody all smarmy and weaselly, like Seann William Scott to play me in the movie, I hope. I don't want to be remembered as Stifler. Or Johnny Knoxville, either. He looks kinda weaselly, too, but even less threatening. I don't want to be remembered as smarmy or wimpy. . . ."

Milo snorted. "Like Hollywood would ever do a movie critical of environmentalists. . . ."

Brandon looked up sharply, some genuine enthusiasm coming into his voice. "Shia LaBeouf. Good-looking . . . earnest . . . innocent . . . yeah, innocent. Yeah, I definitely want Shia. . . ."

Luis Ordoñez climbed down from the ladder in the bedroom of Matthew Barrington's beach house, a Phillips screwdriver and a can of 3-in-One Oil in one hand. Fixing the wobble and squeak in the ceiling fan was almost the last item on the realtor's list of projects that he had been given to do for Mr. Barrington. He dropped the screwdriver and oil can into his toolbox, closed it up, and folded the ladder up. With the box in one hand and the ladder in the other, he trundled down the short hallway to the great room. The house was quiet, except for the gentle hum of the furnace in the basement.

He put down his burdens by the front door and snatched up his lunch cooler, setting it on the coffee table within reach of the huge, leather sofa in front of the giant, plasma television. He picked up the remote and turned on the big-screen. He liked to watch TV while he ate.

He was dismayed to see that his favorite soap opera had been preempted yet again by live coverage of the GreenSword/SUV prison transfer. The shackled and blindfolded members of the trio were being led one at a time into a building on a tropical island. He switched the channel to find crowds chanting pro-death-penalty slogans. He switched again and again and again, but there was no entertainment, just news: graphics showing the dispersal of the current smoke plumes from the still-erupting volcanoes of the Pacific Northwest; the latest estimates of fatalities from the blast; snow falling on a water-slide park in San Dimas; headlines about skyrocketing energy prices; Congressional hearings on disaster relief; glacial coverage maps for Europe; and a schedule for a scholarly conference on "The Coming Ice Age." Finally, he got to The Comedy Channel and sat through a commercial for women's hair spray ("Now in Aerosol Spray!") before settling in to watch Jon Stewart kvetch about pretty much everything.

Luis ate his sandwich and swigged a thermos of hot soup, then thumbed off the remote. He went to the closet by the front door and put on his parka and grabbed the snow shovel from in the back of the closet. He moved through the great room and

opened the drapes on the seaside window. A glare of white assaulted his eyes from the frosty panes, but he unlocked the sliding door and, after a few shoves, got it to slide open. A drift of
snow collapsed as he did so, powdering down onto the parquet
floor, but he ignored it and plowed through the drift onto the
veranda of the house. A thin layer of ice covered the shallow
water near the beach and a group of protesters trudged around
in a circle of packed snow nearby, centered on one of the
property's For Sale signs.

The protesters' signs read "Stop the Glaciers," and "We don't
want to freeze in the dark," and "Just say snow," and the like.
The activists were out there most days Luis came to perform
chores. He ignored them, as usual, and instead turned to look
up at the drift of snow arcing over the roof of the house. He
didn't like what he saw, so he reached into the pocket of his
parka and pulled out his cell phone. Even with gloves on, he
managed to punch the speed dial button for Barrington. He
didn't even know where the country code directed the call
anymore; Barrington changed his number frequently these days,
but the star maintained a manic focus on selling the house to
raise some cash.

When his boss answered, Luis got right to business, fog puff-
ing out from his breath condensing in the cold as he spoke.

"It looks pretty hopeless and downright dangerous, Mr. Barrington, sir. I don't think I should go up on the roof to shovel."

Barrington was cranky and demanding, as always. "The roof's
not designed to support the weight of almost two feet of snow!
You'd damn well better clear it or I'll hire someone who will."

"I'm sure the weather will get better and it will melt on its
own . . . eventually," Luis pressed. Jobs were tough to find these
days, but he really didn't want to break his neck either.

"Look," barked Barrington, "I need action and I need it now.
Extreme action. We just can't wait any longer."

EPILOGUE

Brandon rubbed his arms vigorously to fight off the chill and got back to his task. There was no one to help him. He was all alone now.

He hadn't seen Zeke since that day in the conference room, not even in the distance as he was accompanied to additional legal conferences with his new lawyers. Not even at the trial. About six weeks after he'd quit the group, Zeke had killed himself in his new cell on Kahoolawe. Brandon didn't know the details of how Zeke did it and he didn't really want to know. The little he knew depressed and frightened him.

There was no suicide note, but Brandon had been told by his new attorney that next to Zeke's body was a magazine open to an article about how the rapid temperature drop caused by the ash clouds of the still-erupting volcanoes in the Cascades was threatening to cause a massive, permanent cooling of the earth. Already glaciers were advancing across Canada, Russia, and Scandinavia. The burgeoning amount of whitened landscape was reflecting back sunlight, accelerating the planet's slide toward permanent frost. As the area covered by snow increased, the effect accelerated.

Milo's damn car roofs writ large.

Snowball earth, they called it.

If it got so bad that the tropics froze, the scientists predicted that the world could become an icebound wasteland for millions of years. No rain, no snow. All of the water would be bound up in ice. All of the land animals and vegetation would die and so would most of the life-forms in the ocean. Even animal life deep enough underwater not to be caught in the ice needed sunlight to fuel photosynthesis in algae and other vital links in the food chain. Those vital food sources wouldn't survive because the sunlight couldn't penetrate through more than a few feet of ice.

Nothing would move on the face of the earth. Not the behemoths of yore, not the conquering humans, not the radioactivity-immune cockroaches, not even the single-celled organisms that had given rise to it all.

With no precipitation to help strip the carbon dioxide out of the air, it would accumulate for millions of years, increasing in concentration until the greenhouse effect of the carbon dioxide warmed the planet and life returned. Or so they said.

Of course, there was great controversy as to whether snowball earth was really happening or if the planet was just going through a temporary, artificially-created phase, from which it would emerge, cleansed and refreshed, clear of the scourge of global warming. All of the big money in scientific research was going to snowball earth projects. There were lots of heated discussions about the whole business in the press and certainly in the environmental movement.

Whether Zeke thought he had doomed earth or he was just distraught that nobody praised GreensWord's actions to save the world, Brandon didn't know. All he knew was that Zeke had abandoned the world he had tried so hard to save.

Milo, on the other hand, was defiant to the end, but had been convicted and been given a lethal injection. It was an early evening execution, at six minutes and six seconds after six p.m. local time. A flotilla of boats had gathered off the coast of Kahoolawe the afternoon before the sentence was carried out. Brandon had heard them in the distance as the time to his friend's execution counted down, blowing horns and shouting: "Milo! Milo! Must go! Milo! Milo! Must go!"

The mob cheered when Milo's death was confirmed, high-fiving the annihilation of a life.

After that day, Brandon knew, the name Milo would never be used as anything but an epithet. It joined the list, with the likes of Adolph and Osama, of names you couldn't give a child without your neighbors wondering if they shouldn't call the Department of Children and Family Services to turn you in for cruelty.

The day before the capital punishment was carried out, Milo had been married in a prison ceremony to a very cute girl who had written him after he was incarcerated. Brandon had arranged, through his attorney, to get Milo a fully-loaded iPod for a wedding present, but whether the prison officials actually gave it to him or the guards let him use it that last night and day, Brandon didn't know. He wasn't exactly on good terms with the shaggy guy after he cut a deal to testify against Milo in return for a guilty plea and a life sentence (actually thousands of consecutive life sentences) with no possibility of parole.

Even though Brandon had cried during most of his testimony against his former comrade, he knew that Milo blamed him, not just for making a deal, not just for testifying against him, but for getting them all caught in the first place. Milo never referred to Brandon by name during his own testimony, instead constantly referring to him as "the virgin." At one point Milo declared that Brandon had made a deal and turned on him because "it was the virgin's last chance to screw somebody."

Brandon's attorney said that the government had only agreed to the deal because Brandon was the youngest of the trio and he had been the one who attempted to lead the authorities to the nuke before it was too late. It's not that they wanted to reward him for saving a few of the many lives he had put at risk, but they damned sure wanted to encourage someone to break ranks and tip the authorities should anyone ever try anything like this again.

In retrospect, that quarter from the call at the beach pay phone was the best money Brandon had ever spent. It had saved his life.

And now? Now that quarter was saving the Greensword plant from extinction here on Kahoolawe, where he was imprisoned. Brandon prayed that the Greensword would not go the way of the O'u, the native Hawaiian Honeycreeper that had probably gone extinct. The yellow-headed bird's last known habitats had been wiped out: by lava flow on the Big Island and by Hurricane Iniki on Kauai. The last confirmed sighting of the chunky green and yellow bird with a hooked, pink bill was in the 1980s. But Brandon, always a true believer, hoped that it would reappear someday, like the Ivory-Billed Woodpecker had in Arkansas.

Here on Kahoolawe, Koster's Curse sought to strangle and crowd the Greensword out of one of its limited habitats, but Brandon was fighting back, one weed at a time. That, and the cooler weather on the island that gave the Greensword a chance to expand its habitat range, and the species just might survive after all.

Brandon had already saved the world and he'd been caught doing it. Now, he just wanted to save this little piece . . . and find his own peace.

One person can make a difference in the world.

Of course, three people with a nuke and an agenda can make a big difference.

ADDITIONAL COPYRIGHT INFORMATION

All brand names, trademarks, and service names contained in this novel are the property of their respective owners. Use herein is not intended to convey any endorsement by such owners or their affiliated companies of this book or the political or other views expressed herein, nor is such use intended to convey any disparagement of such products, services, companies, or the employees, officers, or directors thereof. The environmental group GreensWord has no actual members besides the author, is not based on any other actual environmental organization, and most specifically has no relationship with what appears to be a recent United Kingdom based Web site called Green Sword. That Web site at www.greensword.com should not be confused with the author's much earlier Web site at www.green sword.org.

The Discovery Channel® is a trademark of Discovery Communications, LLC, in the United States and its use herein shall not be deemed to imply Discovery Communication, LLC's endorsement or sponsorship of this Work.

iPod®, Apple®, Macintosh®, and Mac® are all trademarks of Apple Inc. in the United States and their use herein shall not be deemed to imply Apple Inc.'s endorsement or sponsorship of this Work.

ABOUT THE AUTHOR

Donald J. Bingle is an oft-published author in the science fiction, fantasy, horror and comedy genres. His first novel, *Forced Conversion* (Five Star Publishing, 2004), is a military science fiction novel set in the near future, when everyone can be immortal in any virtual reality heaven they want, but some people don't want to go. Says Hugo and Nebula Award–winning author, Robert J. Sawyer: "Visceral, bloody—and one hell of a page turner! Bingle tackles the philosophical issues surrounding uploaded consciousness in a fresh, exciting way. This is the debut of a major novelist—don't miss it."

Don has more than twenty published short stories, including stories in a number of themed anthologies, such as *Imaginary Friends, The Dimension Next Door, Future Americas, Front Lines, Fellowship Fantastic, If I Were an Evil Overlord, Slipstreams, Time Twisters,* and *Fantasy Gone Wrong,* as well as in shared-world anthologies for the Dragonlance and Transformers universes. He is also the author of adventures and source materials for various role-playing game systems.

Don is a member of the Science Fiction and Fantasy Writers of America, the International Association of Media Tie-In Writers, and the St. Charles Writers Group. He works as a securities and mergers and acquisitions attorney in Chicago and lives in St. Charles, Illinois, with his lovely and talented wife, Linda, and two boisterous and furry puppies, Mauka and Makai. He can be reached at www.orphyte.com/donaldjbingle or through www.greensword.org.